# GUARDING HIS MATE

## FATED MATES OF THE ATARI
### BOOK 4

## A.G. WILDE

# GUARDING HIS MATE

**All I've ever wanted is a mate. But not just any mate—I long for a female who sees beyond my royal facade and falls in love with the real me, Da'red, and not the prince.**

When a series of unexpected events leads me to cross paths with a captivating human, I can't help but wonder if fate has finally brought me the one I've been searching for. As I find myself drawn to her, risking everything to keep her safe, I start to believe in the magic of the fates.

And when a single touch from her makes my life organ skip a beat...I know that I've found something rare and precious. Every moment with her feels like a stolen treasure. For this female is different from all others.

The thought of her in the arms of another makes me want to defy my kingdom and risk it all for a love that transcends status and power. But can our love truly withstand the weight of the crown? And are we strong enough to conquer the darkness lurking in the shadows?

1

Rissa

The underground network of cages is cold and damp.

A dampness that seems to leech on to me, making my skin itch and prickle.

Bearing down, I hold on to the bars behind me and use them as a guide to the floor, settling with my butt against what feels like cold, smooth concrete.

Even the floor is damp.

That had been my first indication that I'm in some sort of dungeon. It's a place where I have yet to feel the warmth of the sun. All that surrounds me is cold, damp *darkness*.

Off to one side, a constant drip-dripping plays a song that I can hear even when I sleep. Water, I hope, and not some other repulsive fluid. It seeps through the cracks from above, mingling with the heavy, unmoving air that constantly smells of mold and fungi.

I try to even my breaths and relax my bones, but the constant cold makes my body ache in this cramped space. There is no comfort here. But it's that same cold that keeps me alert. That, and the shrill sounds that echo against the walls.

Loud clangs like metal hitting metal. Banging. *Boom. Boom. Boom.* Random shouts that echo from the lips of damned souls. Screams of terror. It goes on and on and on.

The image painted in my mind's eye is a labyrinth filled with various monsters preying on the unfortunates lost within. For I have nothing but my thoughts. Nothing apart from the things I can imagine. The images the sounds create. The horror they incite. It all becomes a churning concoction that only serves to send me to the brink of insanity.

Far off, somewhere in this labyrinth, a scream cuts through the air, bouncing against the walls until it finds its way to my ears. Gripping the bars behind me, I squeeze my eyes shut and wait for the echoes to die down and fade away.

I assume it's only morning, and many more screams are yet to come.

"You'll survive this, Clarissa. You can get through this," I whisper to myself. "You *have* to."

For possibly the thousandth time, I repeat those words. By now the leaders of New Earth would have found the remains of the vessel I'd been on. After all these days, the memory of what happened still makes my heart constrict. Hearing the women around me die as we were attacked...hearing the chaos unfold...feeling their blood paint my skin and everything else around me...and somehow surviving it all...

A shudder goes through me as I release a breath and ward away the tears gathering in my eyes.

I survived for a reason. I have to believe that. Otherwise, I will waste away in this place. I can't dwell on any hope that I will be found. No rescue is coming. I will have to find a way out of this myself.

Allowing my shoulders to slump, I adjust myself on the cold floor.

It's quiet now, the last of those screams fading into nothing, and my ears perk in the silence. Long ago, I'd called out many times, wondering if any of the other humans survived and were down here with me. Long ago, I gave up on that premise. The only sound is that constant dripping that echoes against the walls. It's so quiet, I'm not sure whether the cells around mine are empty or if the occupants are just as broken as I am. But in the quiet, I can relax for a second. I can allow myself to breathe until I hear another sound. Then I'll stand. I'll appear alert. I'll pretend to be as normal as I can.

It's the greatest role I've played in my life. The last thing I want is for my captors to realize I'm different. I don't think they've noticed yet. Maybe because they don't pay much attention. After all, I'm only a slave.

They don't see that my eyes don't focus on anything. That I keep my lids low most of the time and only move when they pull or drag me. They think I'm being meek and submissive when I don't look them in the eye. And it's all well and good that they don't know my secret.

*For if they find out my eyes don't see, I will be discarded in a heartbeat.*

I thank my mother more than anything for her lessons when I was young. For years, she beat into me that I should appear normal, forcing me to mimic eye movements instead of staring straight ahead, forcing me to learn how to track sounds and live like I have the gift of sight.

All those lessons were for her own selfish reasons—an effort to pass me off as a regular child. One that wasn't "defective". For such humans are demoted to the Lower Levels. She tried hard, and for a time, her efforts worked.

I lived as "normal" as I could, hating the fact that I couldn't be myself and that others looked down on the very thing that made me who I was.

Back then, I hated mama's lessons and hoped for the day I wouldn't have to pretend or hide anymore.

It's ironic it's those same lessons I have to draw on now.

It's all that's keeping me going. It's what's kept me alert, even long after I've lost count of the days I've been trapped in this place.

Whenever I hear sounds harkening someone's approach, I put on my best performance. I pretend I can see, and I put my all into it. Because my life depends on it. And I will survive this. *Somehow.*

But existing in the darkness when everything around me is a threat is a sure way to get myself killed. Each day that passes, it gets harder. It's only a matter of time before they figure me out.

*I have to find a way out of here before then.*

*I have to get away.*

A loud clang makes the thick air vibrate and I jerk out of my thoughts, my heart hammering into my chest as my eyes widen.

He's here.

Scrambling to my feet, my ears perk as I listen for any other sound. I'm not disappointed when there is the repetitive scrape of clawed toes scratching against the floor with each step. They grate the air, splintering it as another sound joins in, so jarring it hurts my ears.

*Clang…*

The one I call "the jailer", my captor, approaches.

He travels down the cages, dragging some kind of solid object on the bars as he walks. And that's the one thing that makes me know exactly where he is.

*Clang…*

Those claws grate the floor. Closer. Ever closer.

*Clang…*

I stand straighter, my eyes tracking the sound along with my ears. To him, I'm watching him with some fear visible on my face, but all I feel is unease. In reality, the sounds play with the darkness in my mind's eye, coalescing into a picture of this place and the horrid creature I know I hate.

Long ago, I lost my fear. Maybe in the first few days of realizing I'm stuck here. Or maybe it was when the blood of my fellow humans was splattered across my face, soaking my clothes, my hair, my *skin*, and it was clear survival was dim. I lost my fear sometime between then and now.

The clangs continue painfully slowly, as if the jailer is taking his time walking past the cages. Whenever he comes, whoever he takes screams as they are dragged away, and I wonder whose turn it will be this time. Every visit, I believe my time has come. So far, I have been spared…and I hope it will continue that way.

At least, until I can figure out a way to escape this hellhole.

So far, no opportunity has presented itself.

With bated breath, I wait, my head slowly continuing to turn as the source of the clangs moves, heading in my direction. Gripping the bars behind me, I don't even breathe as the jailer reaches my cell and the clangs begin to vibrate through the bars, reaching even the ones I grip at my back.

He just needs to pass my cell and take whoever he's come for.

But the clangs have slowed…

And suddenly, they stop.

My lungs burn with the need to breathe but I wait, as if my breath will interfere with my hearing. Because I need to listen, it's the only way I'll be able to tell what's going on. *And he's stopped.* He's stopped at what sounds like right in front of me.

A sliver of anxiety begins to crawl along my spine in the silence.

The jailer is there. I'm sure of it. Standing right in front of me somewhere, and he isn't moving. A million thoughts fly through my head.

Is he watching me? Observing my reactions? Has he figured it out? That I've been pretending to see him all along? Is this it? Has my secret finally been discovered? Will he take me now? Dispose of me?

An old wound in my lower abdomen aches as air forces into my nostrils and expands my chest. The need to breathe overcomes me and my chest heaves as I grip the bars at my back.

Maybe he's not looking at me. Maybe he's facing the cage across from mine?

But no screams ensue, and the entire chamber is quiet as if every other creature trapped down in this hole is watching.

Shit.

The silence is only interrupted by the sound of chain links sliding against the metal cage bars, and when the whine of rusty metal hinges interrupts the air, the blood drains from my body, panic replacing it right down to my toes.

He's opening my cage. I can feel the vibrations moving through the metal.

Eyes widening slightly, I stare in the direction in which I think he's standing, hoping my memory of exactly where the cage door is doesn't fail me now.

"Approach, you filthy creature."

The voice isn't a kind one. It grates on my ears and is laced with ridicule and disgust. Every nerve within me jolts, but I don't move.

I could be mistaken. What if he isn't speaking to me? He could be speaking to someone else!

"Approach!"

Still, I stand unmoving, hoping I am wrong. Because if I'm not wrong and I move forward, I'll blow my cover too.

*But the cage is open, Rissa. You're not wrong.* The thought is logical, but I don't get time to argue with myself before the air shifts around me. It's clear something big and monstrous is suddenly in front of me, and I bite back a scream and hold my ground.

A coarse hand closes around my arm, causing me to hiss in pain as I'm pulled forward, but the jailer doesn't care.

"Filthy, ugly thing," he mutters, pulling me so hard, I stumble. He doesn't even pause, content with dragging me as I struggle to stand.

With reality shifting around me, I almost forget my voice. "What are you doing?! Where are you taking me?"

He pulls me so hard, my shoulder collides with the cage door and it swings, slamming into the bars with an ear-cracking clang.

I ignore the pain.

Switching to Galactic Standard, I grip on to the scaly arm that's trying to condense my flesh into bone. "Where are you taking me?!"

He growls in disgust. "For many moons, you have been rotting in my cells. Finally, there is a buyer for you."

A buyer?

What was I bought for?

*Who* bought me?

If I was sold as a slave, I'm about to be killed. There is no way I can perform any duties off the bat. I need time to figure things out. Locations of items so I don't trip or bump into them. How things work, so I can follow the motions without hurting myself or others. I need time! And I don't have that. No one will buy a slave and expect to teach them *how* to survive. My secret will be revealed. They'll find out in the first few minutes of me being there. And who wants a disabled slave when it's so easy to just get another; one that will work just fine? It will be easy to simply...*replace* me.

SHIT!

My heart hammers against my chest, fear slowly consuming me.

What am I going to do?

*Think, Rissa. Think.*

But no thoughts come. Only unhelpful ones that remind me how broken I am. On my own planet, New Earth, people like me are forced to live on the Lower Levels. My disability makes me a target, and one of the undesired. I'm not allowed to do most things. No one would hire me to do any job. I'm not even allowed to have serious romantic relationships or procreate. The Lower Levels are like a prison the human race designed. If my own people treat me so badly…what will another species do?

People like me weren't meant to survive. But we have. *I have.* And I don't want to go out like this.

"Wh-who bought me?"

The jailer owes me nothing. He doesn't have to answer. As a matter of fact, now that it's time to leave this dark hole, I'm actually thankful for him. He'd thrown me into a cell and left me alone. All I had after waking up in this nightmare was this wound in my abdomen. I realize now that he could have done much worse.

He grunts and I don't expect him to answer my question. He never speaks to the captives he hauls away. But he seems to be in good spirits despite his surly manner, for he speaks.

"You've brought me a fair number of credits for all the *zrat* you've eaten. You're to be one of the *Zedeshi's* servants…if you are lucky, you will be part of his harem."

The Zedeshi?

I don't know who the hell that is or even what that species might look like. The Lower Levels don't get much access to information; knowledge of the outer worlds is limited. I have only heard of one species called the Atari, and that was because New Earth got a good trade deal with them trading gold for technology. That's all the extraterrestrial information I know.

I'm walking into this blind.

I choke on a sob, not even able to laugh at my own joke. But I quickly wipe my tears and do what I do best. I pretend.

Holding my arm as inconspicuously as I can at my side, I reach far enough so my fingers travel along the wall. Every nook, every bump, even the slight changes in temperature are like an information highway flooding through my fingertips. The data fills my brain, painting a picture as the jailer continues to drag and pull me.

If anything, I can try and create a map of this place. Maybe there's still a chance for me to save myself somehow.

I grab that thought and hold on to it for dear life.

"Will the Zedeshi be escorting me to his home?"

I sense that the jailer looks at me and I wonder what sort of expression he has. He snorts in a way that sounds like laughter.

"You'll be taken with his other slaves." He pauses. "And if you're lucky, you'll not die when you arrive." He snorts again. "You are an ugly, filthy thing. I'm surprised he has requested you, whatever you are. Impress him, and you may live to warm his furs." He pauses again, his gait not slowing as he pulls me around a corner. For a moment, my fingers lose contact with the damp wall, but a moment later my shoulder collides with it as the jailer sidesteps something in his way. "I suppose I can see the desire of a fleshy thing like you."

The pain in my shoulder is background static as I fight off the sudden urge to vomit the goo I ate last night.

His words do nothing to calm the erratic beating of my heart. If anything, I'm even more convinced I need to get away.

"Here," the jailer lets out a sigh and propels me forward.

I can't stop the momentum and find myself falling, only to collide with leathery skin on the floor.

Whoever is beneath me yelps and pushes me off them.

"I will let in the guards who will escort you to your new owner," the jailer speaks, and from the shuffling about, I get the impression there are three, probably four of us here.

He snorts again, humor filling his voice. "Make a good impression, you worthless beings. I quite enjoy your new master's business."

I only know he's walking away as his clawed feet scrape against the floor in his departure.

Heart still hammering into my chest, I feel tentatively around me, careful to not be obvious as I move with caution until my back is against a wall.

Desolation slowly creeps up on me like a shadow.

How will I escape this, when I can't even tell where the hell I am?

When my greatest asset could be my eyes, but they are useless…

What does that mean for me?

# 2

Da'red

"You there."

I stiffen only slightly at the sound at my back. Glancing over my shoulder, I catch sight of my reflection in a metal shield that stands against a wall and I'm once again impressed by my disguise. Da'red Ystill, the crown prince, the *tanaste* of Atar, is no more.

My golden eyes are hidden by temporary lenses, changing their color to green. My bronze skin is darkened by a cosmetic paste, and the white strands of my hair are darkened the same.

I look like a Uulvian warrior. And that is just as well. The disguise has served its purpose thus far.

"Stand back," the Parsno says when my eyes land on him. "The snizz that owns these dungeons has a habit of setting traps."

Tilting my head slightly in understanding, I halt my steps. Ahead, I can barely make out the lines of a dark door set into the stone. The corridor is damp and narrow, and I wonder for the third time what I am doing here. I have left my *quud*, my only companion on this journey, and my cruiser on a dock far away from this place. I am without my most obvious weapons. And I am alone.

For two moons, I have searched every lesser station I could find, trying to locate one of the human females that was taken after the Khuru hijacked their ship. Seven times I have flown by this station. Seven times I have stopped and searched the bowels of the city it inhabits. I have turned up with nothing. Each poor dreg that I have questioned has given me no leads. Yet, I have been drawn back here, over and over again.

I narrow my eyes, my gaze fixed on the doors before us, and I say nothing.

My disguise was only supposed to conceal me, hide my identity as an Atari warrior just enough that I could sit in the alehouse and listen to henchmen speak of their latest pursuits. But word that a Zedeshi was about to transport a large group of slaves to his palace caught my ears. Females. And he wanted guards to assist. I signed up, and here I am, staring at a door set in stone. Waiting for it to open and reveal the poor females caught in this vicious cycle.

Even if I don't find the Earthkin, I can gather intel from the females behind this door. Only they know what's in the dungeon beneath the station. For I have not yet been able to gain access. The *snizz* that owns it keeps a tight rein on who can gain entry. Even now, standing before one of the access doors, I know the other side only holds a room that is sealed off from the rest of the underground.

A complicated business.

If I don't find the female here, I must return to Atar and get the crown involved. For there's a reason I keep coming back to this cursed place.

There has to be.

Clenching my fist, I wait for the door before me to open. I will rescue these females, learn what they know, then I will send them somewhere safe and continue my search for the human.

At my back, the Parsno and his companion move. They squeeze past me, the narrow corridor not giving much room, to pause only a foot ahead. One of them turns and raps on the wall. A series of three taps, pauses between them. A code.

There's a sudden clang and his comrade cowers as if he expected something else to happen, possibly activation of the trap they spoke about. But all that happens is the lock on the other side of the stone door engaging. The door shudders as if it hasn't been used in a long time.

The Parsno chitter in anticipation. Predators known for their swiftness in battle and their bloodthirstiness, I'm not surprised they're doing work for hire. I can see the glee in their eyes, regardless that these females will not be their own. Their intentions are as clear as a *flebgill's* tail. They'll try to have their way with the females before we deliver them.

The thought makes my fists clench even tighter.

The door jerks but does not fully open, and the two Parsno glance at each other, their gazes flicking to me for but a moment with no consequence.

They don't see me as a threat, and I will let it remain that way. After all, I look like an Uulvian, and the Uulvian are an agreeable sort. The Parsno will not worry about me, and I will use that to my advantage.

One of them stretches forward with his leg, his chitin making a soft grinding sound. He kicks the door, sending it flying inward and, immediately, there are a few screams of fright from the inside.

He's frightened them.

My nostrils flare as I glare at him, but he doesn't even notice. He's too busy laughing with his friend as they both step into the small room, their heavy stomps echoing against the hard floor.

Even without entering, I can already see there are maybe ten females within. For a Zedeshi, this is a large haul. And that only tells me one thing.

He does not take care of his slaves well. They are disposable to him. Where one fails, he will have another.

Taking a step forward, my frame fills the doorway and the females that lay their eyes on me scamper back. They are all of different species, and the Parsno males make a whistle, the sides of their mouths opening, a flap of chitin vibrating with the shrill sound.

I choose to ignore them, my gaze flicking around, landing on each female as I check for the features I'm searching for.

Human.

Earthkin females look like Atari women, minus the white hair and the bronze skin. They are also smaller, rounder, softer looking. But none of these females fit that description.

I have been searching so diligently…and I have come up short once again. None of the humans are here.

I release a breath through my nose, my shoulders sagging, and one of the Parsno glances my way.

They are already rounding up the females, and the looks on their faces trigger that protective vein deep within me. I want to rescue them all *right now*, but it would blow my cover and render this whole operation useless.

"Cheer up, Uulvian. We won't take them all for ourselves. There are many here for you too."

My eyes narrow. "Are these females not for the Zedeshi who hired us?"

The Parsno glances at his comrade and the sides of their mouths open to release that shrill sound again.

They find humor in what I asked? Scum.

"We'll deliver them to him, but they are already so beaten up, he will not know if we have a little fun with them first." His face becomes composed as he levels his gaze with me. "And as long as no being reveals it to him."

I understand his meaning immediately and I force myself to relax my features and nod. "I will not tell the Zedeshi of what you plan to do."

*But you will die before I let you do it.*

The Parsno lets out that shrill sound again. "See, I told you he would be agreeable. He is Uulvian after all."

*Qeffer.*

My fingers itch and I know they will find their way around his throat one way or another if I don't extract myself from this mission.

But I can't leave the females here, and I still need to question as many of them as I can.

The Parsnos' arms are soon filled with females between them, corralling them as if they are meal-flesh and forcing them forward so much, I have to backtrack to let them pass.

"There's one left. A filthy thing. You can carry that one, we'll manage with these," one of the Parsno says to me, dark laughter leaving his throat.

I wait till they pass before I turn to look at the poor being they have left behind. She might be filthy but she will be glad to know it's the one reason they aren't interested in touching her. Which is probably a saving grace.

"Do not be afraid," I say as soon as the Parsno are out of earshot. Stepping into the dark room, my brows furrow as I look around. I almost miss her, huddled in the corner. So dirty, she blends in with the dark wall behind her.

I cannot make out what species she is, but she is obviously a small, soft thing to have molded herself so well to the wall itself.

Stepping forward, I crouch so I can see her better. Dark wavy hair has fallen to cover her face and she is so still, I wonder if she is still alive.

Reaching a finger forward, I brush the tendrils of hair away, revealing her face. Immediately, her gaze snaps to me and shock renders me frozen.

A human?

*One of the humans.*

After searching for so long…I can't…I can't believe it.

My silence probably scares her and she jerks away from me, scrambling to her feet.

My heart clenches as my gaze moves down her small frame. A dark fluid has soaked her clothing, even some of her hair is clumped together where it has dried. But I don't need to press my nose against her skin to know what it is. Lifeblood.

My nostrils flare with the scent of it, but she doesn't seem to be in pain or harmed in any way.

As I stare at her, watching her grip the wall behind her as she averts her gaze from me, I realize a horror that I wish didn't exist.

The dried blood isn't hers.

It's the blood from the massacre.

She's been forced to remain in the same garments all this time. Two moons without being offered relief to wash herself.

My claws scrape against the floor, extended in my anger, and the female winces.

Immediately, guilt consumes me.

I am scaring her, and she has been through the most harrowing experience. I rein in my anger. *This is not the time.* Right now I should be comforting her. Making her feel safe.

"Why are you standing there?" she asks, a tremor in her voice that she pushes past. Eyes still averted from me, she continues. "Shouldn't you be leading me out like they've done with the others? O-or are you just going to leave me here?"

I don't miss the slight hope that lilts her voice; hope that makes my eyes narrow slightly. It's as if she almost *wishes* that I leave her behind.

"I-I might be too d-dirty for your master..." she whispers. "I'm afraid my species does not clean easily. The dirt has stained my skin and will remain there for a time."

My eyebrows lift and a surprised sort of laugh threatens to release itself from my lips.

What on Atar is she saying?

"I might not be the best choice." She lifts her chin a little, but still keeps her gaze low. "You should negotiate for someone else from the jailer."

Jailer? Ah...she must be referring to the snizz that owns this place. Why would she want to return to the bowels of this hell? It doesn't make sense.

"No," I say to her, "I am here to take you away from here."

I do not tell her I am here to *rescue* her. I don't know what state her mind is in after all that she's experienced. I can't lay my plans out too early, lest she let something slip and they are all derailed.

The female fidgets, a shudder going through her. "Ok...how about I make a deal with you?"

My brows furrow. Maybe I was right about her mind being in a strange place.

What sort of deal could she make when she has nothing to barter with?

"I'll do anything you want if you *don't* take me to your master. Tell him I died. Tell him whatever you want and I will repay you handsomely."

Well, this is a turn of events I was not expecting. What is her plan?

"Pay me how?" I ask. It's not the right question, but so many are swirling in my mind, it's the first one that came forward.

"Whatever you want." Her voice gets so soft, so low, that her words almost fail to reach my ears. But the insinuation is clear. I growl without meaning to and she moves a little farther away from me. "T-take me back to my planet and I will make myself do whatever you want for as long as you want." She gulps. "For the rest of my life." She swallows hard again. "Just…please don't take me to your master."

Her desperation is clear and it gnaws at me. She will *make* herself do whatever I want… She is sacrificing herself for a chance at freedom. The horrors she must have endured.

I move forward to pull her into my arms, but when she stiffens, I think better of it.

"H-how many henchmen can say they have their own p-personal whores?" A tear runs down her cheek, as if she's fighting with herself to say the words, and I can't take it anymore. In one stride, I'm before her and she presses her back into the wall. She refuses to meet my gaze and I don't force her to. Instead, my finger brushes against her cheek as I wipe her eye waters away.

The female freezes just as a tingle goes through my arm at the contact—one that has me snatching my hand away from her face.

What in the gods' graces was that?

Frowning, I'm staring at my hand when one of the Parsno appears at the door.

"We don't have all of the light cycle to get off this ugly rock. You can play with the tramp later. The caravan is ready and we are leaving."

# 3

Rissa

He's warm, this henchman. Or maybe the cold in this damp place makes him feel like the edges of a heating cube. That comforting warmth that makes you want to grab a blanket and lie down to watch the holo-embers play. He grasps my arm with such a gentle touch, it's almost as if he isn't holding me there, and with that gentle hold, he leads me from the room.

For a moment, I'm distracted by this new feeling. But everything all comes rushing back in a heartbeat. We're *leaving*! I'm losing my chance to get out of this. But, for the life of me, I can't think of what to do. My heart's seizing. It has forgotten how to beat properly and I wonder how many times in the last few minutes I've died from cardiac arrest.

The henchman leads me through what feels like a winding tunnel, and I forget to even run my hand along the wall to get a sense of the place, too consumed with the chaos and panic swirling in my mind. Too distracted by the feel of this tall henchman walking beside me who has a voice that seems misplaced for the sort of work that he does.

It was…soothing…his voice. As if he didn't want to scare me.

But I know even with a voice like that, I can't let him fool me. He's friends with the scum that's leading the other women, and I heard every word they said. They spoke in Galactic Standard, and I'm sure all the other females in the group who speak the language understood them too.

The moment the jailer took me from my cell was the moment my life got a helluva whole lot shittier. In a desperate attempt, I'd even tried bargaining with the frickin' henchman that's about to lead me to my possible death.

I *offered* myself to him.

Something wrings in my chest like my heart's twisting over itself at the thought.

It feels like an incredible weakness. And to have offered myself and *failed*. My heart wrings some more and my belly turns at the thought of this strange beast touching me. But, in the spur of the moment, it's the first thing that came to my mind.

In this world, two things can work as currency. Galactic credits…or what's between my legs. And I have none of the former.

Many may take the latter for free, like this Zedeshi who has bought me, but I'd hoped the thought of it being willingly given might have enticed the henchman.

I guess not.

I'm well and truly fucked. And not in the way where I could grit my teeth and bear it since it would aid in my survival.

Trying to steady my erratic breaths, I focus on what's happening now and force myself to continue pretending.

Stretching my fingers to the wall at my side, I keep my hands running along it as we walk, painting a picture of the scene around me and a map of the tunnel as we walk through it.

The dampness of the walls slowly fades until my fingers begin to brush against coarse, hard rock, and the corridor begins slanting upward. We walk a few steps before I stub my foot against something hard. Pain shoots through my toes, the simple shoes I'd worn when I left New Earth not much of a barrier between my feet and whatever I just bumped into. I assume it's a step or the beginning of some stairs because as I fall forward, my hand shoots out and I touch the smooth surface.

A warm, strong arm steadies me as the henchman grabs me around the waist, his arm pressing into the wound I have there, but preventing me from face-planting into the floor.

The wind is knocked out of me for just a moment, and when he pulls me up, he doesn't immediately continue walking. I expect him to drag me along and I try to take the first step up what I'm convinced is a staircase, but his arm tightens around my waist, keeping me still.

Panic shoots down my spine as I lower my gaze, trying to figure out what the hell is happening around me. Did I read this wrong? Are these not stairs?

Here I am, faced with one of the greatest obstacles in my living world. If I were alone, I could take my time, feeling my way up the stairs, but now, I have to be brave and take each step blindly.

Again, I can't laugh at my own pun. I'm too terrified to even breathe. Terrified it will become immediately obvious that something's off about me.

But I don't get the chance to expose myself.

The world tilts as I'm suddenly lifted. The surprised sound that leaves my lips is quickly cut off as I slap my hand over my mouth.

I'm cradled against a rock-hard chest and I suddenly realize just how big this guy is. He holds me as if I weigh nothing. Without saying a word, he takes the steps slowly as if he doesn't want to startle me, and even without being able to see him, I can feel his intense gaze on my face.

I avert my eyes, of course, knowing that if I stare in his direction for too long, he will notice they are unfocused. But turning my head toward him causes my nose to press into the leather he wears.

An intoxicating scent, like warm cinnamon, wafts right into my nose and my eyes pop open wide. I'd have never expected a male that does this sort of work to smell so good. I have to blink a few times to clear my head before I turn my face the other way, and the henchman still carries me without a word, taking steady steps in a rhythm I can expect.

My heart, still doing a marathon, hits hard against my ribs as I try to understand what's happening.

I know I'm putting rose-tinted glasses over this whole experience. Imagining that he's walking slowly so as not to startle me. Thinking he's holding me gently because he doesn't want to harm me. Feeling that he's staring at me intently as if he cares.

I know it's all in my head and maybe it's been the stress of this whole ordeal, but I don't fight back, even when the gentle bob of him walking up the stairs stops and it's clear he's walking on flat ground and still hasn't set me on my feet.

"Look, the Uulvian's already getting close to that one." I hear one of the other henchmen say. The way they speak makes me believe they don't have soft, malleable mouthparts. There's a lot of clicking at the ends of the words. Almost like an insect clicking its shell.

"So you've taken our advice," another says, and it's clear they're speaking to the henchman carrying me. So...he's an Uulvian. Again, in my lack of knowledge about extraterrestrials, I have no clue what an Uulvian might look like. "You will mate with that one while we have the others."

I swear a growl rumbles in the Uulvian's chest. Swear I feel the vibration...but his words are a direct contrast to whatever I thought I felt.

"Yes," he says. "This one is mine."

I stiffen in the stranger's arms and force myself to keep in the slow shuddering breath that threatens to release from my nose.

Even his voice has changed. It's clipped and cold, not the deep timbre I recall. Whatever I thought I heard in that room was my imagination. And my entire foolishly-attempted plan had been for naught anyway.

No wonder he didn't reject or accept my invitation.

He was planning on taking what he wanted whether I agreed or not.

The urge to struggle from his grasp and make a run for it swells within me. But what would I do? Release from his grasp only to run into a wall? Or off a cliff? Into the way of a speeding hover car?

There is...nothing I can do.

For the first time in a long while, feelings I'd buried come back to life. As a child, those same feelings plagued me, and here they are again. As fresh as if they'd never left.

If only my eyes worked…If only I was like everybody else…I could help myself out of this situation.

But with maturity comes something else. The ability to cope. For thirty years, I've had these eyes. For thirty years, I've learned how to survive without sight. I'd carved a living for myself even on Lower Earth where the unfortunate go to die. I'm an artist, a complete contradiction to the fact that my eyes don't work as they should. I have never let them hinder me. And I won't let them hinder me now.

If I can survive on Lower Earth, I can survive this too.

So I push those feelings away. I bury them again. And I don't feel.

I squeeze my eyes shut and block out the chatter of the other two henchmen as they discuss just what they plan on doing to the other captives.

They speak of horrible, horrible things, and I know this journey to the demon that bought us will be a long one. If our buyer's henchmen are like this, what is *he* like?

But I ignore them. I block out their words. They won't faze me, and they won't break me down.

I'll get through this, even if at the end, just a bit of me remains.

---

## Da'red

The human's gone still. Almost as if she isn't there.

Eyelids so low she can hardly see where I am taking her, she keeps her hands clasped to her chest as she breathes evenly. It appears to be some form of prayer or commune with her gods, the cosmos, or some other deity.

I can't help but stare at her as I walk. She…*confuses* me.

I expected hysterics, wailing, fighting, maybe even just complete fear, but not this. Not this…resignation. And certainly not her bartering with me for her freedom.

I've been carrying her for some time, up the stairs to the landing, out in the open where there is fresh air and not the heavy, unbreathable one down in the tunnels...but...she doesn't respond.

Before us, the Parsno lead the other females and they chitter and whisper among themselves, their fear obvious, but also their relief to finally be in fresh air once more. Only the gods of Atar know how long they'd been locked in those cells, denied of the star's light. But this female...it is as if she doesn't notice.

She is a small, soft thing, with more places to squeeze than most other humans I met when I visited her homeworld.

It's that softness that squishes against me as I grip her to my chest.

Despite that she is dirty, underneath the grime I can see patches of her pale, rosy skin. It's so thin, her lifeblood is visible just at the surface. And smooth. So smooth. I can feel how smooth it is even though I've been careful to keep my hands on her clothing.

Whatever happened before, when my finger made contact with her cheek, was like a zap of ions. I've never experienced anything like it except once when I visited the *tekuga* homeworld. Water-based life-forms, they emit an electric charge when threatened, and it makes me wonder if there are things about humans that remain undiscovered. We scanned Earthkin for compatibility with the Atari. I don't recall such a defense mechanism in the reports.

As I watch her, I'm not so sure. She doesn't seem to be trying to defend against anything. As a matter of fact, she's hardly even moving. Only the constant rise and fall of her chest tells me she's breathing.

Should I be concerned...or relieved?

Lifting my gaze forward, I spot the caravan that will take us to the Zedeshi's city. It's a series of large open-top compartments, all linked together, and it's already being loaded.

My mouth curls in disgust that I try to hide.

These caravans are known to be the transport of choice for many undesirables. Thieves, beings who con for credits, and malicious scum who survive in the underground of society. I shouldn't be surprised this is what the Zedeshi paid for. No one on this caravan will report that a group of females are traveling with known thugs against their will. The Zedeshi will get away with it, and turn around and do it again another time.

The human in my arms makes a small sound and I wonder if she's thinking the same thing about the transport before us. Her head is turned in that direction and I assume that, even though her world is relatively new on the galactic scene, she knows just what that caravan entails.

She closes her eyes briefly, long lashes fanning over her cheeks and her plump lips pressing together as she takes a deep breath. Almost as if she's preparing herself for what's to come.

I can't help but stare at her, my mind going through a series of emotions far too quickly to process.

She is still drenched in the blood of her people, and her mind does not appear to be frayed. I have only known the warriors who fight alongside me to hold such strength. This female is no warrior, yet her strength to survive this shines bright even though she tries to appear even smaller than she is in my arms.

"Uulvian," one of the Parsno points to the last compartment on the caravan. "We take that one."

I grunt, not trusting myself to answer him in a civil tone. I don't like being in the company of such filth. I need to make a move. And soon.

Glancing at the other Parsno, I note he is occupied terrorizing one of the females. Her shrieks and cries of distress seem to bounce off his chitin as he grabs her and whispers something in her ear that makes her go pale.

His comrade, on the other hand, has his back turned to me as he ushers the females toward the caravan.

Now might be my best chance.

Crouching to set the human down and reach for the blade hidden under the leg of my trou, I keep my eyes on my targets, but there's unexpected movement.

It's almost a blur as one of the females at the front, a velushan-kadrian mix, suddenly darts away from the group. The entire procession freezes, the other females glancing at each other and then back at the Parsno. I can see it in their eyes, the split second when they calcu-late whether they're brave enough to follow her lead or stay put.

But when none of them move, I realize I will not have much trouble rescuing them from this situation.

They're smart. Smart enough to realize that even though one of them seems to have escaped, there's no urgency from their captors. And that…is strange.

The Parsno predators watch the female run before glancing at each other. Their heads tilt back and chitin vibrates with their laughter.

"What is so humorous?" I ask as I rise, my eyes on the female making her way across the distance.

One of the Parsno flicks his gaze in my direction. "You have never worked for this Zedeshi before, so you do not know. There's a tracking device in all of these females."

There are mumbles of surprise from the females and the human stiffens. It's the first real reaction I've gotten from her since I took her into my arms.

A tracking device? That's news to me and it seems to the females as well.

"They ate it in that goo the snizz feeds them. The Zedeshi's moni-toring their location as we speak." He snorts as if he thinks that's bril-liant. A stroke of genius. "She won't get far." He taps a device on his wrist and there's a moving green dot on it.

His companion shrugs. "You get her, before the boss thinks she's been taken and detonates the tracker. Dirty business I don't want to clean up. We'll load the others."

As one of the Parsno heads after the runaway female, my jaw ticks with unease.

Detonate? The tracking device has an explosive component. I should have guessed.

If any of these females escape, they become a liability not only to the snizz but to the Zedeshi himself. There's a reason they deal on the underground market, beyond the reach of the Galactic Union. They can make their own laws.

Qef.

Not only will these trackers interfere with my plan, but it seems these two Parsno have a relationship with the Zedeshi that predates this job. I cannot simply discard them and free the females. I will need to destroy the unit that tracks them, while ensuring it doesn't detonate and kill them all. If I rescue the females now, it will be like handing them a death sentence.

My eyes narrow as I consider the problem, my gaze falling on the humans. I'll have to follow her to the Zedeshi's lair to ensure she lives.

This has gotten complicated.

As the remaining Parsno leads the other females into the caravan, I follow behind. The wooden cart squeaks with every step I take and I know it is past its capacity. In front, the Parsno doesn't seem concerned. He pushes the females, herding them into the caravan and pays no attention to their winces when he grabs them too hard.

With each wince, I want to break one of his fingers, crushing the bones till they are useless. Already I am at the end of my grace. This will be one of the hardest jobs I've ever had to do.

"Give that one here. Throw her in." When he reaches for the human in my arms, I release a growl without meaning to. I stop in my tracks and force my gaze to go low. Uulvian are not hostile. I will blow my cover.

But the Parsno laughs, his chitin flaps quivering in delight. At the same time, his companion returns with the female escapee writhing, her eyes flashing with hatred.

"The Uulvian is getting protective," his friend laughs, gesturing to me with those same fingers I want to break.

His comrade joins in and I allow them the humor at my expense, still forcing my gaze low. The skin at the back of my neck leading down to my spine tightens with the effort and my muscles bunch with restraint.

One of them leans in, his face coming dangerously close to mine as all humor leaves him. "These warm cunts belong to the Zedeshi…*Uulvian*." I clench my teeth but remain silent. "Don't get too attached."

Forget breaking all their fingers. I'll cut their tongues out too and then feed it back to them.

Stepping into the compartment, I watch with clenched teeth as they pull in the female that escaped and close the door behind them.

The cold air that whips around us as the caravan pulls off does nothing to cool the rage beginning to simmer in my gut and I already know, there will be bloodshed by the end of this mission. Lots of it.

There is only so much I will put up with before things let loose. I only hope I can ensure the females' safety before then.

# 4

Rissa

The Uulvian doesn't release me.

I can tell we're moving. There is a slight sway of his body as whatever we are in picks up speed till it's clear we're going incredibly fast.

The wind whips around us, lifting my hair and flinging the strands into my face as it chills my skin. We're on our way, and at this speed, I'm sure it won't be long till we arrive at our destination.

But despite the cold, little shivers go through my body for a whole other reason.

This...*henchman* has not put me down. He's still holding me, bridal carry, and I'm a thousand percent sure his comrades aren't lifting any of the other females. They don't sound like the type of males to do such a thing. Not from the way they chat as the vehicle moves. The things they say about the females make it clear they have absolutely no respect for any of us.

But this Uulvian...

I frown but keep my face turned away from him.

What's his deal anyway?

I didn't miss what his comrade said about him getting possessive over me.

Is that what this is? Possessiveness? ... Shit ... Is he considering my proposal?

My cheeks heat from the thought. Not from anticipation but from embarrassment and pure anxiety.

I try to keep my breaths from betraying any of the panic that's winding its way through me, my mind swirling like the wind whistling around me.

If he's considering my proposal...*fuck*. Why did I even propose to be his whore if the thought sends fear through me like water permeating sand? I don't want to be his whore but either way, I'll be forced to do something I don't want to. The only thing I can probably count on is that he seems to have a strange relationship with his comrades. Almost as if they aren't really friends but are just working together. He seems almost...nicer. Maybe I can use that to my advantage somehow.

The vehicle picks up speed and the wind rushing past us makes my eyes water. I shiver, the cold sending icicles across my body. Without meaning to, I snuggle closer to the Uulvian, pressing that side of my body that's touching him into his scorching heat.

His body's like a furnace, unaffected by the wind around us, and I lean into it, trying not to think about the facts of my reality. That I'm leaning into a male that will probably force his pleasure onto me as soon as he gets the chance.

I grit my teeth, I keep my eyes closed, and I focus on the warmth and not the man. But when the wind picks up even more and I can hardly breathe with the force of it, I know I won't be able to continue like this. I have to do something and I dread doing anything at all and bringing attention to myself. I'd been fine staying motionless in his arms, almost hoping he'd forget I exist. It's clear that's not going to work for much longer.

But as if some kind of guiding spirit is trying to take care of me, the henchman crouches as soon as I'm about to request that he set me down.

The majority of the wind is cut off as we go lower into what feels like the body of a traveling cart, from the rattling of the wheels, and I'm finally able to draw in a deep breath.

The gods are watching over me. They definitely are. Maybe his legs got tired, or maybe he was having trouble with the wind too. Whatever the reason, I'm thankful he decided to crouch. As I squeeze the water that had gathered in my eyes, I use the back of my hands to wipe it away but there's a low rumble. So low, I feel it in his chest rather than hear it, and his fingers grasp mine.

A jolt of electricity goes through me at the contact of his fingers against my hand. Like the nerves at the contact point are stimulated and firing. He pauses when he touches me, just for a moment, before he moves my hand.

My mouth opens, my eyes moving to where I think his face is, and when I feel a soft cloth dab my eyes dry, I'm left speechless and frozen.

"We should stop at the next station," one of the meaner henchmen says. "Take a few of these females and see what they can do."

I freeze, only my heart beating, and the small dabs that were drying my tears stop too, as if the Uulvian is listening intently.

"If you stop, the Zedeshi will not be pleased," he says, his words making a deep vibration I can feel in his chest. "You say these females are all being tracked. So the Zedeshi will know you've stopped for some time. He will not be pleased you have sampled his wares before he does."

There's silence in the cart. Even the other females are silent. Only the wind whistling makes a sound along with the squeaking of the cart itself.

"The Uulvian speaks sense," the other henchman says. There's a rattling that comes from him, as if he's annoyed. "Perhaps that is what happened to Frix. He has not been seen since the last time we worked for this Zedeshi."

"What do you mean?" the henchman holding me says, his deep voice still making his chest vibrate. It is a deep, rich timbre. Once again, I wonder what someone with a voice like his is doing in this line of work.

There's a moment of silence after his question before one of the other henchmen answers.

"Frix took one of the Zedeshi's females for some fun. We have not heard from him since returning from that delivery."

I swear the Uulvian laughs but does not allow it to reach his lips. Instead, I feel it in his chest. A deep rumble. My brows furrow as I extend my senses to take in everything I can about this male, but all I get is darkness filled with mystery.

"We should wait till we arrive at the Zedeshi's city and he has seen his females. Possibly, we can get some time with the ones he doesn't prefer," the Uulvian says.

There is a grunt and then a shrill sound from the other henchmen.

"This Uulvian is smarter than we first thought." There is a shrill sound once more and I get the sense there's a double meaning to those words.

They don't trust him…I don't even think they trust each other. If they're anything like some of the humans that dwell on the Lower Levels, trust is a thing that doesn't exist in their realm.

I tuck this conversation away for later. I may not know what an Uulvian is, but what I can tell is that he is tall and strong. If his comrades turn against him, possibly, I will have a chance to make him my ally.

As he removes the cloth from my face, I realize he must be looking at me and I adjust my gaze, laying my lashes low.

It's the safest thing I can do, and the only way I can be positive I'm not staring vacantly at anyone and drawing their attention.

With only my other senses to help me out, I focus not on my breathing, but on his. The steady rise and fall of his chest tells me he isn't nervous, and I draw strength from that. But as I focus on it, I notice something else. The rhythm of his breaths lull me into a sense of peace. It's oddly comforting, and along with his warmth, I want to lean in and forget about the cold air and the fact that I'm being sold into slavery.

The thought makes me want to slap myself for my stupidity. I'm romanticizing the henchman and that isn't good. He isn't here to help me. So I force myself to think of the most hideous creature I can think of. A demon. A heartless thing. But all that comes to my mind is the timbre of his voice, and I know something is wrong with me.

Maybe I stiffen. Maybe I lean away from him in my efforts to put some semblance of sense into my head, because his fingers tighten around me as he settles me closer to him. Hot breath brushes across my ears and I jerk, my eyes flying open.

"Do not fear, little human." That timbre is deep and low as he whispers into my ear. "I have searched long and hard for you. I will not let them have you."

My ears feel heated, little tingles going through my body as I blink, forgetting for a moment to keep my lashes low. As soon as I do though, I close my eyes and swallow hard.

Did I just hear right?

A spike of anxiety, or maybe anticipation, makes me shiver and, in response, the Uulvian holds me tighter.

*'I won't let them have you'*…

Either my little attempt at sorting a deal with this thug is actually working or I've gotten myself into some deep shit. As I hold myself rigid in his arms, not quick to jump to the solace his words invite, I wonder just who he is…and just what the next few hours of my life hold.

---

## Da'red

The Zedeshi's city soon lights up the horizon as the caravan turns onto the road leading to it.

My chest tightens with unease. This is risky.

Even speaking to the female was risky. But I have somehow become attuned to her life force, enough that I can feel her life organ beating. It thunders in her chest like it's on its own little caravan heading into danger.

She may not display it outwardly, but she is terrified.

She's still rigid in my arms. Still as stiff as cured wood.

When the caravan stops in the middle of the city and the Parsno begin unloading the females, I stand with her in my arms. All around us, high arching towers rise from the brown, dusty ground. They

remind me of the towers of Atar, only that on Atar there is life. Here…
not so much.

The streets are deserted and the few males that walk by are all
dressed in servant garb. They keep their gazes averted from us, not
even glancing over as the Parsno bark at the females. They've
witnessed this scene too many times over.

Still huddling together, the females exit the caravan to stand as one
unit at the side of the thoroughfare, their fear so strong I can almost
smell it.

Setting the human down beside them, I take a step back to put
some distance between us as my gaze flicks up at the towers.

I'm sure the Zedeshi watches us, and if not him, one of his servants.
His eyes and ears are everywhere and the last thing I want is for him to
set his sights on the human.

Seven times I have visited this rock. Six times I failed. But I've
found her now, and I am not about to lose her.

I glance at her, watching as her plump bottom lip slips into her
mouth as she bites on it. Eyes downcast, focused on her feet, I can tell
she's listening intently.

When the female beside her grabs her hand, her whole body jerks
at the intrusion. Her shoulders grow rigid only to relax a moment later
as soon as she realizes the grasp is not a malicious one.

As for the Parsno, they've been noticeably silent. No longer do they
joke about what they will do to the females. Even when the caravan
pulls away and continues its journey without us, their lips remain
sealed. They exchange glances, a few in my direction, and the skin at
the back of my neck itches with wariness. They'll be trouble. I can
sense it.

"Move," one of them barks, and the females all startle and begin
moving as one unit. At the back, the human looks even smaller than
the rest. She doesn't let go of the other female's hand as they hurry
across the street, following the Parsno in front.

I carry up the rear, the other Parsno at the side, as we head toward
a central building. I already know who we will meet there.

My eyes flick around, taking in every detail while I keep my gaze only mildly interested. But even as I scope, my gaze keeps coming back to the human at the back.

The star's fading light hardly hides the stains on her garments. No being deserves to carry around their slain with them on their being. I will wash her myself if that's what it takes to give her that relief.

That unexpected thought has my gaze sharpening on the human, images of my hands running over those soft curves making something stir inside me. Memory of how small and soft she felt in my arms returns. I can still feel her pressed against me...how her body molded to mine...and a sense of guilt almost makes me cringe.

The human is hurt. Traumatized. Such thoughts do not belong here, but trying to push the image of warm oils running down her pink curves only seems to strengthen that stirring inside.

I haven't had a female in a long time. Such pleasures have come to mean nothing to me. Not when those instances often always come from a place of greed. Maybe it's why I spend most of my time away from the palace.

On Atar, I am the crown prince. The *tanaste*. A male who females gravitate to, the promise of queendom making their eyes glow with avarice. But out here, I am no one. I'm not shown respect because it is required, but because it is earned. Out here, I am free. I am almost...alive.

But it seems I have neglected myself for too long.

I can fight the thoughts, and I almost have them under control when the human suddenly stumbles. There is one single step in our path, and she falls over it. I recognize the female holding her hand as the velushan-kadrian mix that had tried to escape earlier, and as the human falls, so does she. They both go down because of the human's misstep and one of the Parsno hisses in disgust.

His arm rises to strike them and the skin at the back of my neck tightens immediately.

His fist never lands.

There is a moment of surprise as his eyes widen when his fist seems to become stuck mid-air. As my hand tightens on his wrist, he looks at me, and so do the females. Everyone except the human. She keeps her gaze down, muttering apologies as she rights herself.

My eyes narrow. Maybe she is clumsy. She hit her foot in much the same way before. At that point, I'd thought she was tired, drained from her ordeal. And perhaps she still is. But even the velushan-kadrian looks afraid, her eyes on the Parsno above who was just about to strike them. The human, on the other hand, is so focused on righting herself, she doesn't notice.

"We are at his abode. I may not know this Zedeshi in person, but I know of his kind. They do not take lightly to insults." I narrow my gaze on the Parsno and his arm relaxes enough that I let him go.

The Parsno huffs, his chitin flaps vibrating as he glances at his comrade. But he doesn't reply.

I know my time is limited here. I'm cutting it really close to revealing I'm no Uulvian, but discretion has never been an Atari's strong point. Sooner or later, I will blow my cover and put every single one of these females in danger. I need to find that tracker and leave this place before that happens.

As the females continue walking, their hesitant steps forced forward by the Parsno's growl, soon we are inside the building.

Large halls, as wide as those in the Atari palace, greet us. The Parsno walk with purpose, leading us through the winding space while I take in every detail I can. Mapping exits, windows, things that can be used as weapons and their locations. It hasn't escaped me that I'm in this alone. My crew, the Atari warriors and my guard, aren't here taking care of any threat at my back while I charge forward.

It's a dangerous endeavor, one that will throw my world in disarray if I happen to be harmed.

I almost smile.

This is a mission only someone with a bit of insanity would under-take. But I have nothing to lose. So when we step into a great room and a sickly sweet scent wafts into my nostrils, I know it's time and the stakes are about to rise.

"Welcome," the Zedeshi says, his gaze sweeping over the group of us before falling on me. "It seems I have someone unexpected in my midst."

5

Rissa

Oh shit.

Ohshitshitshit.

I can tell I'm in trouble the moment the female that holds my hand stops walking and a scent that makes me want to vomit fills my nostrils.

A sense of apprehension floods through me. So strong, goosebumps rise on my skin and I shiver.

There's something malicious here. Something evil. I don't need the gift of sight to see it. I can feel it all around me.

And that *smell*. It's like an overdose of expensive perfume. Too much for my nostrils to appreciate. Instead of making me want to inhale, a headache is blooming in the front of my head.

The female holding my hand groans and shifts, gripping my hand tighter. Her skin is smooth, but not like mine. It's almost as if she has scales and I imagine that she does. I give her hand a squeeze in solidarity. She'll never know how much she saved my ass, *twice*. First when she grabbed my hand as we began walking, and second when she held on to me when I stumbled. I feel a bit guilty for taking her down with me, but she hasn't complained and she hasn't let go of me either.

I grip her hand tighter. Holding on to her is giving me some stability and I'm scared to let go. If I do, I'll be lost in a sea of darkness.

The Zedeshi's voice rings in the room, echoing, the vibrations painting a picture of a great throne room in my mind. He sounds powerful and my heart thunders in my chest as the chances of me escaping this mess get exponentially lower.

"It seems I have someone unexpected in my midst," he says.

The female holding my hand stiffens and takes a step backward.

There are slight gasps and I know something is happening that I'm not aware of. Following the female's lead, I take another step back with her.

I soon realize just what's happened when the Zedeshi's voice becomes much clearer, much closer, as if he is standing just a few feet before us.

The female holding my hand stiffens even more, her chest rising and falling at my side at almost the same rate as mine. Something is freaking her out, and that knowledge only makes me more terrified.

One of the women at the front shrieks and there is a thump as if she falls to the ground. The female holding my hand takes another step back and I follow her, my eyes wide, forgetting to pretend as only terror rules my mind.

"Stand still!" the Zedeshi commands, his voice rising before going back to its usual pitch as if nothing happened. "Yess…yesss…you are good."

I fight to calm my breathing as I take even another step back and bump into something hard that makes me jump. My head whips back, and purely out of instinct and possibly habit, my hand reaches out to touch whatever I'd just bumped into. When my fingers brush over smooth leather and the faint scent of warm cinnamon permeates through the smog of the perfume filling the room, I know I've just bumped into the Uulvian—and I had no idea he was standing at my back.

"Hmmm…you will do," the Zedeshi's voice cuts through my panic and I turn around once more, swallowing hard and hoping he doesn't notice me. I have to mentally shake myself.

Though the perfume is thick, I almost have to remind myself it's not a solid thing. It's not a smokescreen I can hide behind. I erase the clouds I'd painted of the scent in my mind and the room clears. Suddenly, I am even more aware of how out in the open I am.

"You…" The Zedeshi's voice sounds too close. "*Filth*," he spits. Another female whimpers.

Filth. He doesn't want filth. Shit.

I am the physical representation of filth. I haven't had a bath since leaving Lower Earth. I've been surviving in squalor, only the dirt on my skin forming a protective barrier from the many bacteria that should have killed me already.

"And you…" His voice sounds like it's directly in front of me now. As if he is talking to *me*. "How lucky to have such royalty in my midst."

The henchman behind me, the Uulvian, stiffens at my back. The bunching of muscles in his chest whispers like a faint shadow across my spine.

"I will enjoy you the most," the Zedeshi says, the creepiness in his voice pulling my attention once more.

"*I prefer to be skinned alive before I give myself to you!*" The female holding on to me speaks with such conviction it's clear she means every word. My eyes widen, my head turning slightly in her direction. Royalty?

"A hybrid queen," the Zedeshi continues, as if she hadn't uttered a word. "In *my* harem."

Something brushes across my face, causing me to jerk in surprise. Cloth? It's filled with perfume so strong I almost barf.

When the female holding my hand stiffens and jerks back as if pulling away, I realize the Zedeshi must be reaching for her and it's his robe that's brushing against my face. The female holding my hand struggles, her arm pulling mine as her body lurches. Suddenly, she goes still, and the Zedeshi speaks through what sounds like gritted teeth.

"You will yield."

"Over my dead—"

There's a dull thump and her arm jerks in mine. Suddenly, her hold on me slackens and her body sags. I let out a sound of surprise, falling with her, my fingers moving to where her body should be. Smooth scales seem to run up her entire upper body and I follow them, my heart picking up its pace as I realize she isn't moving. But she's breathing. Her chest rises and falls. He's probably knocked her unconscious.

"*You.*"

The word has me freezing. My spine stiffens and I wait. Wait for him to move on, hoping he isn't speaking to me.

"*Rise.*"

Oh God, please don't let him be speaking to me.

"*Rise!*"

I stagger to my feet, keeping my eyes downcast and hoping he's still not speaking to me, even though every hair on my arms and the back of my neck have stood at attention.

"What...what is *this*?" the Zedeshi asks. Something like a rod, or a stick, prods my belly and I quail. I want to run. My feet itch with the need to, but I *can't.*

"It is called a human," one of the other henchmen speaks. I had forgotten about their presence. Even if I could run, they're still here. They would catch me.

"It is *filthy*," the Zedeshi spits. He walks a few steps to my side, using that same prodding device to push against me. I force myself to keep still, to keep my eyes downcast.

"I was told this species is small and soft. Malleable. That they are good for warming furs. Good for breeding. But this *thing*..." He huffs out a breath. "She will not do."

The air moves as he spins, the edge of what must be his robe flicking into my face once more.

"Dispose of the undesirables," he says. "And inform the snizz I need more...items."

I release a shuddering breath. That's it? I'm excused? I'm free?

"Dispose?" The Uulvian asks, his voice booming behind my back, and silence befalls the room.

"Yes," the Zedeshi says after a few moments. "Dispose of them. Cease their existence. Do it in the dungeon in the third tower."

My heart drops. Blood drains from my veins.

"Can we have the ones you don't desire, oh great one?" one of the other henchmen asks.

I get the sense the Zedeshi shoos him away based on the bored tone that seeps into his voice. "It's of no consequence to me. Do as you wish, as long as you dispose of them. The Galactic Union has already placed restrictions on my city." He growls at the last few words as if this has been some sort of disservice to him. "You must cease their existence once you are finished." He pauses. "I will send a servant to ensure this."

Dear God...what the hell am I going to do now? Busy thinking of how I'm going to get myself out of this, I almost miss when the Uulvian speaks.

"The snizz is not known for keeping his captives in good order," he suddenly says. He must have moved forward somewhat because each word vibrates against my skin. "Allow me to clean this female, oh great one. You will see her value...and I promise you will not be disappointed."

There is silence again and I wonder what the Zedeshi is thinking. I wonder what the frickin' *Uulvian* is thinking.

"And what do you get out of that, Uulvian?" The Zedeshi pauses. "What is an Uulvian even doing on a job like this?"

The Uulvian stiffens even more behind me but his voice doesn't reveal any contempt. He's incredibly good at disguising it, and once more, I wonder just who he is.

"I have run into some...unfortunate events," he replies.

There's a moment of silence before the Zedeshi laughs. "You owe someone credits," he says, as if sure. Whatever he sees when he looks at the Uulvian must support his assumption because he laughs loudly, the sound echoing against the walls in this large space. After his laughter dies down, the room becomes quiet once more.

It's obvious this being holds all the power to have such control over everyone in this room.

"Clean the female," the Zedeshi says.

"But—" one of the other henchmen begins.

"And the others?" the Uulvian asks, cutting him off.

There is a sound as if the Zedeshi sighs, but his laughter at the expense of the Uulvian must have put him in good spirits because he says, "Let them wait over there. If you impress me, Uulvian...I will give you a chance to impress me some more."

So...he didn't think of giving us all a bath before he decided who he wanted to keep and "dispose" of? Like those affluent beings who don't wear the same underwear twice, he sees us as nothing but... items. Our lives mean nothing to him.

I've only heard of humans on the Upper Levels of New Earth living like this. To be in the presence of a being so callous highlights that my reality has changed completely.

"If you can make that one presentable...I will consider the others undergoing the same treatment." The Zedeshi's words sends an uncomfortable feeling crawling across my skin. The other females' survival now depends on whether he will like the way I look after I bathe? Their lives are worth much more than that, and suddenly, it's all on my shoulders.

I wish I could pin the Uulvian with a glare. I hope he has a plan, because I'm not sure right now whether he is ally or enemy. But, at the Zedeshi's decision, I hear when the Uulvian releases a smooth breath.

"The human is very dirty," he says. "Human flesh absorbs filth and it will take time for me to get her clean."

I choke on air and force myself to swallow it. Did he really believe me when I said that to him? Holy shit, maybe that stupid lie wasn't so stupid after all.

"I'll begin at once." He leans forward over me, the top of my head brushing against his chest. "At no extra cost to you, oh great one, but at the request that you consider me in the future."

He pauses in the bow, and his cinnamon scent envelopes me.

Breathing hard, I can't stop myself from inhaling that comforting scent, and I stare ahead, wishing I could see his face.

The Zedeshi laughs, breaking the silence. "This! This is what I love to see, you qeffing unworthy Parsno. A guard like this Uulvian is always welcome to do my bidding."

The Uulvian slowly straightens and I don't miss the low rattling of what sounds like insect shells clacking together.

The other henchmen aren't happy.

"Come," the Uulvian grasps my upper arm and turns me with him, leading me from the room. And as he walks with purpose, me by his side, it feels like a thousand eyes are boring into my back.

Whatever this Uulvian is doing…he's just spared my life. I have to admit that at least. But that doesn't tell me what his deal is…only, I'm pretty sure I'm about to find out.

# 6

Da'red

A servant comes and leads us to a room on the lower levels of this extravagant home. I remain silent the entire way, the human tucked into my side as we walk. She remains silent too, walking stiffly as if unsure of what is next to come, and I hope I'm able to speak to her in private once we arrive at the bath house.

The servant takes us into a dim room and retreats as if her life depends on it. And judging from the way that Zedeshi is, it probably does.

As soon as the door closes, I inhale deeply, enjoying the fact this room is not heavily perfumed.

"Qeffing Zedeshi and their scents," I murmur.

I expect the human to dart away from me and demand answers. Instead, she faces me and takes a step backward. A hesitant one, her shoulders stiffening as she waits.

When my hand rests on her shoulder, she jumps. I remove it immediately.

I have been liberal with my hands on her body up to this point. But now, when we can breathe for a moment, I will give her some distance. Some space.

I keep my voice low, mindful of the door behind me and the absence of sound in the hallway.

"Do not be afraid." At the sound of my voice, the human takes another hesitant step away from me, almost as if she's afraid to fall. My gaze slides over her legs. Is there something wrong with them?

Her eyes search the floor, moving back and forth as she keeps her head down.

She refuses to look at me and a part of me winces at that fact. She is so afraid. Of *me*.

It is unusual for an Atari prince to experience such a feeling coming from a female, and I realize I have not once experienced it from *any* female on Atar.

But *this* female...my life organ wrings as I watch her fight her natural urge to tremble.

Her chin tilts slightly upward, bringing her plump little lips into my view.

"Why shouldn't I be afraid?" she asks, and despite the way she appears, there is no tremor in her voice. Not even a whisper of it. "Why did you bargain for my life? What do you want...Uulvian? Are you...are you considering my offer?"

Her voice goes almost to a whisper and it feels like the air is charged while she waits.

Her offer...

The one about giving herself to me in exchange for freedom...

"I guess that's a yes," she whispers, her hands fisting at her side. She squeezes her eyes shut and releases a steady breath.

"I can do this," she whispers, another steady breath releasing from her lips. Fisting the edge of her tunic, she begins to lift it, revealing a soft belly.

"No." I stop her, and she freezes. "I didn't bring you here to—" To what? To take from her something she obviously doesn't want to give. "I didn't bring you here to use you."

Her brows furrow as she releases her tunic and a few moments of silence pass between us.

"If that's not why you brought me here," she says, "then *what the fuck do you want?*"

I smile slightly, the sudden fire on her lips surprising me, but she doesn't notice. She's still not looking at me, her gaze probably locating every detail on the textured floors in this dim room but dutifully avoiding mine.

"Your Earthkin," I begin, not sure how to bring up the tragedy that befell her people. "You were attacked by Khuru two moons ago. I've been searching for you since."

Her throat moves as she swallows hard, her hands fisted even tighter at her side. For the first time since meeting her, she lifts her gaze to mine and I am blessed with the deepest brown eyes I've ever seen in my existence. Even with all the dirt marring her face, those eyes suck me in.

She is…staggeringly beautiful.

"You…how do you know…who *are* you?"

"I am—" I pause. I do not want to tell her who I am. *What* I am. So I settle with telling her half the truth. "I am Atari. We were sent to haul your ship back to our world."

She swallows again, as if a lump constantly rises in her throat, her head shaking. Her gaze zones out as if she's seeing the terror of what happened behind her eyes.

"Atari? I—I don't understand. I was on a cruise. We were hijacked…"

"By the Khuru," I say, checking behind the door that no one is passing by. "We found what was left of your ship. We saw the security feed. We've been searching for you since. You are the fourth to be found."

When I turn to look her way, she's still shaking her head. "But you said…you said you were to haul our ship back to your world? That doesn't make sense."

"Aqnar mentioned this." I remember this part at least. "He said your Earth leaders seemed to have tricked you. You were not on that ship to attend a luxury cruise."

"What?" More head shaking. It's all too much information at once. "What do you mean?"

"You are part of a bridal gift to my world, Atar. A vessel full of potential mates. Females for us to love and care for."

Her expression falls and her gaze darts to the floor again. I'm not sure what I said wrong.

"M-mates?" she whispers.

Ah. That explains it. Humans don't have mates.

"Do not fear." I move toward her, closing the distance. My hand stalls halfway in the air to her face.

I stare at it.

I was about to clasp her cheek. Pull her toward me.

Even as I snatch my arm away and force it to my side, it itches with the urge to touch her. To comfort her.

I frown at myself.

"Your kind is compatible with mine," I finish, my gaze moving down my arm as it trembles in place at my side. It's an effort to keep it still. What in the qef?

"So you want to force us to mate with you?"

My brows dive immediately. "Atari are not scum like the Zedeshi and Parsno."

I say it a little too harshly and she visibly flinches. My tone softens all on its own.

"It was a contract. A deal between the Atari and your world. We believed all females on that ship knew what they'd signed up for. It was never our intention to force you to come to Atar." I pause watching as her shoulders shudder with every breath and she slowly turns away from me. "I understand if you don't want to honor the contract," I say. "But at least let me get you off this cursed rock first. I will make sure you are safe, then you can decide what to do once I take you back with me."

"Take me back with you?" Her head turns as if she's looking over her shoulder at me again, only, she isn't. Her gaze focuses to the side and I get the impression she's only turned her head so she can hear me more clearly.

"To Atar." I pause, studying her. "I cannot return you to your homeworld. You belong to Atar now. It is…it will be…your home."

I know it's a lot to take in, and in other circumstances, I wouldn't have dropped all the information on her so quickly and suddenly. But we don't have the luxury of time.

To my surprise, the female nods, still turned away from me.

I glance around the room, taking it in fully for the first time. Not far from the human, part of the floor is depressed and smooth. Water swirls in the center of the small pool. Off to the side, a fresh tunic sits.

I nod to myself. "I will leave you to wash and clean yourself. I'm sure you wish to do so." As much as I'm sure she'll want some time alone to digest everything I just said.

"Th-thank you," she says, almost inaudibly, and once again I get the urge to approach her and pull her into my arms. The urge is so strong that I take a step toward her before catching myself. I clench my fist at my side and force myself to halt. This compulsion to comfort her…it can only be a result of the trauma she's experienced.

She is a small, delicate little thing and I wish she was in my quarters, being tended to. Her tears being washed away; her skin being cleaned. Her sorrow being comforted. I would remove all threats and storm out of here now if I didn't have that tracker to find.

But I will give her space. I'll stand guard on the outside and I will give her privacy. My muscles strain as if that is not the right response.

"I will be outside. Call for me when you're finished."

She nods but doesn't move, probably waiting for me to exit. Earthkin have stringent morality laws. I'm sure she doesn't want to be bare before me.

Turning, I open the door to exit the room. Only then does she tilt her head even more to the side as if listening. But something about the way she stands…something about the way she pauses, makes me wait.

Releasing the door, it shuts with a soft sound.

When she remains still, I wonder what she is doing.

Her soft brow is slightly furrowed, her gaze staring at something on the floor off to the side, her head tilted my way.

"I know you're still there," she says, but her voice is low. Low enough that it's difficult for me to hear even though I'm still in the room with her.

I open my mouth to apologize when something stops me. Maybe

it's the way she says it. That she *knows* I am still here, not that she can still see me standing right here in front of her.

A few moments pass with her still looking over her shoulder. It is so still, so quiet, that the soft sound of the water swirling sounds like an angry whirlpool.

When the female's shoulders suddenly slump, a large breath leaving her body, my eyes narrow.

She slowly falls to her knees, placing her hands on the floor as she exhales again, as if she'd been holding a ball of tension within her the entire time.

"God," she whispers.

Once again, I open my mouth to say something, but I stop short. It's the first time I haven't seen tension stiffening her shoulders. The first time she has let her barriers down.

On hands and knees, she crawls slowly, running her hands over the surface and feeling every inch before her. She does it as if she is completely alone, her entire focus on the movement of her hands. But…surely, she is aware I am still here.

A sinking feeling starts to grow in my gut as I watch her move, and when she finally finds the edge of the bath and releases a sound like a sob mixed in with a breath of relief, that feeling in my gut only intensifies.

She dips her fingers into the water before easing back on her haunches.

When she grips the edge of her dirty tunic and pulls it over her head, revealing pink skin underneath, I hold back a groan.

Her modesty laws…

That sinking feeling reaches up into my throat as if it has claws that are gripping me from within.

I've been a fool. How did I not notice? The fact she's never looked at me except for the one time. The constant stumbling. The fact I've never seen her walk on her own—I carried her half the time and other times, she was holding hands with the other female. A ball of tension rises in my chest as I take a quiet step forward, disbelieving that my hunch may be right.

As I move, I don't make a sound. I don't even breathe. If I'm wrong and the female turns around and sees me, she will be livid. But if I am right…

I walk along the edge of the bath, watching her as she strips her upper undergarment off. A lump promptly bounces into my throat much like the two large mounds on her chest that bob as she lifts her arms. Their center is a deeper hue than the surrounding skin and I cannot pull my eyes away from them, even as they pebble with the brush of cool air. My fangs lengthen and I almost nick myself with how hard I'm clenching my teeth.

Those soft-looking mounds bounce as the human rises to her feet and strips off her trou, revealing light-colored undergarments. She strips those off too and suddenly she is standing there, completely bare before me.

Deep in my groin, something stirs and my cock awakens. I force the feeling down, try to push it away, but it doesn't budge, just like the thick rod hardening in my trou.

The lifeblood freezes in my veins when the female looks up and right at me. She stares into my eyes as she sighs, and for the first time since encountering her, I see her lips shift into a ghost of a smile.

When she slowly lowers into the swirling water, eyes still on me, my cock swells so hard, it aches. Her eye contact is like a challenge. Seduction that is drawing me in. But even with her eyes on me, that sinking feeling that's swirling in my gut swallows me whole.

How could I not have realized? How had I been such a fool?

It's all clear now. It all makes sense. Though, I can admit, she's very good at hiding it. Smart, actually.

As she carefully slips into the pool, eyes still on me, I look into those brown depths. Facing her on the other side of the pool, I crouch with her, keeping her gaze, and realizing that my fears are right.

She's staring right at me…but there is no recognition in those eyes.

I wave my hands before her, just to make sure, and there is no change.

I stare at her, frozen, a thousand thoughts flicking through my mind.

This beautiful, soft little female…cannot see.

She has been through all this, and the entire time, she's had no sight? The thought of a creature experiencing such a thing blind almost makes a comforting purr develop in my chest.

I must have made *some* sound because the female freezes in the water, her head tilting slightly as she listens. Every beat of my life organ sounds like thunder. For what feels like ages, she remains frozen, listening.

When she finally goes back to washing herself, I stand silently. Reaching for the clean set of tunics on my side of the pool, I take them with me and set them close to the human's discarded clothes. With one last glance, I creep from the room, careful to not let the door make a sound as I exit.

I realize now why the fates kept leading me here. If I had not come, the Zedeshi would have discarded this female already, even before he realized she was different. Whether he would have kept her when he found out her secret is a question I'd rather not answer. Zedeshi like to have their females as helpless as possible.

If anything, her lack of sight will make her more desirable to him. And that is something I will not permit.

7

Rissa

I might've stayed longer in the bath than I intended.

Maybe because the feel of the water on my skin is like heaven…or maybe because I dread what will happen when I finish cleaning myself.

As I climb out of the water, dreading what's to come next, my fingers brush over something at the side of the pool.

I freeze before reaching for it and my fingers brush over fibers that I know I haven't touched before. The material is crisp. Clean. *These aren't my clothes*. And I don't remember these being here before I went into the water. I'd made sure to feel along the pool's edge.

Panic sets off through me like a warning bell as my other hand taps frantically at the edge of the pool. It takes me a moment before my hand closes over my filthy garments and I release a breath. Maybe I'd reoriented myself and misjudged where I'd left my clothes? Maybe these clean clothes had been here all along?

I choose to believe that because any other reality is concerning. Pulling myself up from the pool, I smile, eager to get dressed in something that doesn't stink. But as my fingers move over the tunic and I bring it to my nose to smell if it really is clean, a new thought enters my mind, causing me to pause.

These are garments I've no familiarity with. I know my clothes inside out. I'd customized them just for me. On complex garments, I have little buttons placed at specific parts so I know which way is up, which way is inside out. But these clothes are new.

Gripping the clean tunic between my fingers, I wonder if I can wear it without looking suspicious. I don't have a choice but to wear it. Putting on my old clothes is out of the question.

I could call the Uulvian, no, the *Atari*...I could call him to help me, but the thought only makes me blush. Turns out I'm not messed up in the head to have been romanticizing him.

While in the water, I had time to think, and I believe him. He knew too much information about how I came to be here. And he's also my only hope. I either believe him or reject his help and end up with that cruel Zedeshi scum.

That whole thing about New Earth trying to ship us off on some bridal program doesn't surprise me. The "luxury cruise" had come out of the blue. An initiative from the newly elected World President, they'd said. I should have known better than to sign up for it. I should have stayed my ass at home.

All my life, my own species has treated me as an afterthought. Why would they suddenly care about the disadvantaged like me?

I only feel stupid that it's taken so many near-death experiences for the truth to finally hit me like a brick.

Shaking myself, I try to get as much water off me as possible. Feeling around doesn't reveal any towels, so I air dry as well as I can. And then I tackle the tunic.

It feels like a simple thing that would probably fall to my knees once it's over my shoulders. A modest little dress. Not what I'd imagined the Zedeshi would provide. Thought of him only makes me shudder, and, after about seven tries to put on the tunic, I finally succeed.

My shoes are stiff, the soft outer fabric hardened by the blood that soaked into it, and I'm not sure I want to wear them again. But I hold my breath and fight past the desire not to. I don't have any other footwear...and I don't know what happens next.

From what it sounds like, the Atari is up against everyone in this city. The odds are against us and I might have to run. I take a deep breath, trying to steady myself. I might have to *fight*.

Steeling myself, I feel around slowly, my hands moving through air as I try to find my way to the door. I bump into something that sounds hollow and metallic as it falls to the floor, causing a loud clanging noise.

I freeze just as the door flies open so hard it hits the other side of the wall.

I fix my posture, standing straight as I avert my gaze.

"Are you alright?" That deep timbre of the Atari floods right through and over me. It is like a warm beckoning that makes me want to go closer to him, to feel the vibration against his chest, to run my fingers across his skin.

I clear my throat, *and* my thoughts. "Y-yes. I didn't see that...that um..."

Shit. I have to be careful with my words.

"The *zichrin*..." he supplies and I jump on to that.

"Yes. The, the uh, the *zichrin*." Whatever that is.

He seems to accept it.

"Come," he says. "The Zedeshi waits."

I swallow hard. Moment of truth. I have to walk directly to him. Slight fear goes through my bones, but the few times he's spoken, I'd honed in to exactly where he's standing.

"Where is he?" If he continues to speak, I can listen and let his voice guide me directly to him. I'm confident.

"In his chambers." I begin walking as soon as he speaks and when his words end in a low growl (...or purr...he purred?) I stop walking. I can almost feel his heat in front of me, another thing beckoning me to touch him once more.

I frown at my thoughts and try to think of something else to ask that will allow me to get an idea of where I am and what I should do next.

"I want to say thank you...for all you've done." I keep my voice low.

"I have done nothing yet, human. Things are about to get much more difficult."

I swallow hard at his words and nod. "Rissa," I say.

I sense that he shifts and I take another step forward, looking off in the direction that he's not.

"I don't understand," he finally says. When my shoulder touches lightly against the side of the wall, I lift my hand to touch it.

"Rissa," I reply. "My name is Clarissa, Rissa for short."

He doesn't reply for a few moments. "Do you know anything about my people?"

It's a strange question to ask but I answer him anyway, as long as it keeps him talking.

"No. Nothing."

"Nothing of our kingdom... Our king?" He pauses. "The prince?"

I shake my head. "No. Nothing. Should I?"

I wish I could see the man this voice belongs to. Wish I could see his expression because his voice almost sounds relieved when he speaks next.

"My name is Da'red. But do not speak it while we are in this place."

I nod again, surprising myself at how easily I've put my trust in this male.

"This way," he suddenly says, and I hesitate.

I do the only thing I can think of doing. I turn and reach for him. Seconds later, I'm gripping on to smooth muscle. Heat radiates right through the contact and my mouth falls open in a gasp.

Da'red grunts before clearing his throat and begins moving, me at his side, my hold on his arm making little shivers go through my frame.

We walk in silence, me too afraid to say anything lest my words be heard by someone else, and him silent as a rock. When the sickly sweet scent begins to permeate my nostrils again, my steps falter.

Da'red's hand closes over mine and he pats it for a moment in comfort before flinging his hand away as if my skin burned him.

"Ahh, I took your word, Uulvian...and you have delivered." The Zedeshi's voice rings out, making goosebumps rise on my arms.

Da'red doesn't respond, but he stops walking and I come up at his side.

"You must have scrubbed the human well for her to shine like this." I can tell the Zedeshi moves closer to us as he speaks because his voice gets incrementally louder. Standing still beside the Atari, I refuse to show any fear, so I lift my chin but keep my gaze low.

"She is ready for you now, your grace." Da'red says. There's a low vibration. The same kind I heard before. Like insect parts rubbing together and I turn my head slightly in that direction. The other henchmen, they're still here? Shit. "I trust you have now seen that my words are true."

I swallow hard as Da'red speaks and force into my mind that he is on my side. This is all an act. An act I'm a part of. All I have to do is continue pretending. Just continue, until I am safe.

The Zedeshi hums something in his throat. Probably approval. He is now so close that I feel the slight brush of his robes against my skin.

"She is a docile female," Da'red says. "She will not try to escape."

Why do I get the sense those words were for me?

The Zedeshi laughs. "Escape? If she tries she will die. I made sure of that before I purchased her."

Under my palm, Da'red's bicep stiffens.

"The tracker?" he asks.

The Zedeshi stops circling us for a moment, the brush of his robes stilling against my skin. I fight the urge to shrug them off me.

"You know of the tracker?"

Da'red jerks as if he shrugs. "The Parsno mentioned it."

There's a moment where I think the Zedeshi won't continue that line of conversation, but he completes the circle around us, his voice sounding again in front of me.

"There's a device burrowing into your belly even as we speak," he says, right in front of my face. I stop inhaling at the first hint of something distasteful on his breath. Like rotten cabbage mixed in with whiskey. "I've decided to keep you," he declares. "Run from me, and with one press of this button, you will die."

Da'red stiffens some more. "That's all?" he asks.

I can tell the Zedeshi leans away from me when I breathe again and that disgusting scent isn't so close.

"What do you mean?" the Zedeshi asks.

"That device in your hand is all that keeps the females from running?"

"It is *miroshi* tech. Small but reliable. This control device keeps all my servants in line."

Da'red seems to release a breath. "So that is why you have no guards," he says. "You control everyone…everything, yourself."

The Zedeshi laughs again. "You wish to join my guard? Ah, that explains your interest to serve me. A job like this would do well for an Uulvian who is in trouble for credits."

"That's true—" As he speaks, Da'red turns to me and gently takes my hand off his arm. My heart thumps, panic gripping me as I hold on to his hand. I don't mean to do it, but my eyes widen on him, communicating, even though I can't see him, that I don't want him to let me go.

I'm lost. Fucking lost in a sea of darkness and unsurety and instability here. I didn't realize how much I'd leaned on him for the entire walk to this throne room, but I suddenly don't want him to let me go.

He holds my hand and leads me to a wall, pressing my hand against it.

"Wait here," he whispers.

*What*? I don't even get to ask the question before he' s gone again.

"—but I'm not here for a job," Da'red finishes what he was saying. My heart swells a thousand times in panic. He's doing it *now*? Making a move *now*? *Here*?

I'm not ready. I don't know the layout of this place. I don't know where the exits are. If I have to run I'll be like a headless chicken!

I can hear the slight confusion in the Zedeshi's voice. It cuts through the panic that's quickly overtaking me as I try desperately to get a sense of the room before Da'red makes his move.

"What do you mean, Uulvian?" the Zedeshi says. "What are you here for then?"

"*That.*"

I wish I could get a sense of what Da'red gestures to, or what he's talking about.

"This?" the Zedeshi says. "My tracker control? Why would an Uulvian want this?"

Da'red laughs. I swear he does. No way someone else in this room has a deep flowing timbre like his that demands such respect. His laughter seems to make the air chill and I swear everyone in the room stops breathing.

"I am no Uulvian."

"I told you!" one of the other henchmen hisses in a harsh whisper.

"I see," the Zedeshi says.

His voice betrays nothing. Not even slight fear, and I wonder if Da'red is really on my side or if he's just insane. We're outnumbered. Alone. And there are at least three enemies in this room alone. He surely won't be able to fight them all off and I can't see for shit.

"If you are no Uulvian," the Zedeshi says, "then what are you?"

There's a moment where no one says anything and I wish they would speak so I'd know what's going on. I gulp, gripping the wall so hard, I hurt my flesh.

"What are you *doing*?" the Zedeshi asks. "What are you taking out of your eyes?" There's another moment of silence and then a gasp.

"Your eyes," the Zedeshi says, and it's at that moment that I hear some fear seep into his voice. I almost feel it. Almost as if the air changes. Whatever Da'red just did, turned the tables. "Your eyes, they are arzentus…like the Atari."

The last word is almost a whisper before I hear a curse, a shuffling of movement, and then a male guttural scream.

"Atari, yes." Da'red says, his voice cool as if there's not someone gasping for breath as if they're choking on their own saliva. "And you just messed with one of our brides."

There is a loud crack, metal twisting, before something is tossed in my direction. It lands on the floor near my feet, sliding the rest of the way till it touches the tip of my shoes.

Still holding on to the wall, I reach for the item and my fingers brush over a metal device with sharp edges where it's been bent so much it's broken in two.

As the male scream continues then suddenly stops, I hear other sounds. Tousling and grunts.

My fear almost reaches a new height. If he is hurt…

When there's a shrill sound from one of the henchmen, I know Da'red might be in trouble. And I feel useless just standing here, doing nothing. He's come all this way to find me, to get me to safety. He wouldn't be risking his life right now with these degenerates if it wasn't for me.

Waiting is like agony. And the sounds. They make my imagination go wild and I imagine the worst. When there's a loud crack, like plywood breaking, I think someone might have hit him over the back with a board. But the hiss that comes next makes it clear it's one of the insect men that's taken damage.

There's a shrill sound, probably from the one that's hurt, or maybe from the other, and that sound gets louder. I don't have time to react before I feel cold, hard hands close over my own. My heart nearly lurches from my chest.

These aren't Da'red's hands. And if it isn't Da'red, then it's my enemy.

"*You*," the henchman growls, and I do the only thing that comes to my mind.

I beat the shit out of him.

8

Da'red

I turn just in time to see the second Parsno charge for Rissa. A roar rumbles from my chest, echoing in the large chambers as I go after him. But even though the little female cannot see, she realizes that it's an enemy that has his claws on her. And she does the most unexpected thing.

Instead of screaming and trying to escape, she twists the broken controller in her hand and uses the sharp end to stab the Parsno repeatedly. One of her blows manages to go deep enough to draw the thick green fluid that's his lifeblood, and he screeches in unbridled rage.

Lifting one claw and about to strike her away from him, he roars. But I'm already there. I recognize him as the one who'd told me not to get "attached"…that Rissa's warm slit belonged to the scum that's the Zedeshi.

The thought only makes my gaze burn with rage, fury consuming me.

Gripping him before he can land his blow, I pull him away from my female and slam him into the floor.

"You cursed Atari!" he screams. "What are you even doing so far away from your world!"

My nostrils flare. "Even at death's door, you cannot hold your tongue."

He sneers. "You want me to beg you for forgiveness?"

I can only see red as I stare down at him.

"No," I growl. "Not me." I pull his head toward me, glaring into his eyes. "The life spirits of all the females you defiled."

And he was going to do it to Rissa too. If I had not been here, he would have had his way with all these vulnerable females.

Slamming his head back into the floor hard enough for a fissure to spread across the hard surface, I grip his maw with both hands. He struggles against my arms, not able to throw me off as I force his jaw open. He gurgles something, but I don't care to hear his final words. All I can hear are those despicable things he'd said before. All I can see is the image of him defiling the soft female behind me.

Something more than hours of training in the barracks is flowing through my veins, giving me strength I never knew I had, and in one movement, I pull his jaws apart, ripping the muscle that keeps his maw together and dislodging it. He gurgles, choking on his tongue before I grip his neck and twist.

There's a sickening crack before his body goes limp.

"D-Da'red?... Oh my God. Oh my God. Please don't be dead." A soft voice seems to pull me from a deep dark hole and I glance over my shoulder at Rissa. Tremors rack through her frame that she can't seem to control. Still gripping the broken device in her hand, her chest heaves as she clings to the column I'd left her standing beside.

"Please don't be dead. Please don't be dead. Please don't be dead." Her lips move, repeating the words, but she appears to be unharmed. It takes great effort to calm my breathing, to quell my rage. I cannot go to her like this. I will scare her.

Qef me.

I'm scaring myself.

I turn my gaze back to the Parsno I just killed. His death was unnecessarily brutal. That is...unlike me. I've killed many beings. Death is a consequence of war, and Atar has been fighting alongside its allies for many revolutions. But never had I reveled in taking a life, snuffing it out from existence, as I did just now.

Something overtook me that made me lose control…and I have no idea what it was.

"Da'red?" Rissa calls my name again, her voice so soft, almost like a whisper, and something inside me spasms and swells. "He's dead…" she whispers, her chest heaving even harder as her chin tilts downward, her eyes wide. Gripping the broken control device in her hand, she squeezes it so tight I fear she's going to cut herself with the sharp end. "He's dead, and it's my fault." Disbelief registers across her expressive face.

Her sorrow finally pulls me from the far reaches where my mind had gone, and I shake myself before rising to my feet and turning toward her. She stiffens at the sound of my movement, her hands going up in a defensive stance as she readies the broken controller in her hand. I ignore it as I step up to her and pull her into me. I don't even flinch when she reacts at the invasion and slams her weapon into me, causing it to dig into my skin.

Rissa jerks, a shriek on her lips. I think she will fight me for a moment, shock and fear overtaking her. But the moment her body presses into mine fully, she seems to realize it is *me* and not a foe.

And she does the strangest thing.

Rissa inhales deeply before burying her face into my chest.

"You're *alive*?"

I grunt. "I've only just met you, little bloom. I am disappointed you believe I would leave you in this dreadful place. I haven't the chance to get to know you yet."

She releases a slight breath through her nose, her soft body rising and falling against mine.

"I thought…" She shakes her head, releasing her weapon. It clangs as it falls to the floor and those delicate fingers of hers grip me tight. I freeze, almost too scared to move as a sense of warmth rises within me, filling me completely with that simple touch. It feels like we are sharing something precious. Something discreet. Like a wall I didn't know existed between us is falling and I've known this female for eons. Even after we leave this place, I will remember this moment for ages to come. Remember how her small fingers dig into my leathers as her face presses into me. How her body heaves with unrestrained emotion. How she leans into me as if I am her strength.

I…like this.

Ripping that Parsno apart was worth this reward.

"If you'd died…" she whispers.

I shrug. I'd learned a long time ago not to fear death. "My only thought was destroying that cursed device that held you trapped in the Zedeshi's claws."

She nods as she chokes on a sob she tries to hold back, and I realize that despite the strength she'd displayed, she was afraid. *Terrified*.

And I made her worry.

If I'd died, she believes she would've been stuck here, despite my efforts.

"Do not worry. Even if something happened to me here, my cruiser has a tracer. Qhenno, my helmsman, would have known where to look. You would have been found, one way or the other. He would have come for you." Which reminds me. I need to update him so he can send message to Atar.

Rissa pauses and eases off me, wiping her tears away with one hand. "I don't care about that." She shakes her head. "Well, I do. I want to leave this place. But I also didn't want you to die…because you don't deserve it. *They* did." She gestures off to the side with her hand. "But *you* don't. You're not…you're not like them. You sacrificed yourself to free all of us. Since I was taken, I've found no kindness in the cosmos. You…you're the first person to have shown me any grace in this nightmare. You're…*different*. "

I huff a short laugh through my nose. If only she knew how different. When she sniffles once more, burying her face into my chest, that warmth within me grows even further.

She's so vulnerable with me right now. It only makes me want to shield her and keep her safe. And with that thought comes another.

She might be open to me now, but when she finds out who I am, she will behave differently. No one reacts the same when they find out my lineage.

Soft whispers at the far end of the room suddenly draw my attention and I look toward the sound. Females, captives all of them, peek from behind the pillars. They must have run and hid when the fighting began.

One, the velushan-kadrian hybrid, steps forward, her gaze on the lifeless body of the Zedeshi. She approaches and spits on him, giving him a kick for good measure, her tail swishing right round her to slice him across the midsection.

"Zedeshi filth," she says, before her gaze finds me and Rissa. She smiles slightly, her reptilian eyes zoning in on us with interest.

"Thank you, brave warrior," she says. "I suppose we are all lucky this fool decided to purchase your mate. Otherwise, we would still be trapped under his rule. We are all truly grateful."

I give her a slight nod and she glances toward the other females that have come out of their hiding spots. For a second, I wonder why I don't correct her that Rissa isn't my mate. For a male who has side-stepped many forced matings, the thought surprisingly does not offend.

Reaching into the side of my trou, I take out my communicator and fit it back onto my arm. I'd removed it for this mission in an effort to look less suspicious, just as I'd left my cruiser on the other side of the station, as well as the *quud* that travels with me in it. Both would have blown my cover immediately.

Activating the communicator now, I first initiate contact with my mothership, the *Zarzenius*. Qhenno picks up the communication imme-diately.

"You found her," he says, his voice immediately ringing from the device and echoing through the hall. Looking up, I realize the other females have come closer. In the short time since their master's death, news must have spread because more and more of them seem to be coming out of the walls.

"How did you know?"

"I've been tracking your cruiser. You keep returning to the same station. Aqnar believed it must be the fates leading you there."

"Did he really find her?" The voice of Qhenno's mate is so similar to Rissa's that my brows rise. It's the first time I've heard her speak and by my side, Rissa's head snaps up.

"Trudy?" she whispers.

"Oh my God! Rissa! Is that really you?!"

Rissa's chest heaves with a swell of emotions. "It's me. Where are you? I can't believe I'm even hearing your voice."

The female on the other end of the line releases what sounds like a breath of relief. "I'm safe. Don't worry, you'll see me soon."

Rissa gulps, nodding her head as her fingers tighten on my leathers. Whether she knows she's doing it or not, she's clung on to me as if I'm a lifeline. And, for the life of me, I don't have to urge to pry her fingers away.

I can sense she wants to speak with the other human a little longer, but that will have to wait. We need to leave this place quickly before the Zedeshi's allies arrive. If he has any, that is. His species is not only cruel, but selfish. I wouldn't be surprised if any Zedeshi that arrive only come to take this one's throne and captives for his own.

"Rissa is with many other females that need rescue."

Qhenno releases a breath of relief before he pauses. "More females? Human?"

My gaze flicks over them all. "No."

He pauses again. I know what he's thinking. Of the three males that make up my crew, he was the one who wished the most for a mate. His need went past the urge for procreation. It was almost an obsession. I never discovered why. But Qhenno is no anomaly.

Many other like him live on Atar. Males who would give everything to find a mate for their own. And all of these females could form potential matehoods with our brothers waiting on Atar.

"That's wonderful news," he says, his caution almost dripping through the communicator as if he's worried he'll scare the females with his voice. "I see now why you had me send a transport ship to wait in orbit. You knew there would be females to extract."

"Lucky guess."

Qhenno releases a soft laugh through his nose. "As for you...."

"I have my cruiser."

"No. I mean, as for your *wellbeing*... I know you have the *quud*, but if your father found out you've been traveling without the *Zarzenius*—"

*"He won't."* I cut him off, glancing at Rissa. Thank the gods it doesn't appear she's understood any of those keywords Qhenno just dropped. I don't mind the other females knowing exactly who I am. As a matter of fact, I don't care. But Rissa...she thinks I'm normal...has treated me as such. I don't want that to end. Not just yet. I don't dare to dissect why that is. My mission is to get her from this nightmare and back to Atar.

That's all.

"Initiate the transport ship's descent. Send it to my present coordinates. These females need extraction immediately."

"Aye," he replies.

The line clicks off and I'm left, for a moment, with only the uneasy thought that my life is about to go back to normal the moment I leave this place.

And I hate that normal.

Still holding Rissa against me, I turn to face the females slowly gathering around us.

"You are free now. The Zedeshi no longer has control over you," I tell them. "A transport will shortly arrive with enough space to take you all to Atar, my homeworld. There we will remove the tracking device the Zedeshi implanted within you. Afterward, you are all welcome to stay on Atar for as long as you like. Our refugee services will attend to you and provide you with all that you need." When their gazes fill with hope, some of their eyes shining, I know this day has been a more than successful one.

"As princess of Kadria, I would like to return to my tribe," the velushan-kadrian says. "I have a duty to my people," she pauses and a knowing look comes into her gaze. "As I am sure you understand."

My brows furrow only slightly, but I dip my head in a nod, acknowledging her words. It's clear she knows my true identity, probably as a result of Qhenno's hints. Not everyone travels with a quud and even though she hasn't seen mine, mention of the beast alone draws attention. I appreciate her not disclosing her conclusion to everyone else.

Giving the other females a slight nod, I lead Rissa over to one of the steps below up to the dais.

"Sit here."

Reaching out with her hand, I see uncertainty flash across her eyes for a moment but I lower myself with her till she touches the step. Realization dawns on her features and she smiles before bracing on the step with one hand and then sitting.

Once again, I am awed by her will and trust in me.

"Is it really over?" she whispers.

I can't stop the small smile that tugs at my lips. "Yes, little flower. You are safe now."

But the joy and hope that is reflected on the other females' faces is hardly reflected on Rissa's. Her expression is tight. Guarded. As if she expects more misfortune to come. She won't be eased until I have removed her completely from this nightmare.

"Wait here," I resist the urge to brush the back of my hand against her rosy cheeks. "I must check whether there are any captives locked away in this place."

She nods immediately. "Yes. You must. Go. I will keep watch here."

A small smile tugs on my lips as her cheeks grow even rosier. She's still pretending. For her own survival, it must come naturally to her. I hesitate, not willing to walk away just yet. I want to tell her she doesn't have to pretend around me. That I know her secret. That she can let me take the weight from her shoulders.

But those are probably words I'd like to hear myself.

As Rissa sits up straighter, her unseeing eyes move with what's now obviously practiced precision.

Leaning a little closer, I watch as the corners of her nostrils flare and the movement of her eyes suddenly stop dead center, almost as if she is looking right at me.

"I thought you said you were leaving…"

For a moment, I wonder if I was wrong. Maybe her sight is only impaired. I hesitate a little longer before standing straight. I will find out later. After all, I have all the time on our trip back to Atar to find out why I was so drawn to this place. Drawn to *her*.

Shaking my head, I clear my thoughts. "If you become distressed, scream. I will hear you." My brows furrow. I should take her with me. Just the thought of leaving her in this chamber while I scout the palace for threats is now making me uneasy. "No. You should come with me."

Rissa...*giggles*.

It's a soft, quick sound. One that catches me so off guard that I can only stand and stare at her.

I want to hear it again. I want to hear her joy.

"I'll be fine here." She smiles. "Just like the other females. You've given us the courage to protect ourselves."

"Have I?" Why do I even ask? I already know the answer. But I want to hear her speak. I want to hear her voice once more.

"You have." She smiles, her eyes dipping till her lashes fan over her cheeks. "You've given us something we didn't know we'd lost. At least...something *I* didn't know I'd lost."

Her voice dips at that, going to almost a whisper, and my ears perk.

"And what's that, little bloom?"

"Hope."

# 9

Da'red

Activating the communicator on my arm, I walk from the Zedeshi's home out into the open with the human in my arms. The world outside is a sea of orange as the star the station orbits falls across the horizon.

The steady hum of the transport ship as it lifts from the ground and takes off toward the stars is all that fills the air. Checking the Zedeshi's cursed rooms for hidden females had revealed three more, all chained and on the brink of mental breakdown. None of them even resisted when I led them from their quarters.

None showed a semblance of this hope Rissa believes I've given them. Their eyes were dead. I cannot imagine the horrors they endured.

Horrors this little bloom would have endured as well.

Tucked against me, I look down at Rissa. Getting her into my arms had required making an excuse about her possible exhaustion. I am thrilled it worked, but she lies with her hands clasped together, her shoulders somewhat stiff as if she's tense. Uncomfortable.

Unsure.

It's hard to believe this is the same female that dug her fingers into my leathers and wept in my arms.

I fight the illogical sense of loss that brings.

"My cruiser should find us shortly," I whisper, not sure she is listening, but the moment I speak, her head tilts slightly in my direction, telling me that she'd heard.

Her lips move, going inwards for just a moment before plumping out again and I watch her do the movement one more time.

I could not be staring at her like this if she was aware of it, and I take the liberty. It's the first time we've had alone since I found her in that dungeon, and with the muck and grime washed off, the star's low light casts a warm glow over her pink skin.

Rissa is utterly beautiful.

I have the urge to run my finger over her soft cheeks, moving them slowly down over her pretty lips.

"You didn't want me to go on the transport ship with the others," she says. "Why?"

A question I have no answer for, because the simple truth is a selfish one. I just...*didn't want to.*

I like her company.

But I cannot tell her that. Because it is inappropriate.

I should have placed her on that transport with the other females. I've completed my task. I have rescued her. This...urge to keep her with me for just a bit longer is uncharacteristic. Puzzling even.

"My cruiser holds two passengers and is faster than the transport ship." Half-truth, but truth enough. "I've engaged the autopilot. It will be here soon."

Her lips move once more, thinning and plumping as she brings them between her teeth before releasing them again. Eyes downcast, she's thinking about something.

"Do you trust me?"

Rissa releases a slow breath. "Can't you tell?"

I watch her face for cues, anything to tell me what she's thinking, but I can't decipher it.

"I don't go around letting tall, muscular men carry me everywhere, you know." She suddenly smiles and I'm enraptured by it. "I'll let you know it's a privilege."

A laugh bubbles up through my throat, and I grunt, humor stretching my lips. The action almost feels alien and I freeze. When was the last time I laughed?

Genuinely?

"So…you were telling the truth…" she whispers, eyes still downcast, her lids low. "You're taking me back to your planet. New Earth really tried to get rid of us."

I cringe at her choice of words. "It would be tragic to think they meant to discard you—"

"That's exactly what they meant to do." She sighs. "You don't have to soften the blow. It doesn't surprise me. I'm just sorry I was such a fool to sign up for their stupid cruise." Her breath stutters and even with her lids low, I see the water lining her eyes. "And those other women." Her breath stutters again. "They didn't deserve it. The way they died."

With utmost care I lean so the hand supporting her shoulders can reach and I brush a finger against her cheek, wiping her tears away. She startles, surprised, but allows me to wipe away her sorrow. My finger trembles as another one of those strange electric jolts goes through me at the contact, and I frown, staring at her.

Is it her tears that's causing it? Was she weeping the last time I touched her and that strange charge happened? My gaze slips to my fingertips as I stare at my skin.

"I'm sorry we didn't arrive sooner," I say, still staring at my fingertips. "It pains me that such a soft creature had to experience what you did." My voice is hoarse as I speak and I frown again. It doesn't sound like my voice at all.

For the first time, I'm startled. Clarissa huffs a laugh through her nose, her body jerking in my arms. "Soft? I am not *soft*."

My lips part as hers do, revealing a set of flat teeth as she full-on laughs. Her joy is like a drug that I suddenly need more of.

"You *are* soft. You're full of curves. You fit into my arms nicely, and when I grip you, you mold against me. You are to be treasured and wrapped in expensive soft furs. Delicate…soft…warm…" I only stop when I realize the humor has disappeared from her face, to be replaced by something else. Her cheeks grow rosy, the hue making her look even more beautiful.

"Is that why you're carrying me around? Because I'm like a pillow?"

My eyes widen, just as my cruiser zooms through a cloud and begins its landing sequence above us.

"I—" Qef. Is she happy or offended? My brows furrow again as I try to figure a way out of this mess I've put myself in. It was going so well…I got carried away. I didn't mean to go into such descriptive detail. But it was all the truth. She feels like heaven in my arms.

When Rissa chuckles, the panic swelling within me lessens. She's not upset at my words.

Taking a step toward the landing cruiser, I…smile.

I cannot remember the last time a female's banter came without her wanting something in return—a written declaration of our matehood, in most cases. It has made me wary.

Murmuring to Rissa that the cruiser is here, I walk toward the opening doors and only glance behind me one last time. The Zedeshi's palace rises from the dirt like a skeleton. I am happy to be leaving this place.

"Time to go home," I say, a heaviness rising in my chest. My excursion is over. Back to reality.

"Home?" Rissa whispers. "I have no home."

I don't know why I say it. Maybe because it feels right. So as the words tumble from my mouth, I let them go free.

"You do with me."

---

Rissa

My heart's thumping like it's forgotten how to beat properly anymore. There's a hum in the air, the sound of his cruiser, and as Da'red takes a step forward, my heartbeat picks up the pace.

Squeezing my hands together even more tightly than before, I try to calm myself. But it doesn't help that Da'red suddenly stops walking and freezes.

"Qef," he says, before there's a strange sound in the air. A combination of a deep bark and a whine, so strong the sound vibrates the air around us.

It's a beast. A fucking huge beast of some sort from the sounds of it, and I think it's right in front of us.

"What the fuck is that?" Fear seeps through my pores as my heart begins thumping even harder. At this rate, I'll go into cardiac arrest in about two minutes. "Should we run?"

There's another deep bark, like the air is squeezed through large, tense muscles before escaping through the cracks of sharp teeth, and I jerk in Da'red's arms. Why the hell isn't he running?! Is it because he's carrying me?

"Put me down. I can...I can fend for myself while you fight it." Because I can't fight it and he sure as hell won't be able to do anything with me in his arms. Our best bet is for him to have both arms free.

Da'red stands still and I can feel his muscles bunch. "Horrible plan."

Well, it's a plan! He's not doing anything!

The thing bellows again and it sounds like those extinct creatures they used to call "lions" on Old Earth, mixed in with those breeds of large dogs the elites of the Upper Levels use for guards.

Oh God.

Suddenly, Da'red turns with me, spinning so his body twists to the side and I only feel the whoosh of air as something flies by us.

Oh shit.

"Da'red!"

"Apologies, little bloom. But someone has forgotten their manners."

What the fuck is he talking about?

"Bee. *Sit.*"

My pulse is raging in my ears so hard I almost don't hear the soft whimper as something big plops down on what I assume is the ground. What the hell is happening?

Da'red sighs and takes a few steps forward before he hoists himself up and the low hum of the engine changes to a different tone.

"Welcome to my cruiser. I apologize for Bee's behavior."

"Bee?" I'm still as Da'red sets me down on what feels like a chair or some other sort of seat.

I hear him release another sigh. "That snarling thing is my *quud*, and he knows better than to go around scaring females."

What the what now?

"I'm sorry…what?"

"My quud…" Da'red says again, his voice a little farther than it was before, telling me that he's moving around the ship. I grip the seat beneath my hands, ears perked for any sound. "I'm sure I saw them when I visited your planet," he says, his voice coming nearer. "Your world president has one."

He must see the confusion on my face because I am *certainly* confused. I have no idea what it is he's talking about…

There's another whimper and Da'red releases another sigh. *"Fine,"* he says. "Bee, you can come apologize."

I freeze again, my eyes going wide. Usually, I rely on every sense I can use. Smell, touch, taste, hearing. Right now, I rely on my ears mostly, because I don't want to reach out and touch the snarling lion dog thing that's clearly hopped into the cruiser from the vibration as it bounds into the space. I can't smell it…and I am most certainly not licking it.

"Bee, this is my hu—" Da'red stops. "This is Rissa," he says. "She will be traveling with us back to Atar."

There's silence and I wish more than anything that one of them would make a sound. When Da'red's fingers close over my wrist, my whole body jerks just as I feel a brush of fur. I sputter an apology. The entire circle of warmth underneath his fingers feels like it's tingling and spreading through my arm. I try not to focus on it. There are more pressing things. Like lion bear. I'm pretty sure it's a bear now, not a dog.

It's frickin big.

"Hold your hand out like this…" Da'red guides my hand, holding it in his with a gentle touch.

He asked if I trust him. I guess this is the test of that trust.

Squinching my eyes tight, I allow him to guide my hand forward. There's only a moment's pause before my entire hand is enclosed in something warm and wet. Sharp teeth graze along my skin as a tongue wraps around my arm.

I shriek at the same time that Da'red shouts, "Bee!" and it takes me more than a few moments to realize he's still holding my hand in what must be the beast's mouth.

My hand is promptly expelled with a whimper as Da'red mutters a curse and admonitions under his breath.

"I must apologize. I don't know what's gotten into him," he says, releasing my hand slowly, just before a coarse tongue flicks over my palm. I fight not to pull my hand away, but when a cool muzzle is pressed into my palm, I suddenly have second thoughts.

"It's too much too soon, Bee." His voice is gentle, not as if he's talking to a killer beast and I freeze, allowing the creature to sniff me. When it makes a strange sort of contented whimper, my shoulders sag. Da'red guides my hand along the creature's maw and I fight my heart to calm.

The creature's fur is thick but soft. Softer than I expected. Enough for my fingers to dip into the layers as they run along its maw and upward. Its long tongue flicks out and laps at my arm again when my fingers reach higher and when something twitches underneath my palm, I startle a little. An ear?

"He doesn't feel like a bee," I whisper. Da'red chuckles. It's a rich sound. One that fills the shuttle and warms my skin.

"He's only called that because he reminds me of my friend, Bhihan."

"Your friend also likes to lick girls he's just met?"

My cheeks warm immediately. What the hell is wrong with my tongue of late?

"Only ones he likes," he responds. "So far, only one female has been able to melt his cold, unfeeling being. A human, like you. His mate."

His words surprise me enough that I forget I'm touching a strange creature. Another human has mated with his kind?

That's two now that I know of. How many more are there?

When Da'red suddenly releases my wrist, I freeze, reality returning swiftly. Hand still on the beast, I don't know what to do. The confidence I was gaining while he was holding my hand suddenly dissipates.

"I've never seen Bee take toward someone as quickly as he has taken to you," Da'red murmurs.

I almost scoff. Fingers still frozen on the animal, I'm scared to remove them lest the beast try to eat my arm again. At least it isn't moving while I'm touching it. And it's really big. I can tell with my hand just on the head alone. If I was standing, it would probably reach the center of my chest. Maybe it *is* a lion dog after all.

"I disagree. He tried to eat me."

The beast whimpers and I wonder just how intelligent it is. Can it understand Galactic Standard? Me?

Da'red chuckles again. "He was just excited. I haven't seen him for many cycles...and then, he was also intrigued by you. Obviously, I must train him better."

I don't openly agree but Da'red huffs a laugh through his nose as if he knows exactly what I'm thinking.

"We should go," he says.

The seat readjusts itself while I am on it and I feel the restraints slip over my body before snapping in place.

"Bee, take position," Da'red says from not far ahead. "Was all well while I was away?"

Something makes me smile as I listen to him talk to his animal. Almost as if they're lifelong friends. It's a very different male before me now than the one who just fought to set me free.

Bee lets out a whimper that sounds like the negative to me, but when Da'red doesn't respond, I decide I'm no expert on lion-dog talk.

"Ready, Rissa?" Da'red asks.

I nod. "Yes."

And with that the ship hums and rises.

This is it...I'm finally leaving this nightmare.

"Finally leaving this deathtrap of a station," he mutters, probably to himself. I smile, my own anticipation building.

Speaking with Da'red is…nice. I can already tell he's an honorable male and he didn't need to rescue me and almost risk his life to prove that. The few times he's made me laugh so far have already lifted a huge load off my chest.

He's like…the exact type of male girls like me who live on Lower Earth dream of.

I fidget in the seat, my eyes widening on the floor, as the thought paints pictures in my head that shouldn't be there. Spending such a long time in isolation, I'm obviously getting too attached to the first person that's shown me any kindness. And that's bad.

If I can't go back to my little apartment on the Lower Levels and I have to survive in this new world, I'm going to have to bury any soft feelings I have and suck it up. Life's about to become a thousand times harder and my little secret's bound to be discovered the moment I set foot off this ship. That alone deters any romantic thoughts that were forming in my head as dread takes their place.

As the ship evens out, I assume we're in the void when the sound of the engine peters down to a low hum.

Da'red moves from his position, little sounds he makes carrying in the small space as he moves around, and when he comes near me, I keep my gaze low.

"It will be a bit of a journey," he says. His voice travels over my skin like a smooth wave that makes me want to shiver. "You should rest."

He leans closer and that sweet cinnamon scent fills my nostrils as he reaches across the back of my seat and activates something.

The seat tilts slowly and I try to keep my features schooled as it reclines, the restraints that were holding me seated disengaging and sliding back into their brackets with a soft click.

Da'red hovers over me. Far too close. Enough for me to feel the slight brush of air that comes from his every breath and I can feel his gaze moving over my face with such an intensity that it affects the way I breathe.

Every nerve ending traveling across my epidermis feels like it's firing just from his proximity. As if his fingers are skating lightly over the surface of my skin and a breath stutters in my chest.

I'm definitely romanticizing him. Definitely turned on just by the picture of this male that I've painted in my mind.

Trouble is, I can't seem to rein in my emotions.

And when the air shifts and I'm sure he's moved away, a part of me wishes he'd return and touch me the way my body's begging him to.

But that's a result of all this trauma, right?

I'm leaning on his kindness. And I don't want it to end the moment we land on his planet.

Swallowing hard, I turn on the now reclined seat and pull my legs up to my chest.

When the large body of what can only be Bee settles at my back, the warmth from his thick fur spreading through my frame, I don't even jerk away.

Being with this Atari is comfortable. And comfort is bad.

Because no matter what, it always gets ripped away.

## 10

"Rissa?"

A deep timbre tickles my ears as my eyes flutter open.

That trickling of water that usually greets me when I wake in this cold dungeon is nowhere to be heard.

And that's because I'm not in that cold, damp place anymore.

I'm surrounded by warmth. And *weight*.

I grunt, stretching underneath the heavy fur that's on top of me, only to freeze a moment later.

"Bee insisted on keeping you safe." Da'red's voice is the best thing I've ever woken up to. It sends a shiver right through me even as it strokes across my skin. "He would not release you."

I try to stretch again only for my mind to come online and realize that two huge, furry legs are draped over me. One across my breasts and the other over my legs. This dog-bear-lion thing is spooning me.

I can feel when Da'red attempts to lift the animal's leg so I can get free, only to get a whimper from the quud that's so deep, it makes my ears hurt. The dread I expect to feel is quickly replaced by a chuckle that bubbles in my throat.

"He believes you are ours."

As soon as he says that and my eyebrows rise in surprise, Da'red makes a sound as if he clears his throat.

"We've arrived at Atar. Bee, back to your position."

That's enough to make me forget everything else and I shuffle once more, trying to rise. Luckily, the quud acquiesces and lifts its legs as it climbs off my makeshift bed.

As soon as he does, warm cinnamon fills my nostrils, signaling that Da'red's come closer. I'm not prepared for his sudden proximity and a sharp inhale rises in my nose as my hands automatically thrust forward, plastering against his hard chest.

There's a low rumble that goes through his chest at my touch. One that vibrates through my arms. But it is so sudden and so short that when the seat begins to go back into its original position and the restraints move across my body once more, I wonder if I imagined it all.

"I will take us down now. It might be a little bumpy...my cruiser went through a bit of a fight on our journey to find you."

He moves away and I force down a lump that's trying to rise in my throat. I owe so much to this male.

"How did you know where I was?"

Speaking to him now, I keep my gaze pointed at my lap, letting my voice carry in the ship. I have no clue which direction he went in.

"The aliens that hijacked our ship and killed all those women, they'd been growling about finding somewhere to stash me off where the Galactic Union wouldn't look."

"I searched over fifty stations. I searched the one you were on seven times."

"Seven?" My brows pop up and so does my head before I push my gaze back down. I hope he wasn't looking at me then. Throughout this little time we've been together, I've no doubt slipped up my act more than once. I keep forgetting this male is still a stranger and not someone I've known for years. I keep forgetting I have a secret to protect. "You searched seven times?" It doesn't make sense. *Why?*

Seconds pass before he answers. "I...don't know," he says. "Something...kept calling me back."

I'm not one to believe in superstition. The world's been far too harsh and far too real to allow me to, but I nod anyway.

The shuttle gives a marginal jerk before evening out.

"Beginning descent," Da'red says, and I nod again as I grip the edges of my seat.

It's not as bumpy as I expected it to be. Each time the shuttle jerks and I expect to be thrown about by some horrible turbulence, it evens out only moments later until it feels like we're simply floating on soft air.

"The city of Gwar. My home," Da'red's deep timbre breaks the silence and warms me immediately.

If he knew what his voice was doing to my insides, would he continue to speak to me?

I offer a ghost of a smile in case he is watching me, and then I realize I have no clue whether there's a transparent screen at my side that I can see out of...or whether he's only looking through the viewport at the front of the ship. I can't pretend to look and be amazed.

Slight panic rises within me. The last thing I want is for him to think I'm being disrespectful by keeping my gaze on my lap while he's showing me the sights of his city.

"It's mostly white. Most cities on Atar are. We have an affinity for it. And arzentus," he says. "Or gold, as you call it."

I lift my head slowly as I listen to him.

"There are winding transport tubes. The smaller ones carry walking traffic and you reach almost anywhere around the cities using them, if you want the exercise. The larger tubes are for hover vehicles. There's an underground network you can use to travel Atar in half the time it takes to do so above ground. It's a project my father worked on for years." He pauses and I blink, my heart beginning to do that thundering thing it does in my chest. "We're passing over the markets right now. Many colors sail on flags in the wind. Most refugees trade there and the Atari females love to spend their mates' credits gathering exotic items for their homes and their nests."

The shuttle swerves as he navigates.

"Before us, towers rise from ground level into the heavens. Those are where most of the refugees, females who can be mates for our kind, live."

Mates. There's that word again. But it passes through my mind without consequence. The reality of what's happening right now too much to ignore.

"And in front of us is the palace. A tall, vacant thing. Much too big for the crown family. They only have one son and he has no mate. No heir to take the throne after him and no other direct kin except his father, the king." He releases some air through his nose. "The walls of that abode are cold…lonely…lifeless…devoid of warmth."

As Da'red stops speaking, I can hardly breathe. And possibly, I hold my breath until I feel the shuttle lowering.

Fear tingles across my spine as I wait. Hoping that what I think isn't true.

Because Da'red just did something only my mother has ever done for me. Without any prompt, without a request, he just described every scene he saw with his own eyes as if he knows that mine cannot see.

As if he knows my secret.

Da'red grunts and I swear he murmurs something about going back to reality before I hear movement. Stiffening, my eyes widen as I stare in the direction of the sound, no longer hiding the fact there is no light within them.

"You know," I whisper when I sense him before me.

There's a moment of silence before I hear more movement and I feel that he's crouched before me.

"I do," he whispers.

My heart lurches. "For how long?"

"Since you were taking your bath…"

I force myself to take a deep breath. "You watched me?"

There's a little pause and I know what his answer is even before he says it. "I did…for a little while."

That lump in my throat becomes the size of a football. "You saw me naked?" I whisper.

Another pause.

"I—you were so beautiful that I stopped and then I noticed something strange. I could not leave after I witnessed you using your hands as your eyes...but I only stayed long enough to confirm my suspicions."

I gulp again, my cheeks growing warm at the fact that he'd been creeping on me. And it should make me livid. Instead, warmth pools in my center at the fact he was watching me. I have problems. Problems I will deal with when I get the chance to hammer some sense into my skull.

"But now that you know...that means..." A new fear crawls up my spine. "You will send me to the Lower Levels...won't you."

There's a slight growl and I startle when I realize it's come from him and not Bee. I startle again when the warmth of his palm suddenly cups my cheek.

"Atari are not like your Earthkin. There are no lower levels here."

My eyebrows shoot up at that, but it doesn't dispel my fears.

"Am I to be a servant? You know my secret now. You know...it will be difficult for me to survive here." I swallow hard. "But I can learn."

When he says nothing, I hurry on.

"If it's too much trouble, you can take me back to my apartment on Lower Earth. But please give me a chance first."

Shit.

I never imagined myself living on his planet, but now that the option is right here before me, I can't pull my thoughts away from it. And I can't pull my thoughts away from him either.

Ugh.

I want to scream at myself.

Am I really letting the influence of a hot man sway my decision? My future?

I swear he growls again.

"A mate," he says. "He will take care of your every need. You will not need to worry. You will not suffer. You will live the way only you decide and your mate will take care of your every desire." He pauses. "He will go wherever you wish. He will do everything to ensure you are happy."

A *mate*.

The word makes me ache.

Such a thing wasn't an option for me on New Earth. Sure, I've had two partners in my lonely existence, but they were temporary things. Never meant to be more than that. Because, on my homeworld, I am broken.

The thought only makes me ache some more.

This poor male. He has no idea. His *people* don't.

I decide to just rip the bandage off right now.

"I have been designated as unfit for any unions. I guess the New Earth World President didn't tell you Atari that. From what I know, every woman who was on that cruise was like me. From the Lower Levels and, therefore, designated as unfit even before we reached puberty. There's an implant inside me that proves that fact. I'm not allowed to procreate. So if it's children you Atari want, I'm afraid you got a bad batch." I force away the wry, sour laugh that threatens to bubble to my lips to soften the blow of my words. "We can't be mates. We are banned from doing so."

"Why is that?" Something's changed in his voice and I wish I could see his face, his expression. No. I wish I could *feel* it. I wish I could run my fingers over his skin and paint a picture in my mind.

"Because," I smile but there is no mirth in my voice. "Because, as you have discovered, I am broken. I cannot *see*, Da'red."

I point to my eyes and a warm fist closes around my wrist, gentle enough that I don't feel any pain.

"Broken?" he asks. "I have already judged…and you are perfect."

I blink. What?

"I—" I don't know what to say. I can't even rely on the idea that he doesn't know my secret and he's being naive. But he's seen *me* now. Everything. Literally.

"Let me tell you this," he says. "I will personally smite any male who comes to bond with you and makes your lack of sight an issue." His words make my eyes widen, tears that won't fall finding its way in them. "Though, there is little chance that will be a problem. As soon as you are entered into the bridal register, you will have males flocking at your door, desperate for a chance for *any* of your attention."

He says the last sentence with a growl, as if the thought displeases him and I take that moment to do what I have been yearning to do from the first time his warm cinnamon scent wafted into my nostrils.

I lift my hands and move them to where I think his face is. He stills, not moving, his hold on my wrist tightening a little and when my fingers make contact with his skin, he inhales deeply.

So smooth, silky smooth, his skin feels like heaven underneath my fingers. I move them over his forehead, his brows, down to the slant of his eyes. I run them over his straight nose and down to the plump limps perched underneath.

My heart picks up the pace as I go lower. His chin is strong, and so is his jaw. I move up a little, taking in the sense of his high cheekbones, my own cheeks warming as his face is painted in my head.

He is gorgeous. I expected a nice face to go with the voice, but this…what's underneath my fingers right now is certainly not what I'd imagined. His feels like the type of face belonging to someone from the Upper Levels. Someone strong and powerful with good looks that make women fall to their knees. I try to pull my hands away but he grabs hold of my other wrist and keeps them there.

For a moment, he just presses my hands against his skin and my heart picks up the pace, little strings of electricity flying between me. *Us*. It feels like there's a web of tension slowly winding around him and me.

But surely, that's just in my mind. I already berated myself about this. About developing feelings for the first person that shows me kindness.

"Feel here," he says, his voice deep and octaves lower than it usually is. "Be gentle. I do not wish for you to harm yourself."

My eyes widen slightly as he guides my fingers down to his lips and they open. Using one of my hands, he guides those fingers to the side of his mouth. At first, I don't know what he's showing me, and then I feel it.

They descend from his canines in sharp, hard points.

"You have fangs?" I whisper.

"Aye," he says. "For biting you with."

He makes a sound at those words and pulls my hands away from his mouth.

"For biting me?"

There's another sound he makes in his throat. A groan? A purr? I can't tell for he suddenly pulls away.

"Why would you bite me?"

There's another sound. Almost like a whimper as he takes a deep breath.

"Forget I said that, sweet flower. We must go now. They await."

I blink.

Everything's suddenly happening too fast.

"They?"

———

Da'red

Gods of Atar be with me. It's all clear now.

For someone who studied with the best tutors Atar could provide, I am woefully brainless.

I stare at Rissa wide-eyed as I watch confusion, fear, anticipation, and worry flick across her face.

I want to bite her. *Mark* her. *Claim her as mine.*

Qef.

It's all clear now. The fact I was drawn to that station seven times. *Seven* times. The fates knew all along and had led me there for a reason. For me to find and rescue my mate.

Clarissa of New Earth is mine and *I have no idea if she will have me.*

My fingers itch with the need to have her hands on my skin again. So soft...I want her to touch me everywhere.

Movement in the corner of my eye catches my attention and I run a hand through my hair. My people, workers, attendants who live in the palace, are waiting patiently outside my shuttle to unload it. I cringe at the thought, even as Bee pushes his muzzle into my back, impatient to get out of the cramped confines of the vessel.

Even he's taken to Rissa, sleeping with her in much the same way as he does with me. As if he knew she was mine from the start.

Qef. Me.

I haven't even told her who I really am, much less to let her know that I will, in fact, *not* be putting her name in the bridal register *because she is mine.* The thought of any other male even trying to get her affection makes the skin at the back of my neck tighten with displeasure.

More movement outside the cruiser and I know the attendants are getting restless, wondering what's happening and if I am, indeed, alright. They'd hustled to the cruiser the moment it landed and have been waiting since.

Groaning, I run my hand through my hair once more before turning to the door and releasing a breath. Rissa's gaze finds me immediately, and I swallow hard as I look into those eyes. They may not be able to see me, but they are so soft and expressive. I wonder just how long she has been without sight.

Does she know just how beautiful she is?

Opening the door, I'm not surprised when the first thing I hear from the attendants is a loud, collective gasp. I still appear as an Uulvian, my skin marred by the dye I'd rubbed all over it.

"Master—"

I don't even have to glare at the one who speaks. Perthru, one of my most trusted friends and the attendant who basically raised me, promptly frowns as she steps forward.

"You won't be able to stay with the senior attendants if you can't remember one simple thing," she says to the new attendant. "When in his service, the prince prefers to be called by his name."

Perthru turns to me then, her gaze leveling with mine. "I have told the prince many times that playing in mud pits and wallowing with scum in the outer reaches will never change who he is, but his skull is thick and he does not listen."

I can't stop the smile that spreads my lips, even as the other attendants gasp, glancing at each other at Perthru's harsh words.

Little do they know, she's being nice.

"Good to see you again, Perthru."

Her eyes narrow slightly. Not a hair out of place, she stands tall and strong, belying her actual age.

"The pleasure is not mine," she replied. "Usually, your presence causes some ruckus in the palace and I have only just settled your father for the day." She gestures to me. "And here you come looking like an Uulvian. The exact species that couldn't choose a side and started the war between us and the Gaizon." She frowns. "*Where* have you been? Your father has been worried to the point of almost sending himself into the medic's chambers for good."

I shrug. My father wasn't worried about my wellbeing. Perthru knows that, even though she refuses to say it. He was worried about the crown.

"I was searching for someone." *My mate.* Even the thought sends warmth through me.

"They had better be someone special to have you traveling without your guards to the outer reaches." Perthru's frown increases and I groan. Qeffing Qhenno. He told them I was alone.

"Well…? Did you find them?"

For a moment, two different emotions crash through me at once.

One: I have to protect Rissa. She's new to this world and she does not know who I am. Well, she probably does now, with Perthru's loud declaration of my station.

Two: I want to spend more time with her. Ease her into this. Not throw her into the chaos that is my life at the palace.

"She—" I begin, just as Bee loses patience and bounds from the ship, crashing into the nearest attendant who barely manages to remain on his feet.

Perthru shakes her head. "I see you've been teaching that quud your version of manners."

Before I can reply, she brushes past me. For a female that could be my mor's mor, she's still of good health. Strong and fit. She freezes the moment she sees Rissa, her eyes widening in her uncrinkled face.

"You brought a *female*?" She turns to me. "Is she a mate for one of your guards?"

I bristle at that, a soft growl escaping my lips before I can stop myself and Perthru's eyes narrow.

"Well, she could certainly not be a mate for *you*."

Surprise makes my mouth fall open. "What? Why not?"

"She has no mark and you're not trying to fight us away so you can rut her." My eyes widen at her words, darting to Rissa for a moment. But thankfully, all I see is confusion on her face. "Gods of Atar know I have tried to hammer some decorum into you," Perthru continues, despite my glare for her to stop speaking. "But you are a wild thing. Just like your mor was." She says the last words softly, a smile threatening to soften the thin line of her lips as her eyes warm.

With a huff, Perthru brandishes a wide smile. "Apologies, my dear. Welcome to Atar. I am sorry you have had the displeasure of extended time with our surly prince."

"Prince?" Rissa whispers and my heart sinks. When Perthru shoots me a glare, it sinks even further.

"Ah, I see, he didn't tell you. Da'red is the crown prince of Atar. He is next in line to the throne and should not have been off on his own doing *missions*." She frowns in my direction. "However, I am very happy that he found you. You are a beauty to behold. I am very sure you will find many males here who will wish for your matehood."

I fight the urge to snarl at Perthru and instead, rub the sensitive skin at the back of my neck. It's heated, growing warmer by the minute.

"I..." Rissa begins. Her gaze searches the floor at her feet, more in confusion than because of anything else.

I move over to her, the urge to touch her strong, but I manage to keep my hands to myself.

"A prince?" she whispers.

"I..." What can I say? That I lied to her for my own selfish reasons? "Yes, that is my station. Prince Da'red of Atar."

Even saying the title makes me want to groan.

When has it ever brought me favor that I wish for? Never. It has taken more from me than it has ever given. And now, a new fear sparks up my spine as I stare at Rissa.

Will it take her away from me too?

"I hope you can forgive me for that." I search Rissa's lowered gaze, hoping with all hope that I don't see anger or disgust there. But all I see is a twinge of sadness floating among the many other emotions that float in her eyes.

Rissa nods, her movements jerky, and I know I have already been a bad host. Reaching for her, she startles only a little when I wrap my arms around her and lift.

"You don't have to carry me," she whispers.

"I *want* to."

As I hop from the cruiser and my feet land on the smooth white floor of the landing pad, I hear Perthru muttering curses behind me.

"Her name is Rissa," I say to all the attendants. "She will be staying in the palace with me. Ensure everything is prepared for her comfort." Tilting my head to Rissa's ear I whisper, "Do you mind if I tell them your secret?"

She hesitates for only a moment before shaking her head slightly, her lips pressing in, and that soft fear whispering across her skin.

"And Rissa is unseeing. Make adjustments for that fact."

She stiffens somewhat in my arms. "I may be blind, but I'm not incompetent," she hisses and I grunt with some laughter.

"I know that, my flower. You are anything but incompetent…but *they* can be."

Rissa

The halls of the palace are quiet, almost like there's no one within them, but years of having to use my ears have tuned them so much that I hear the whispers of feet tapping softly against the floor as servants pass by us. Even the soft clicks of Bee's sharp claws as they hit the floor lightly alongside us.

"Where are you taking me?" I whisper, as if whispering will make me smaller and less obvious in what I can't believe is a palace. A palace! And I'm being carried by a *prince*.

Holy shit.

"To my chambers." The words roll off his tongue quickly, as if natural.

"Your *chambers*?"

He stops walking suddenly and it's almost silent enough for me to hear my own breaths that slide through my chest.

He makes a sound in his throat. "I assume you will want to have your own chambers for a while."

For a while? And why is he saying those words as if they bring him sorrow? I don't understand.

"I—I can't stay here. You weren't serious about me staying here, were you?"

He begins walking again, slower this time. "I was. This is where you belong."

I assume he's speaking about Atar. "Well, I...But refugees aren't usually housed in the palace, right?"

I don't know why I'm pulling away, or trying to. Maybe because I know I will have to sooner or later. Despite that I was beginning to enjoy this Atari's company, I'd known all along that this was a temporary arrangement. And that was *before* I knew he was a prince.

"You told me of those towers that house refugees. Why not bring me there?"

For a moment, he doesn't speak. "You need a medical assessment first," he says, and maybe it's me wanting to spend more time with him, but it's almost as if he's using that as an excuse. "And I need to be sure that you are well."

Is that what he usually does? As a prince, doesn't he have other things to take up his time rather than tending to a single lost female who's been discarded by her world and left to drift?

Or is he doing this for me?

My heart thumps hard, wanting more than anything for that to be true. And at the same time, afraid that it is.

I'm drawn to this male.

Where his fingers brush against my skin sends tingles right through me and the warmth of his embrace feels like a safe place I can lean into. For a moment, I can imagine myself as one of those damsels in books held in the archive libraries of New Earth. Stories of princesses and princes. Of love despite differences.

Hoping the seed of warmth that's been growing inside me ever since I met this male can grow into something more.

But that's all I'm doing. Imagining things. Still yearning for things that don't exist. *Can't* exist. He is a *prince,* and I am no princess.

I gulp, trying not to focus on the warm cinnamon that seeps from his skin. Trying not to get lost in that voice that will send tingles straight down to my center if I let it.

I close my eyes, and I focus on what I know. That I've been rescued from a nightmare and this is a new beginning. I don't focus on the strong male who's carrying me like I'm something precious.

At the thought of that, I stiffen in his arms.

"I can walk," I say to him. "I can hold your arm, if you allow me to, just so I can…you know…follow you…but I can walk."

"Is the thought of me holding you so disconcerting?" His question makes my cheeks warm.

"I just…"

"You don't want to depend on me." He says it as if he can read my mind. "But please allow me to take care of you. You have been through much."

I bite my bottom lip at his words and try to quell that warmth that's been growing within me. This isn't going to last much further than him making sure I'm alright. Then he'll be gone, and I refuse to pine after something that wasn't even real to begin with. I feel so stupid even fostering the thought.

He's a prince and someone so gallant, who went through so much just to rescue me, tells a lot about his world and his values. I'm sure he will be a great leader one day.

I settle against him, accepting his assistance, but I can't help but wonder what he thinks of me. He let me touch his face…

Even thinking about how intimate that moment was makes me shiver with something other than delight.

"Here we are," he says. "I've brought you to my chambers for now."

He walks into the room and sets me down gently. My hands brace back into something that sinks just enough to accept the pressure I put on it. His bed? I resist the urge to feel around to get a sense of where I am, but moments pass and I realize there's an uncomfortable silence between us.

The only thing that breaks the silence is Bee's loud huff as it sounds like he flops down in the corner.

That prompts the prince to clear his throat. "I will wash myself. Remove this dye…" he murmurs. "Walking around looking like an Uulvian will probably give Perthru a seizure. Though, nothing seems to faze that female."

I smile a little. "She doesn't seem afraid of you."

He scoffs and grunts a short laugh. "I promise you. She is afraid of nothing."

There's a rustling sound, then more sounds like leather hitting the floor. Eyes pointed in the direction of the noise, I know I should turn them away out of respect for his privacy. He's obviously getting undressed, but I stare in that direction anyway, an image of him being painted in my mind's eye.

It only makes my cheeks grow warmer.

He makes another sound as if he's cleared his throat again. "I will wash now," he says. "Please remain in my chambers. The palace is safe but…"

"But what?" I whisper.

He's naked now, isn't he.

My throat's gone dry, carnal thoughts filling my mind.

"I would rather give you a tour myself."

Heat from an outside source comes close to my cheek and I freeze. I can feel the warmth tickle my skin…but that's all that happens. I must be imagining it. I was sure he was just about to touch me.

"I will not be long," he says.

As he moves away, I gulp, squeezing my eyes shut as I try to steady myself. The room goes silent, not even Bee makes a sound, and I'm left with these intrusive thoughts.

"Are you gone?" When there is no answer, another large breath shudders from me. Shit, I'm really getting flustered over nothing.

Standing on shaky legs, I brace myself off the bed and inhale deeply. This room smells like him. Spiced with cinnamon. I inhale again, a soft smile coming to my lips that makes my eyes widen as I tear the smile from my face.

Good God. What is wrong with me?

One hand outstretched, I keep the other on the bed as I move around it. Unlike what I thought, it's not a typical bed. It's round. And *big*. On the other side of it, my fingers brush against wooden furniture set into a wall. I turn, my fingers gliding over books. Many of them.

So he reads.

I don't know why I find that surprising. I guess I painted him as the type that went to gladiator fights and partied hard afterward with many women.

That thought creates an uncomfortable feeling in my chest that I push away.

Backtracking, I continue feeling around the room, painting a picture of its size and the position of things as I go. I move carefully so I don't bump into anything and don't accidentally push anything over. Luckily, it seems he's kept his place clear of low objects. My bane. The last thing I want is to fall over some floor object and go flying into some priceless memento of his. The thought makes me move even more carefully.

When I circle the bed and my toes bump into a large furry body on the floor, I smile.

"Bee," I whisper. "You could've given me a heads up about this royalty business."

Bee makes a low purr in his throat. It's so soft, I can't believe I was afraid of this gentle beast.

When he leans forward and licks my ankle, a soft laugh huffs through my nose.

Retracing my steps, I'm surprised there isn't more to this room. It seems almost...normal. Too normal for who he says he is. Or maybe, my imaginings of the heroes in all those books from the archive painted pictures that aren't entirely true. Of rooms that breathe opulence and luxury. Of royalty that dwell among only regal and showy items.

In contrast to all that, this room seems grand, but not overdone.

Comfortable. Like his *actual* personal space.

And he brought me inside it?

I don't know why that makes me feel...good? Relaxed?

Taking my time, I feel against the wall, following it until I find an open doorway. I hesitate. He told me not to leave the room, but this doesn't feel like the door to the hall.

Stepping inside, I tilt my head, listening. There is no sound, just the faint scent of cinnamon-vanilla that fills the air in his space.

Running my hand along the wall, I continue on, wondering if I should turn back. I don't know why I continue. Curiosity? Maybe. But there's an old saying on New Earth. One that goes "curiosity killed the cat."

Only, there's only one cat here and she'd been packed and hidden away a long time ago. I shrug. I'll just go slow down and retrace my steps if I become unsure. But as I continue walking, a frown develops on my brow.

This room is nondescript. I can't tell where I am. It's almost as if I'm in a corridor, and when my fingers brush against a wall in front of me, I stop walking, my frown turning to one of confusion. I've met a dead end.

A closet? Is that where I am?

Turning slowly, I feel in front of me for the other side of a wall when my fingers brush against smooth hardness.

Skin. Muscle. A chest?

There's a low rumble, a growl, and I pull my hand away in shock. Or, at least, I try to pull my hand away. A warm grip encloses my wrist and I swear my heart darts up into my throat.

Oh shit. This isn't a closet. This is the bathroom!

"I'm so sorry. I didn't know you—I was just looking around and wandered too far."

He doesn't reply. I wish he would say something. Anything.

Instead, he pulls me toward him, plastering my body against the hardness that's his. Water soaks into the tunic I'm wearing and I wonder whether he'd turned off the shower just before I entered. I didn't hear it.

Well, he's turned it on again now, or maybe by pulling me toward him I've bumped the tap, because water's suddenly raining down on us.

Da'red growls.

"Rissa," he says and his voice is...unholy. There is no other explanation for the depth his timbre has gone, nor the feelings it immediately incites. He said my name and it sounded as if he said something filthy. Something dirty that would make a queen blush.

"I—" I make an effort to pull away, to apologize once more for interrupting his bath, but he only pulls me closer.

His skin is so hot it's like he's burning up and a moment of clarity disperses all the thoughts in my head. I stop trying to pull away, alarm filling me as my other hand finds his chest.

"Da'red, you're, you're burning up. Are you okay?"

Is he ill? Had he been hurt after fighting those henchmen and the Zedeshi? I hadn't even thought to inquire about that. I'd been completely selfish.

At the touch of my fingers against his skin, he growls again and there's the thought that I should pull away from him. Except, self-preservation has gone out the window because I don't. I don't pull away and I don't know why. Instead, I let Da'red pull me tighter against him, the water running through his hair, down his face, and dripping on mine. The heat emanating from him almost turns it to steam.

"You're ill, aren't you? You have a fever. I need to call the doctor." My heart's swelling in my chest with something other than fear. Maybe it's the way he's tilting his head, pressing his forehead against mine. Or maybe it's the way he's moving it now, his nose tracing a path that water follows down my cheek, before he presses against my neck, inhaling deeply.

I swallow hard.

Maybe I can get the doctor for him. This is a palace. It has attendants. I'm sure I can find my way back to the bedroom and find the exit from there. There's bound to be someone walking by in the hall outside. I could get their help. Take him to the medic.

But when I feel the sharp tips of his fangs brushing over my neck, I lose all sense of what I was thinking. My thoughts stutter and disappear. All I can feel are the tips of those fangs. I quiver, wondering if he's going to bite me, but doing nothing to stop it.

What the hell is wrong with me?

My heart shouldn't be trembling with anticipation... Heat shouldn't be pooling between my thighs.

*Heat's pooling between my thighs!* I can't deny it, even though a part of me wants to run away from it. I'm turned on. Turned on more than I have ever been in my life.

Da'red inhales deeply and groans against my skin.

"Rissa," he growls, "why did you come in here?"

He still has his fangs against my skin, so close that if I move he'll draw blood. I'm sure of it. So I stay still, forcing my throat to move as I speak.

"I…I was just…" What had I been doing again? Oh, that's right. I was being nosy. And now here I am. Can't say I don't deserve it, except, I'm not even sure what this is.

I only know that I *want* him to bite me. The fuck is wrong with me?

And he'd mentioned biting me before. In the shuttle. Only, he hadn't explained why he'd said that. Was his species some sort of primal race that bit to assert dominance or something? I delete that thought because it doesn't make sense. I wasn't trying to dominate him in any way, so he wouldn't have been trying to do that.

Plus, this castle, the way his attendant, Perthru, spoke, even the way he described the city…the Atari don't exactly seem like primal beings.

"You shouldn't have come in here," he says, voice so low, I feel the vibration against my skin.

My chest heaves with each breath I take, causing my skin to brush against his fangs. Da'red growls again and moves his mouth a fraction away from me, making enough space that his fangs aren't pressing against my skin anymore.

But then he does something that I didn't expect.

Warmth and wetness bloom across my neck as his wet tongue caresses my skin. My body jerks with surprise, heat filling my core. When his tongue extends, swiping over my neck once more, my knees almost buckle.

"What—what are you doing?" I grip his chest. That hard, muscular chest that immediately sends images of this naked god bracing over me while he fills me with his cock, my hands against this same chest as he plows into me.

When he licks my neck again, I full-on whimper.

Da'red growls and it's not tame like the other times he's done that same sound. This one rumbles right through me, causing me to gasp when he suddenly tilts my head back and his lips crash against mine. Something throbs between us, pressing into my belly, and my eyes widen as I feel *all* the sensations. Like having a permanent blindfold, I don't know what to expect, and my body tingles with anticipation as need overcomes me.

I whimper against his lips as his tongue dives into my mouth, opening me to him.

One of his hands reaches down as he bends to grip my ass. Now completely wet, the tunic presents no barrier between us and it's as if I am naked before him.

He kisses me like he's a starving man. Like I'm his lover and he hasn't seen me for years. Like I'm a drug that he can't get enough of.

Reaching for my tongue with his, he wraps it around mine and sucks, eliciting another moan from me before he pulls his mouth away to suck on my lips.

"You shouldn't have come in here," he growls again.

"Why?"

*Stupid question. Very stupid question, Clarissa.*

I've walked unwittingly into a very horny male's bathing chambers and I wonder why he's acting this way. He probably thinks I knew he was in here and decided to come in anyway.

The thought puts some sanity back into me and this time, when I pull away, Da'red lets me move just an inch.

"Because something's happened to me that I wasn't prepared for... and I..." he pauses. "I don't want to hurt you."

I gulp. Why would he hurt me? He hasn't hurt me yet, and I don't know why, but I have complete trust that he won't.

"You don't feel it," he says. "You don't feel it, do you?"

"Feel what?"

I wish I could see his expression, or at least get a sense of it because he doesn't speak. Doesn't make a sound. I can't tell what he's thinking. Or maybe he doesn't want me to. So, when I lift my hand and he doesn't stop me, I'm surprised.

My fingers brush across his face only lightly and a tremor goes from their tips right through my arm, almost as if his fever is spreading to me.

My other hand presses against his chest, feeling his heart thumping, his breathing rate rising as I run my fingertips slowly across his face.

He blinks. I feel his long lashes brush over my fingertips and I'm suddenly aware that he's solely focused on one thing. Me. But his face is serious. There is no softness to it. Almost as if he is clenching his teeth and when my fingers move over his jaw, I know that's exactly what's happening. Is he angry? Pissed? Annoyed?

"Do you mind when I touch you like this?" I whisper.

Da'red groans. "No," his voice is hoarse, almost unclear.

"I'm sorry for intruding," I whisper, and when a breath shudders from him, I don't know whether I've gotten it right or wrong.

"Not intruding. Never intruding," he says, and as if to punctuate that, that hard thing pressing into my belly throbs again.

I'm finally drawn to the thought of it, and my fingers hesitate over his face.

His cock. His cock is pressing into my belly.

I don't move. But I *want* to. I want to slide my belly along it to feel its entirety. I can tell it's big. Thick. And warm. Oh so warm.

My cheeks flush with heat at my wanton thoughts, at the same time that my core fills with need.

This is unlike me. Every second in his presence is making me act like I have no control over myself.

"I should—"

"Stay." He clears his throat. "Please."

My hesitation is clear because he continues. "I will not take advantage of you, Rissa. I would never do that. No matter how much I want to."

"What?" I whisper. What the what now? That whole speech is so loaded, I don't know what to focus on. "You want to take advantage of me?"

That shouldn't make my nipples harden. Shouldn't make that bud between my thighs grow and throb in tune with his cock against my belly.

Shit. I need to leave or…

Or I might end up having *sex* with this male.

The idea does nothing but make my breasts swell like they want to be touched, my body buzzing like it wants to be manhandled, taken *advantage* of.

"Yes. More than anything," Da'red says. "You have no idea what you're doing to me."

I can't reply. I can't speak. Shock makes the words stick in my throat. That part of me that says things that shouldn't be spoken out loud wonders why he doesn't go ahead and do it, *take advantage of me,* while the sane part of me looks on in horror.

Da'red turns with me in his grasp and my back presses into the cool wall behind us.

"But I won't. I will wait until you see the medic."

My heart drops. He's worried about me giving him an STD or something?

I open my mouth to tell him that I haven't been with a man in years. That the only thing that's found itself inside me are my own two fingers and a toy that lives in my bedside drawer. That the thought of being rammed in the shower right now is making me all sorts of excited and scared. But that I *want* it. I don't know how, or why, but I'm sure I want it. Even if it means nothing to him now and will mean nothing to him tomorrow. I want it. For myself. Because it would mean something to *me.*

I just want to…live.

"I—"

"Rissa…" He tilts his head forward so his lips brush against mine. "Even your voice is making me lose my sanity. Every time you speak, I want to hoist you up against this wall and bury my cock deep inside you. I want to hear you whimper my name with those same sweet lips. I want you to weep as pleasure overcomes you."

My mouth falls open, only to be engulfed by his lips.

This might not mean anything to him, but it means the most to me. He's giving me something not even my own people could give me. He's making me feel human. Making me feel *alive.* Making me feel wanted, and even though it's only a temporary feeling, it's given me enough confidence that I moan into his mouth and forget everything else.

For these few moments, I will breathe.

# 12

Da'red

Qef me if I haven't put myself in a situation I can't seem to retract from.

Rissa is in my arms, soaking wet, her soft body pressed between the wall at her back and my chest at her front.

She feels so soft. I have one thought and one thought only. I want to sink into her. The image is taking over my mind with each second that I hold her near.

She whimpers into my mouth, a sound that sends all my instincts into overdrive, the need to mark her, to claim her, pushing through me so hard I have to fight not to hoist her into my arms and expose her soft flesh to my needy cock.

"Rissa," I groan and gods be my witness, she groans back at me.

I can't take it any longer.

Dropping to my knees before her, I know what I am going to do even before the thought fully registers.

Rissa makes a small sound of surprise, her hands shooting out for me and landing on my head. Her fingers lace through the tendrils before she grips my skull underneath her palm.

"What are you doing?"

Her voice.

I wasn't lying when I said it was driving me crazy, and in this position, looking up at her, I am driven even closer to the brink of insanity.

It's the heat. I know it's the heat. The need to secure the mating bond.

If Rissa was Atari, she'd be feeling the same thing. She'd know exactly that she needs me. She'd beg me to seed her and I would do so gladly.

But she is human. Her species do not have mate bonds. This ache in my fangs, this need, it is just my own, and I feel that I will lose my mind if I don't taste her sweetness.

Lifting one of her legs, I set it over my shoulder, causing me to get a peek at that juncture between her thighs. Slick glistens on the dark curls that cover her slit, making my fangs drip at the sight.

"D-Da'red?"

I dip my head closer, inhaling her delicious scent. "Oh Rissa," I groan. "I want to taste you." I pull my gaze from her wet slit to look up at her. She's a goddess. Soft and beautiful. And all mine. Only, she doesn't know that yet. She will soon, however. And I will make every effort for her to understand it.

Her eyes are pointed down at me and I am partially glad she can't see the desperation in my eyes. The fact my fangs have extended and are dripping. The fact I look crazed.

I would scare her.

It's a fight to keep my voice level.

"You want to taste me?" The leg on my shoulder trembles and even though the water is raining down on us, I can smell the fresh slick that has seeped from her entrance. My cock bobs, slapping against my leg.

"More than anything." My gaze falls back to her precious cunt. "Can I?"

Rissa swallows so hard I hear it. "Y—"

The word isn't out of her mouth fast enough before I dive forward, my tongue already lengthened and stiff as I slip it between her waiting thighs and into that warm, hot, welcoming triangle of sweetness.

Qef me. A groan barrels through me at the taste of her, my fist punching into the floor, cracking the smooth carbon that lines it. At the same time, Rissa cries out, her hands tightening in my hair, yanking the locks so hard, she might pull them from my skull. But I can't even feel the pain that should bring. There is only one sense, and it is the taste of my mate on my tongue.

I push my tongue deeper, seeking her very end, unable to get enough. Her moans greet me as my tongue presses into a soft bud at her center, her scent enveloping me as more slick coats my tongue.

Qeffing yes. This is it. This is what I have been searching for all along.

All my life, never feeling like Atar was my home. Never feeling like I was meant to stay here and rule it. Always feeling like there was something missing. It was all because of her. This female.

She is what I'd been searching for this whole time. She's the home I have longed for.

This sweet, sweet pussy is a place I could live in forever.

I can't stop the rumble of pleasure that rolls through me as her juices, her slick, coat my tongue. I swallow and burrow for more, only to fill my mouth enough to swallow again. I can't get enough.

And her scent…

My eyes roll back as I inhale her.

*Rissssssaaaaaaaa.*

She whimpers above me, her hands relaxing and tightening in my hair. Her hips jerk forward involuntarily, rubbing that sweet little bud against my nose as she cries out, pleasure consuming her.

It is the sweetest sound. One I want to hear again and again. So I lift her other leg, forcing her back against the wall as I support her hips with my shoulders and I spread them, opening her up to me. She shakes in my grasp, her body betraying her need, her pleasure.

Groaning, I close my eyes and enjoy the taste of her. My cock hardens and lengthens, so ramrod straight it's almost painful. But still, I can't get enough.

Burrowing my tongue deeper, I roll it inside her as I use my nose against that bud. Up and down, I make love to her sweet pussy with my face, taking my every breath from within her folds, intoxicating myself with the heady drug that is her scent.

"Oh…oh…I think…Da'red I think…I think I'm going to—Da'red!" The last word screams from her lips as she shudders above me. Warm, wet slick coats my tongue, her sweet musk intensifying, as she screams my name.

The sound of my name on her tongue as she experiences such bliss is something I didn't expect and the base of my cock tightens. That's the only warning I get before spend shoots from the tip, coating the wall before me. It comes in streams, my cock bobbing with each jet, and Rissa's whimpers of pleasure milk me for more. I didn't even touch myself. It's a first-time occurrence but it only solidifies for me that she is the one.

Taking more of her into my mouth, I finally roll my tongue from her depths as I lap at her sensitive flesh. She shudders above me, whimpering my name, and I know I will never be the same again.

Rissa

Holy fuck.

I feel like I've just ridden a wild ride in one of those Lower Earth underground parks where the rides aren't safe but the thrill of the danger gets you high.

As Da'red licks and laps at me slowly, moans I can't hold back escape from my tongue. Those wet sounds as he laps at me make me shiver as he takes his time, his tongue running over every inch of me, lapping up every bit of my slick, before he slowly retreats.

My chest's heaving with every breath and I hear him breathing hard too.

What the hell just happened between us?

My body shakes, unable to deal with all the pleasure still shooting through me, and I grip on to his head as he slowly rises with me still perched on his shoulders. When he's finally on his feet, he reaches up, his hands closing around my waist as he lowers me. I slide down every inch of him on my way to the floor.

He braces against the wall, leaning into me and his body shudders too, as if he's also unable to control the feelings shooting through him.

"Da'red?"

"Rissa," he answers.

I shuffle against him, and he groans.

"Don't move. By the gods, Rissa…keep still." He bends, pressing his forehead into the top of my head.

I want to ask what just happened, why he's not demanding more… He just brought me to my peak and he's not demanding that I return the favor.

As if it can hear my thoughts, that thick rod between his legs jerks against me, sending heat right down to my core immediately.

Da'red groans. "If you get slick again, I'll have no choice but to lick that sweet cunt of yours once more," he whispers.

My legs almost buckle at his words. Not even the cool water raining down on us can dampen the heat spreading through my entire being.

Reaching up, my fingers tremble as I find Da'red's chest. Following an unknown path upward, I paint a picture of him as my fingers slide up to his neck and I do something daring. Gripping the back of his neck with one hand, I pull him down toward me, tilting my head back at the same time.

A groan rumbles through him as his lips crash against mine.

"Rissssa," he groans. "You know not what you're doing."

I mumble into his mouth. He's right. I don't know what I'm doing. I don't know what this is. I only know that I want him to continue. I only know I want this more than anything I've ever wanted.

I want *him*.

The skin at the back of his neck is warmer than the rest of his body. Pulsing, almost beckoning me to rub it. So I do, my fingers threading up into the hair at his nape as I moan into his mouth.

Da'red growls against my lips and I feel his fangs descend, my tongue flicking against the side of one, as he lifts me once more.

He moves with me gripped to him, not breaking the kiss and I'm only aware that he's heading out of the shower because the water has stopped falling on us. His wet footsteps smack against the floor before

I'm suddenly being placed into something soft. The bed. He's taken me back to the bedroom. Crawling over me, the bed depresses on both sides as if he's pressing his fists into it as he braces above me. When he finally pulls his lips away from mine, he's breathing as hard as I am.

"You must see the medic," he whispers, as if speaking to himself. "And you must be told of the program first. You must do the orientation. I can't…"

"Can't what?"

He doesn't answer. The only reason I know he's still there is because I feel the gentle rise and fall of his body from his harsh breaths.

"What if I want to?" For the first time in my life, I reach for something I've been told I don't deserve. For the first time, I'm taking a risk, even though I already know the repercussions will tear me apart.

I've been rejected all my life. But if Da'red rejects me now…I…I feel as if it's something I won't recover from.

"You shouldn't say those words to a male who's pining for you," he whispers, going still.

Pining? For me?

"I crave you, Rissa."

Me?

His words…they're…almost unbelievable. Yet still, my ears tickle. I want to hear them. They make something deep inside me wake up and bloom.

"Da'red…"

His lips find mine again and so do his hands. With one jerk, my tunic rips down the middle, my breasts bobbing without the tension holding them anymore.

Da'red inhales deeply, one hand moving up to settle over a breast, his slightly roughened palm teasing the sensitive hard nipple.

Ripping his lips from mine, he trails his fangs down my neck before he sucks at my skin, his mouth a heated furnace that makes my body arch toward him. Da'red groans, easing up so he can knead the other breast in his palm before he takes the nipple into his mouth.

I cry out something, words I can't decipher, as his tongue flicks over my nipple. He sucks the little bud, flicking his tongue, playing with my nipple as the other hand slides down the center of my body to nestle into the curly dark hair covering my center. With a moan against my breast, he slides one finger through my slit, his finger playing with my clit before he dips further and slides the digit in.

I clench on it, but it's not enough. *I need more.*

My body trembles with each stroke, needing that sweet ache. Needing to be stretched and filled.

When his finger retreats, I whimper. He pauses his ministrations on my breast for only a moment and I hear a sucking sound as if he's licking his fingers.

Da'red growls. "I told you not to get slick again," he whispers, his voice so low it sends vibrations right through me. "I'm afraid I'll have to clean you up again."

"Da're—"

He dips then, sliding down me as he pushes my legs apart, opening me to him as his hands slip under my ass, gripping the cheeks as his hot wet tongue swipes through me. Da'red laps at my entrance to the sound of my cries, his tongue swirling through my folds, playing with that tight little bud, until every drop of my slick is no more and all I can do is shudder in his arms. But he stops far too quickly. Setting my ass back down, I can hear him breathing hard as he stares at me.

"Do it," I whisper.

I know what I'm begging for. I know he knows what I'm begging for.

I've been locked up in a cell for two months. If that's taught me anything, it's that life is short and fleeting. It can change at any minute and this, this is heaven. I don't want it to end...and I want him to go all the way.

"Do it," I whisper again.

Never would I have thought I'd be one day telling a prince to fuck me.

Da'red makes a sound that almost startles me. Something between a groan and a roar as he climbs between my legs. Sweet honey drips from my core, the anticipation tightening the peaks of my nipples, making that bud between my folds swell and ache.

As he lowers himself over me, Da'red places a gentle hand against my jaw, turning my head to him as his lips descend to mine once more. As I feel the head of his thick cock press against my entrance, my eyes roll back in my head.

It feels big. Far too big, the head flared over that tight little hole that's my entrance. With a grunt, he pushes softly against my slit. He's so gentle. Far gentler than the deep groans echoing from his lips into my mouth as he grips my ass with the other hand and tilts me so he can access me better.

He kisses me, moaning into my mouth as he finds the perfect position. I only get a moment where there is no sound between us before he surges forward.

My lips break away from his as my head tilts back in a scream of pleasure as he pops through that line of resistance. Sweet mercy. Far too big. Far too big. But oh so good.

Da'red tilts my head back and from the soft brush of his breath against my face, I can tell he's looking at me. He pushes into me slowly, watching my every reaction, before he pulls back and enters once more, going an inch further than before.

He works me on his cock, getting me used to the width, the length with each slow thrust and I forget all sense of time and space. All I can feel is the heat of his body. All I can hear are the sweet words of encouragement that he whispers as he gets me used to his godlike shaft.

"So sweet," he whispers. "So tight, Rissa." He kisses me before releasing my lips to dip his forehead to mine. "So warm," he whispers. "This pretty little cunt is *mine*." He thrusts in hard with that declaration, burying my ass into the bed as he retreats slowly, only to slide in hard again. "You're so beautiful...like a goddess...and you're mine, Rissa." He thrusts in hard again, so much that I feel when my entrance meets the base of his cock.

A groan rumbles through him as he shudders against me, enjoying the feel of stretching me to my fullest. My pussy lips quiver around his length, warm honey flooding through me as he withdraws and thrusts forward again.

Slowly creating a rhythm that renders me speechless, Da'red fucks me. His hips pull back to slam forward again as he begins to piston within me, while he gently sucks on my lips. The sensation of both the gentleness of his kiss mixed in with the carnal sounds of our bodies slapping against each other makes me whimper.

"All mine," he declares again.

"Yours?" I whisper, not even sure what I'm asking.

"Mine, Rissa. You're mine. My mate."

His words don't register. Not until he murmurs them again, his face dipping to my neck as his fangs brush against my neck.

"My beautiful mate."

Pleasure crashes through me and I scream his name, riding the wave of something I've never felt before.

And as Da'red shudders against me, thrusting so deep all I can feel is the twitch of his cock as spend shoots deep within me, I'm lost to the world.

It isn't until clarity begins to return that his words pull me back to the surface.

*You're mine, Rissa. You are my mate.*

I would love for that to be true. And maybe it's a thing he says to get himself off. But we both know it can't be true for me.

He's a prince and I'm a reject from Earth.

We were never meant to be together. No matter how right his cock feels nestled deep within me...or how much my heart feels like it's bleeding and yearning for him.

# 13

Da'red

Holding Rissa in my arms as she sleeps, it takes every effort I have to release her gently as I slip from the bed. There are many things I must attend to and her arrival here at the palace is one of them. I will have to assume my duties as crown prince…and I will have to go to see my father. I can't use the excuse of being off-world for my absence any longer. At least, not while I'm actually on the grounds of the palace.

Sighing, I slip from Rissa's side and she makes a little soft sound in her sleep. Pulling the furs over her, I watch as her face relaxes.

I wasn't lying when I told her she was a goddess. Her face is so soft and delicate, I'm partly happy the snizz kept her in such horrible conditions that her beauty wasn't displayed. I might not have found her in time if he'd realized just how priceless she is.

Thinking about that, I make a mental note to get the attendants to give her everything she needs. She will need days of rest and proper food. She will need someone to tend to the lingering aches that must be in her muscles. She will need someone to treat her delicately.

At that thought, I groan inwardly.

I shouldn't have pushed myself on her. She wasn't ready. Not after what she'd been through. But after she wound up in the washing room, I couldn't resist. Not after she touched me.

Her touch was like a beckoning call that I couldn't resist.

Pulling a clean tunic over my frame, I slip into clean trou and rake a hand through my hair. With one last glance toward her sleeping in my bed, I smile.

I didn't realize how empty it was without her there.

As I leave the room, I jerk my chin at Bee, who simply lifts his head. He doesn't make any effort to rise and follow me like he usually does, and I know it's because he's taken guard over the female that's come into our lives so suddenly.

She's mine, and he knows it. He'll protect her as he would protect my life.

With one final glance at my mate, I slip from the room and tell the attendants by the door to keep watch. If she wakes, they are to notify me immediately and take her to Perthru if I cannot return to her side swiftly.

They nod, slight glances toward the door and I'm sure they'll be discussing the fact there is a female in my chambers as soon as I'm out of earshot. After all, it's not a regular occurrence.

It isn't an occurrence at all, and though they are trusted attendants, I know they gossip among themselves.

Perthru will soon be at my back the moment she hears.

Sighing, I head down the hall toward my father's quarters. Far across the palace, on the other side on the east wing, the king of Atar resides. Slipping into one of the secret passageways that will take me there without having to walk through the main halls, I run a hand across the nape of my neck. The skin there is still heated, almost itchy.

I need to mark Rissa. I almost did it. Came so close to sinking my fangs into her neck several times. But I couldn't. She doesn't even know I'm her mate yet. She probably doesn't understand it. I said it. Sure I almost roared it as her sweet cunt tightened down on my shaft, but Earthkin don't have mate bonds. She possibly doesn't understand what the declaration even means.

That she is the only female for me. That the fates have decided it. And that there is no other that will make me whole.

She'll only understand once I mark her and my life spirit seeps into her veins.

But that will have to wait. My trusted friend, Aqnar, almost lost his human after he marked her. The life spirit interfered with some device implanted in her womb. I will have to ensure Rissa gets hers removed before I even attempt to mark her.

But, I will have to convince her to remove it first. I have no clue how she will respond to that news. A part of me…fears it.

And if I mark her and lose her…I won't be able to continue living.

I already know I can't live without her. The thought alone makes me ache. And not a good ache. Not like the one pulsing at the base of my cock, wanting me to return to my quarters and sink into her again.

No. That ache is a dark, lonesome one. One that will rip me apart if I allow such a thing to happen.

The dim corridor winds as I travel through the tunnel. As a kit, I used to play in these tunnels with Aqnar. He was like a brother to me. Still is. After my mor died, he was like family. The only other true kin apart from my father…a male who is only family because we share the same lifeblood. Before mor's spirit went back to the gods of Atar, he was hardly a father. After she passed, he was even less so.

As I reach the door that will open into the eastern wing, I pause and release a breath. Popping it open, I'm happy to see that no one is in the corridor. I slip out and head toward my father's chambers.

This will be a quick visit. Just an update on the status of our trades with small worlds like Rissa's New Earth, and mention of her too. I will tell him she is my mate and let him know that I intend to secure the bond. I doubt he will be very concerned with either matter. He has not cared about the small trades with what he sees as non-threatening planets, nor has he ever much cared about what is happening in my bed.

Just a quick visit then I can be back with Rissa. Then I can take her to the medic and sort everything out.

"Da'red!" I stop in my tracks as I see the female who has stepped out of my father's chambers. Dressed in expensive white robes that drag against the floor, Sylsylla is a rare velushan female that has taken residence in the palace.

"Sylsylla," I give her a tight smile as I move to walk past her so I can enter my father's chambers, but she blocks my way.

Freshly oiled, her green scales glisten as her slitted eyes move over my face. I can never tell what she's thinking with those eyes. They never betray her emotions. "I didn't know you had returned from your excursion off-world," she says.

I smile again. "I have only just returned, Sylsylla. I am sure the attendants would have notified you sooner or later."

She does a fake pout, her thin lips hardly managing to complete the action. "It would have been nice to hear from you, my dear prince." She smiles, those eyes of hers twinkling. "I would have made myself available in your quarters to ease your aches and pains. You do work ever so hard for Atar. We are all so truly grateful."

I smile again but don't respond. The last thing I would have wanted is to find her waiting for me in my chambers. And that's even before I found Rissa.

My eyes narrow only slightly as I regard her. Dipping my head in an almost bow, I smile at her again. "I am sure that wouldn't have been necessary, Sylsylla. But as always, your kind heart warms mine."

She has always been friendly...I don't know why I constantly feel the urge to be out of her presence. Like now. I want to end this conversation and return to my mate. There are things I need to discuss with Rissa. Things that can't wait for long.

Sylsylla smiles at me, turning to hook her arm underneath mine. With no cartilage above her nostrils, only the holes appear on her face and this close to me, I see them flare as she inhales my scent.

I resist the urge to shake her off my arm and instead continue moving forward toward the door.

"I was just telling your father that you should arrive from your excursion any day now. How coincidental that you arrived so soon, just as I said." She bats her long lashes up at me, and I remind myself that she's a sought-after female on Atar. Why she decides to dwell in the palace instead of seeking a mate among the many unmated and eager males on the outside is beyond me.

From a planet where the males force-mate their females, she is one of a few that have survived unscathed. She is a treasure, in her own right, and the way she carries herself tells me that she knows this. A female like her will give any male lucky enough to woo her many kits.

I assume that is why she has latched on to my father and hasn't left the palace grounds.

I haven't found the time to care.

"You are very wise, Sylsylla."

She giggles at my praise and follows me into my father's chambers, her arm still wrapped around mine. Turning to close the door, even though it slides shut on its own, I take the opportunity to slip my arm from hers. She pauses twiddling her fingers as if waiting for me to take her arm once more, but I pretend I do not see it.

The room smells like expensive balms and ointments. By the window overlooking the city leading to the coast, my father sits with his back turned to us.

"Sylsylla, have you returned so soon?" he asks, not even bothering to turn and look at who has entered his private space. His voice seems to echo and move up the high columns decorating the room, right up into the transparent ceilings high above us.

Arzentus trim is everywhere and on everything, even the chair on which he sits.

Looking at him now, one would never know that he is ill and has been for some time. An illness that has no name. One that baffles even the greatest healers on this side of the universe.

"Yes, my king. And I have brought your son." Sylsylla releases a sound of laughter that breathes through her nose rather than her mouth. "I told you he would arrive soon."

My father barely tilts his head to look my way. Not that I expected much else.

Better to just get this over with. "I have returned, father." I keep my eyes on his back, and refuse to let his usual disregard affect me. Instead, I pull the image of the female I left on my bed in my mind. I remember her sweetness and how she felt around my cock as her tight cunt milked me just hours before. The thought is so strong, so vivid, that I harden in my trou.

"Our trade partners remain loyal. There is nothing to report on that front." I stare at the back of my father's unmoving head. "I am sure

Aqnar has reported the trade arrangement with New Earth was interrupted by rogue Khuru."

"Yes," he says. "And I have also been told that you have been searching for one of the females…"

My spine stiffens. Already, I do not like his tone. These matters are usually of no interest to him. "I have."

"And you have been successful?"

My eyes narrow, that heated piece of flesh at the back of my neck thrumming.

"I have."

My father releases a large breath. "It puzzles me why my one living kin, the person set to rule this magnificent world after me, would risk his life for a refugee."

"Their ship was ravaged by Khuru. They are innocent females with no home. You expected me to leave them in the hands of such scum?" I can't help the fury that drips from my words. Already I wish to be out of this chamber.

The king makes a sound in his throat. "You are like your mor. I always seem to forget that." He releases another breath and sits upright. "There are many refugees who have not yet found mates here. If you are so inclined, you can have any one of them that you want. Risking your existence for a female you don't know—"

"I didn't risk my life. I followed the fates."

For the first time, he looks over his shoulder at me. Golden eyes now faded as if they are losing their light study me.

"What did you say?"

At my side, I swear Sylsylla stiffens.

"I followed the fates."

I know he knows what that means. Every Atari does. I followed the fates and they led me where I needed to be. They led me to my mate.

"You have found a female?" he asks. "One of your own?"

I don't know whether it is shock or disbelief I hear in his voice. There is no way to change the fact of what I am about to say, so I say it outright.

"Yes. A mate. *My* mate. I have finally found her."

Sylsylla releases a sound I can't quite determine, but solely focused on my father, I do not turn to look at her.

He watches me, surprise in his eyes, before that emotion finally settles.

"You will bear an heir then…" he says.

My brows furrow, my fangs lengthening. Is that all he cares about? That I find a mate and breed? It is no wonder he has been inviting females like Sylsylla here. In the hopes I will bed one and breed them. After all, you don't need a mate bond to create a kit, but those unions rarely last. It is heartache for many. Which father would wish such a life on his kit?

"Isn't that what you have Sylsylla for?" I ask, finally turning to glance at her. The expression on her face is unreadable and she makes that sound again, only I have no clue which orifice the sound escapes from because her mouth remains tightly closed.

"Sylsylla?" my father asks.

"You know I would gladly abdicate any claim to the crown if you fathered a second heir."

My father looks at me incredulously. "I have never intended to mate with Sylsylla." There is a glint in those eyes that I do not like. "But now that you have found a mate…you can bear heirs—"

"No." Annoyance mixed in with rage fills my veins. "My mate will not be a breeder for you. She is not an item to be owned and used."

His lips tighten before he turns to face the view once more.

"Have you marked her yet?" he asks. "Have you made your claim?"

I stiffen.

He wants to know whether I have bred Rissa or if we have yet to succumb to the rut. The moment I mark her, I won't be able to keep my hands off her. And in his mind, that's the most likely time that she will breed.

"Where is she?" he asks when I do not answer. "I would like to meet her."

Right now, he is the last person I want Rissa to meet.

Something like fear crawls up my spine as my mind flicks through all the possibilities. He knows I haven't marked her, from the fact that I am standing here and the fact that I didn't answer him. If he thinks he can dissuade her from taking my mark…manipulate her somehow…

Qef.

This is all more complicated than it should be. Rissa has no idea about mates and marking. I don't even know if she will have me. But if the way she cried out while her tight channel gripped my shaft is any indication, there is hope. It is not usual that females reject the mate bond…but Rissa is not just any female. She is not Atari and her life up to this point has been obviously difficult. She may not want to be queen of a planet she has no connection to. It's a burden I would never impose upon her. But if my father speaks to her before I can explain all of this…that's the angle he will take. That she will one day be queen. That she will one day rule. And that it is her duty to produce many heirs.

Qef him if he thinks he's going to laden my mate with the same burdens imposed upon me since my birth. I do not wish that life upon anyone, especially not Rissa. I will not let them spoil the one light I have seen in my life all these years.

I've only just found her too.

"You will meet her in time. Give her some space to settle in." *Give us some time to just be normal together for qef's sake.* "I am sure you will adore her."

Because who wouldn't? Just looking at her beautiful face had opened a gentleness in the center of my being that I hadn't known existed.

Sylsylla makes another sound at my side and I turn to look at her. I had almost forgotten her presence there.

"If you will excuse me, your grace," she says, before her eyes dart to mine, "and prince…"

Prince? In all her time in the palace, she has never used my title.

"You are excused, beautiful one," my father says and without hesitation, I swear she rushes from the room as if there is a fire at her back.

Frowning slightly, I watch her go before my father's voice catches my attention once more.

"Come here, son. There is much we must discuss."

My lips tighten into a thin line and I open my mouth to tell him I have other things I need doing. Namely my mate. Taking care of her that is. But he beats me to it.

"You have been gone for many moons. You would deny your dying father of your presence."

Swallowing hard, I look toward the door, my shoulders falling somewhat as I release a breath.

The two attendants waiting there, basically blending in with the wall, are looking at me.

"Notify Perthru that my mate is asleep in my chambers. She will know what to do."

# 14

Rissa

My eyes flutter open at the same time that silence greets me. I lie there for a moment, just listening, and then I remember. I remember *everything*.

I bolt upright, my heart hammering against my chest.

"D-Da'red?"

Silence greets me. Had I imagined it all? Dreamed it all?

But that can't be right. I'm in a warm bed. Warm enough for me to know I haven't been here by myself all along. Da'red must have left not too long ago.

Slipping from the bed, I reach my hand out as I feel for the wall. A low rumble near my feet reaches my ears just as my fingers brush against the smooth surface shortly after.

"Bee," I murmur. The *quud*'s presence is oddly comforting.

Following the path I took before, I feel my way to the entrance of the bathroom and pop my head in.

"Da'red?"

No answer…and I don't think he's just not answering because he's caught up in need and might growl at me instead of using words. He's really not here.

Releasing a breath, I find my way back to the bed and plop down on it.

Had we really had sex? I…I can't believe it.

But my body's singing, my belly feels packed with butterflies, and my core feels tender and used. I dip my finger down there and the moisture of our mating is still right there between my legs. It makes me groan, my core clenching as if ready to go again.

We'd really had sex…and it was the best thing that's ever happened to me in my life. Holy fuck. I've never been loved like that before. It makes my heart swell and sing.

Falling back on the bed, my fingers brush over some sort of fabric that's been laid there and I grip it in my palm. It's soft, like cotton, and smells exactly like Da'red.

I bring it to my nose and inhale, aware that if there were other people around, I'd probably look like a druggy of some sort. But his scent calms me and makes my insides quiver. Just smelling this, I can remember everything that happened between us the night before.

It's everything I dreamed about when I was a girl. And, as I fall back onto the bed, gripping the piece of clothing to my chest, I realize something else. I lied to myself.

In the heat of things, I'd convinced myself that if this was just a one-time thing, I'd be okay with that. After all, my only two instances of intimacy were the same.

Men on New Earth don't make lasting unions with females like me. Labeled as having damaged DNA, females and males like me have no hope of ever finding a lasting union that involves a family and children. That's just a dream.

And I'd told myself that sleeping with Da'red would be the same temporary thing. Only now, lying here in the aftermath, my heart wrings at the thought.

Even if I assimilate into this society…I'll be pining for him. Always. He has spoiled me for other males…because now I only want him.

And he'd called me his *mate*.

I cringe at that.

I don't know what the mate systems are like on Atar, but if it's anything like New Earth, then he's in for a nasty revelation. If my planet really tried to trick another world and ship us off so they could get rid of us... A bridal gift with females they don't deem as worthy... My heart aches at the thought and the memory of all those other females dying around me just because of New Earth's stupid ideals.

There's a dull sound at the door that has my head snapping in that direction. Sitting upright, I grip Da'red's clothes to my chest. There are more sounds, muffled, and a slight thump that goes through the door frame as if something, or *someone*, bumps into it.

"Bee?"

But even as I call the animal's name, I know he isn't the source of the sound. It's not coming from in here. The sound's coming from the outside of the room.

Swallowing hard, I stand and my tunic falls open from where Da'red had ripped right through it. Slipping the torn robes off, I fumble with Da'red's clothes in my hand and manage to find an opening. I slip my head through that and fight for a few seconds to find the armholes. The thing falls awkwardly across my body and I'm pretty sure I'm not wearing it correctly, but it's big enough to hide my nudity.

The mumbling rises and it sounds like whoever is on the outside is trying to get in but is being stopped by...guards?

Being as careful as I can, I head towards the sound, my fingers falling against a textured wall that I soon realize is the door itself, judging from the fact the sound seems to be coming directly from behind it. I fumble for the doorknob but whoever is blocking the other side must hear my attempts because the door cracks open.

"Princess?" a male asks, a question in his voice. "Is everything alright? We were ordered to keep guard and inform the prince when you wake."

Princess?

I blush at the title. "I'm not a—" I sputter. "Call me Rissa." I smile, hoping I'm directing it at his face and not the wall or some other embarrassing thing.

"Princess Rissa." It almost sounds as if he's as embarrassed as I am.

"No, I mean—" A furnace ignites on my cheeks before I force my throat to clear. "Was that what the commotion was? You were wondering if I was awake?"

"N-no, princess," he begins.

"Is that her?" That voice that rings out, the feminine one, has me stiffening. It's not a threatening voice, so I don't know why I have that reaction. But picking up on slight cues in people's tone has helped me more than once before, and something about the way this female speaks has my senses honing in.

I've never met her before. At least, I don't think I have. This voice is new. I would have remembered it too. There's a slight hiss at the end of her words. So indistinct it's almost easy to miss.

"Is that Da'red's mate?"

I blink at the words, my mouth falling into an 'O'. I'm about to deny that when the guard speaks.

"Yes, Sylsylla."

There's a moment's pause before the female's voice rises with what sounds like fake glee to me. "Oh, by the gods! Aren't you a beautiful thing?"

Cold hands suddenly close over mine and I jerk backward. She's brushed past the guards and I hear them grunt as they try to prevent her from entering the room.

I'm torn in two. I don't know her, but I'm not sure she's here to harm me.

"Are you one of Da'red's friends?" I ask.

I swear she stiffens.

"Oh, we are far closer than that," she says. "I've lived in this palace for quite some time and have grown quite close to the prince and king. It is…nice to meet the female who will be the keeper of his life spirit."

My eyebrows move upward a little.

"I am Sylsylla, a refugee like you," she says, then her voice dips as if she turns her head toward the guards. "Da'red will be very unhappy when he discovers you are preventing me from meeting his new mate. He has never prevented me from entering his chambers."

Her words make something deep inside me tighten and twist. A frown threatens to lower my brow and I fight it away.

It's not my business who he takes to his bed. I have no claim on him. He's not mine and for all I know, a prince like him has many wives.

A cold, cold air feels like it breathes over my spine. Is that what he meant when he said I was his mate? Does he have a harem like the Zedeshi? Does he want me to just be one woman he sleeps with?

I don't know why, but that thought hurts me more than it should, and I already know that if he asks, I will reject his offer. Probably it's selfish, coming from a female who was designated as "unmateable". A mate bond of any kind should make me fall to my knees in thanks.

I guess.

Warring emotions rise within me that I fight to control.

But one thing's clear. Even though I haven't known this male for long...I don't want to share him with anyone else. Which is silly. I have no claim over him.

The woman before me grunts in annoyance and her hands jerk on mine as if she's still fighting against the guards, snapping me from my thoughts. "It's okay. You can let her enter," I say.

I can tell when they release her because her body relaxes. She releases my hands then and brushes past me into the room.

Bee growls immediately, and the woman lets out a slight sound of surprise.

"I was wondering where he left you, you...big animal."

Bee growls again and I shift closer to his side for some reason I can't yet determine.

That sixth sense that compensates for my lack of sight twinges in my brain.

"Please leave the door open," I say to the guards, before thinking quickly of an excuse. "I'm not used to closed spaces."

I cringe at the reason that came to my lips. It's just as bad as that lie I told Da'red about my skin holding on to dirt. But the guard grunts in acknowledgment and I don't hear the door close.

I don't know why, but something about this woman makes me want to guard myself. From her.

Turning to face the room, I note it's gone silent. I dip my gaze low, not sure where to direct my attention, because the female within is not making a sound.

"So," she finally says, and I finally lift my head toward the sound, "it must thrill you to be the mate of the crown prince. It's a coveted title...one many refugees and Atari females have vied for over many moons. But the fates chose *you*."

I smile at her, not allowing my thoughts to flick across my face. "What makes you think I'm his mate?"

She makes a sound I can't determine. Surprise maybe? "He declared it to the king!" Her voice moves as if she takes a step farther into the room. "I was there."

Unable to hide my reaction, my mouth falls open. "He *what?*"

There is a slight whisper of cloth over the flooring as the female moves. "Oh...you were not aware?"

I blink in her direction.

"He visited his father's chambers and declared the next queen has been found."

I almost balk at her words. "Queen?"

"Of course, your grace. You are the next queen. As I said, I am sure you're thrilled. After all, the title is coveted by many."

The way she says that makes me frown a little. "Like you?"

There's a moment of silence before she scoffs. "Oh, never *me*. Such a title requires grace and elegance. Strength and leadership. The queen will have to bear the next generation of kings and princes." She scoffs. "Oh, look at me. I am sure you already know all this."

I can only blink in her direction. Her words are sending my mind into a spiral. Queen? Mate? Children?

"But...he doesn't appear to have marked you. How curious." Her voice appears right in front of me so suddenly that I jerk back.

"Wh-what do you mean?"

"Well, if the prince has truly accepted you as his mate, he would have marked you already. Wouldn't he? That is how it is done."

I sense some truth in her words. At least, the last part of what she said.

"How do Atari mark their mates?"

The female scoffs as if it's something I'm supposed to already know. And maybe she's right about that. I feel grossly ignorant and unprepared.

"He sinks his fangs," she says, her finger moving up to my neck. "Right here."

Her touch sends an uncomfortable shiver across my skin at the same time that flashing thoughts, images painted in my mind of what Da'red and I shared, reappear. Of his fangs brushing against my neck. Of how he licked the skin there as if he was tempted to sink his teeth in...but he didn't.

The woman must see the loss and confusion on my face because she almost coos. "Oh...I'm sure it's nothing for you to worry about. After all, why would he deny a bond with you? The only way he would do that is if..."

"If what?"

"It isn't my place," she says. "I shouldn't even be having this conversation with you...*Princess*."

I clear my throat, my shoulders stiffening slightly.

"I assume you are truly Da'red's friend, right?" The female is silent and I continue. "I'm sure he wouldn't mind you telling me, if that's the case."

That's a great stretch. A liberty actually, but I'm grasping at straws in a world that's become even more confusing than before.

The female makes a slight hiss.

"I'm new to this world, as you know." I smile. "Mating laws are different where I come from. Why would the Prince refrain from marking me?"

She makes another sound, probably in her throat.

"Well, dear Princess, that would be if he intends to use you for breeding his heir, but not to officially claim you in front of Atar."

She caved so easily, but that doesn't stop the fact that something wrings in my chest as her words settle in my brain.

"I must be off now." She blurts it, as if she's just set off a bomb and needs to evacuate posthaste. "It was a pleasure meeting you. I'm here if you wish to have a guide in this new palace life. Or a friend." There's a smile in her voice that I don't return. "We all need friends, and it seems you are all alone." There's a pause and I can almost feel her eyes moving over me. "Take care now, *Princess*." I can only stare in her direction as she leaves, only for her to be stopped at the door by another voice.

"Now what are *you* doing here, Sylsylla? Shouldn't you be in the company of his grace?" I know that voice. It's the attendant, Perthru. "I hope you haven't been scaring Rissa with your attempts at dominance."

Sylsylla makes a sound in her throat, but Perthru doesn't seem affected.

"Growl at me all you want. You can kiss your threats of you one day being queen goodbye. The prince has a mate!"

There are heavy footsteps as if Sylsylla storms away and I hear low chuckling as if Perthru is enjoying every moment of it.

So she *did* want to be his mate. She was lying to me.

Still doesn't deny everything else she said, though. A mate to the Prince is the future queen. And we had sex...but he didn't bite me. He hasn't claimed the mating, even though he's told his father about it.

Perthru walks into the room, and it's almost as if I can feel her presence as she enters. Even as an attendant, I can tell she carries a lot of power.

"I hope that serpent didn't offend you, Princess."

"Please, call me Rissa."

Perthru laughs a hearty laugh. "Perfect for the Prince you are. Come now, let's get you cleaned up."

# 15

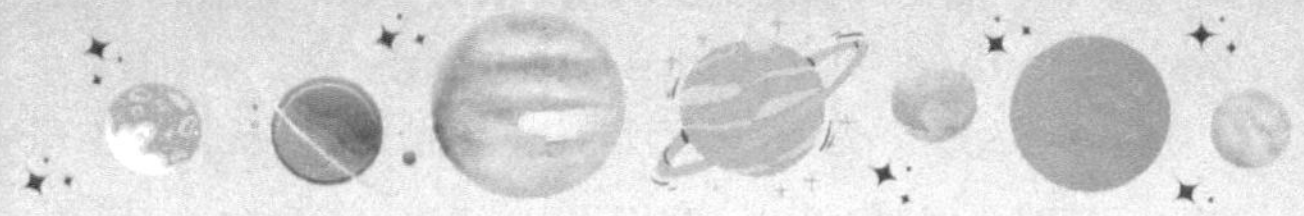

Da'red

It takes far too long to extract myself from my father's clutches and by the time I leave his chambers my mood is in a dark place.

I mentally shake myself and decide to take the main halls back to my quarters. By the time I reach there, I should be in better spirits and able to tend to Rissa the way she deserves. She must have awoken by now, but I trust Perthru with my life. I know she will take care of Rissa until I can return to her presence.

As I stretch my limbs, the communicator on my arm dings. I lift it to see it's a message from Aqnar. I pull up the communication without hesitating and his face appears on the screen.

"So, you made it back to Atar alive," he says.

Humor makes me grunt. "Seems to me you were worried. Yet you didn't come to my aid?" I feign disapproval and Aqnar grunts, pulling a female into his arms. She yelps and swats at him, but she's overpowered. The pure joy on his face has me aching for something I never knew I needed until Rissa appeared in my life.

"Blame it on this treasure," he says. "My Marion has intoxicated me. I could not leave."

"Don't believe him, Da're—, I mean, your Highness." Marion, Aqnar's mate, grins and swats at Aqnar again. "I told him to leave me here and go help you guys. I've been very worried about the other survivors."

I smile at her, careful not to flash my fangs.

Her features are so similar to my Rissa's, yet so different.

"If I can give you any assurance, I have found one of your Earthkin."

Marion freezes, her eyes going wide. Her dark hair reminds me of Rissa's, except hers is straighter, shorter. And her eyes, though seeing, are not as warm as my Rissa's. She's also not as round as my mate. She is beautiful but perfect for Aqnar. Like how Rissa is perfect for me.

I can't help but smile at that thought, my mind going back to the warmth we shared in each other's arms.

"Da'red." Aqnar's voice pulls my attention and I realize they must have asked me a question. "Which female have you found?"

"Her name is Rissa," I reply. "And I have found more than a female."

Aqnar's brows dive. "What else have you found?"

"I have found my mate, brother."

Both their eyes widen, her pale ones and his golden ones. They look at each other with disbelief before the female squeals and wraps her arm around his neck.

"You were right!" she shouts, gripping Aqnar's jaw as she stares at him with wonder.

"Right?" I ask.

Aqnar hums. "Mm. Yes. Once I heard you visited that station over five times and still kept returning, I believed the fates were at work." He grins at me, his fangs baring.

"Have you marked her yet?" In her excitement, his mate almost pulls the communicator from his grasp.

It's strange, having a female ask that question, but I shake my head to indicate the negative.

"Good, because I almost died when Aqnar marked me." Aqnar pulls her closer at those words, as if the memory is still fresh and I understand. The thought of Rissa nearing death turns my insides into dust. "Tell her she needs to remove the implant first. She'll know what that means. It'll interfere with the bite."

Aqnar had warned me of this from my third visit to the station. He'd always been good at following his instincts and, as he told his female, he was right about me finding my mate.

His warning and now his mate's is why I fought all instincts that told me to bite Rissa. That and the fact that she isn't yet aware of all this. A mate bond isn't easily explained to a species that doesn't naturally experience them.

When I inject my life spirit into Rissa's veins, I'll be adding a chemical component that will change her very cells. I need her to understand this before I take her fully. I need to know she wants it too.

With a few well wishes from Aqnar and his female, we bid each other farewell and the communication clicks off as the line closes.

"Is something wrong, my Prince?"

I glance up from the device to see Sylsylla standing not far from me. Why does she always seem to appear when I least want her presence near?

"I was just heading back to my quarters."

"I see."

Something glints in her hands and I catch sight of it just before she puts her hands behind her back. A seemingly innocent gesture, but I saw the communicator before she could hide it. *If* she even was hiding it…why would she need to hide a communication device? She's not a captive, nor is she a slave. She is free to communicate with whomever she wants.

"That's where your mate is, isn't it?" she says. "Your quarters?"

Mention of Rissa has my senses sharpening. "It is. And the reason you know this?"

"Because I know you…Da'red." She says my name with some emphasis, before softening her features with obvious effort. "Is it that you don't want her to stay in one of the many guest quarters?"

Her question is a strange one.

"Rissa is free to stay wherever she wants." *Preferably within my quarters, warm on my bedding.*

As I stare at Sylsylla, something doesn't seem right but I can't pinpoint exactly what it is.

She smiles at me. "I'm...just wondering."

As Sylsylla steps forward, her hips sway as she approaches. "I simply found it interesting, my Prince."

My eyes narrow a fraction before I grant Sylsylla a tight smile. "I'm late, Sylsylla. If you could excuse me..." I brush past her and she lets out a soft sound of frustration, her breath blowing through her nose.

It's almost as if she isn't happy with my answers. But her questions are strange ones that don't warrant a response. Whatever game she's playing, I don't have time for it.

"Da'red!"

I pause, glancing over my shoulder and failing to dispel the frown that's deepening my brow.

"You *don't want her to*, do you?"

She's incredibly interested in this. My frown deepens. "I don't want her...to what?"

The slight look of frustration that was on Sylsylla's face suddenly dispels like it was never there to begin with.

"Nevermind, my Prince," she smiles. "You have only just returned from your journey. We will have plenty of instances to talk at a later time."

A beat passes between us before I jerk my chin at her, turn, and continue walking. I just want to see Rissa. Hold her in my arms. Feel her softness melt against mine.

Turning the bend, I only glance back once to see Sylsylla's heading in the same direction as I am.

Ah, right. Her quarters are this way.

Pushing the velushan from my mind, I focus on the one I want to think about instead. Rissa.

She should be with Perthru right now, and hopefully, Perthru will explain some things about Atar. I'm sure my mate will be interested.

As soon as she's settled in, I'll take her everywhere. I want her to experience everything with me. And for the first time, I'm excited about actually traveling on my own planet. Seeing Aqnar's joy, I can't wait to spend time with the being that will keep my life organ beating.

As I head down the hall, passing the bend and Sylsylla's quarters, I frown as I notice the person coming in my direction.

Perthru should be with Rissa, so why am I seeing her hustling before me now?

"Perthru?"

Perthru's mouth sets into a thin line as she glares at me.

"Do you know why I'm here?" she asks. For the first time, a tendril of her hair is not in place on top of her head. It's almost as surprising as the fact that she seems to have walked here in such haste. As a kit, she always scolded me for running in the corridors.

"Are you not going to tell me?" I glance behind her even though I know Rissa won't be there. "Where's Rissa?"

Perthru's eyes narrow. "I warned you about Sylsylla. Warned you she's not to be trusted."

I stiffen at the sound of the velushan's name. "What has she done?"

Glancing behind me in the direction Sylsylla is supposed to be appearing from any second, somehow she is nowhere to be seen.

"She went to your chambers."

My gaze snaps back to Perthru. Surely, she's mistaken.

"Your mate is of the impression that you and Sylsylla have a history together. I think she believes Sylsylla might have been the one you wanted to be your mate."

The air feels like it loses all moisture and goes dry.

Perthru only stares at me, that hardness in her eyes deepening. "Sylsylla pointed out that you have not yet marked your mate, Da'red."

I try not to growl at Perthru as annoyance and rage begin to stew in my gut.

"She told Rissa that it's her I want?"

"In not so many words, but I believe she did."

For a moment, I see red.

"By the Gods of Atar...why would Sylsylla do such a thing." I release a breath, just as Sylsylla comes around the corner. The way she appears, the delay in it, tells me she was already listening and waiting for an entrance.

She approaches me, ignoring Perthru's grunt of disapproval at her arrival. Her complete focus is on me, those slitted eyes boring into mine.

"Sylsylla…you went to my chambers?" I try not to speak harshly. Even though I'm finding out by the minute that I cannot stand this female, she is, after all, still a precious thing.

She is female, and should be treated gently.

But she has planted seeds in my mate's mind that I will have to squash and burn. She has made a process that's already tenuous even more difficult.

And if her actions so far have told me one thing, it's that I can't leave Rissa alone. Bee, at least, has to be there to guard her, because like me, that quud will guard Rissa with his life.

"I had to see the female that took you away from me," she whispers. When she lifts her hand toward me, I catch her by the wrist just before she tries to grasp that sensitive spot at the back of my neck.

The thought of her touching me there makes me want to retch.

"You were destined for me," she whispers, still trying to touch me there, even with my fist stopping her wrist.

I frown at her, my gaze searching hers. She's speaking nonsense.

Her other hand that's gripping the communicator rises and I barely see the numbers ticking on the screen as if she is on an active call. She's ignoring whoever she's speaking to in order to do this?

I grab that wrist as well before she can touch me at the back of my neck. It's almost as if she's intent on doing it, struggling against me.

The back of an Atari's neck is his weakest spot. Often, when mates touch each other there, they go into immediate need. But maybe she does not know the other aspect of such a touch because she's not Atari.

I already have a mate. One I want. One I am realizing with every second that I *need*. If Sylsylla touches me there, I will only grow vicious with her.

She will only incite my rage.

"You were destined for *me*," she says again, with more emphasis this time. "For many revolutions, I've waited in this palace, saving myself. Saving myself for *you*. It cannot go to waste. I know you want me too."

I glance at Perthru but her livid gaze is only on the velushan female who is now trying to push her body against mine.

"Sylsylla...I don't know why you believe this. You had many chances to join the mate register. I'm sure you would have found a worthy mate by now."

She grunts and if her eyes could water, I think they would be watering right now.

She seems completely different from all the other times I've seen her before. This isn't the poised, calculating Sylsylla that usually roams the halls. This female before me almost appears manic.

I glance at Perthru once more and even she seems confused by the change, but she sets her shoulders and looks at me with that same hardness in her eyes.

I can't be soft and gentle. I know Perthru would have tried to calm Rissa, but I need to be by her side. She is, after all, my priority, not Sylsylla.

"Sylsylla...you are wrong."

She pauses, looking up at me with eyes that scream sorrow. "You don't want me?"

Those words are harsh. They are not words I want to say.

"Tell me, Da'red. Tell me you don't want me."

My lips thin, but she needs to hear it. "I don't want you," I say to her. "Sylsylla...I have never wanted you. When I rescued you and brought you here to the palace, it was only because you'd been through too much. No female should have experienced what you had. You were almost forced to breed...you would have been just one female in that scum's harem and you would have eventually died. I took you here because I knew your life would be better." I release a breath, but at least she's stopped struggling against me. In fact, she seems enrapt with my words. "That was all. Nothing more. I know on your homeworld the males are different. I am sorry to have misguided you in any way."

She relaxes then, her hands slowly dropping and when they reach her side, I release her.

I study her as she studies me and it seems she recovers because her mouth thins somewhat, almost like a smile.

"It was my mistake," she says. "I will go to my chambers now."

She moves so quickly I don't get a chance to say anything else. At my side, even Perthru seems perplexed.

But Sylsylla isn't my concern. Turning, I give Perthru a jerk of the chin before I rush down the halls to my mate.

# 16

Rissa

The door slides open so fast it makes a whooshing sound.

My heart jumps into my throat, but I don't startle. Sitting here on my own in silence with Bee's warmth by my side has given me time to think and calm myself.

"Rissa."

Goddamnit. The walls I've built around myself crumble at the sound of his voice and I fight to put them back up.

"You're back," I force a smile onto my face. "I'm just about ready to leave now. Your attendant, Perthru, gave me fresh clothes."

"Leave?"

I swear I hear his voice break, but I steel myself. I've been acting like a love-struck teenager and I am far from that. I'm a grown woman and I should take control of these disorderly feelings and—

It's the warm cinnamon that I scent even before I know he's moved to stand right before me. I can't help but smell it. With every inhalation, he's there, permeating my space.

I can tell he crouches before me when the hard muscles in his chest press against my knees.

"You want to leave?"

I gulp. I open my mouth to say yes, but the word feels dry and hard to utter.

"Perthru told me Sylsylla came here. She may have said some things to you. Things that aren't true."

I gulp again.

Yea…I want to believe that. But she said some things that *are* true. Like the fact that he needs a *queen*.

"I…"

"Sylsylla may have been somewhat deluded. And…I've only just found you, Rissa. I know not yet how to convince you that what I say is genuine."

My heart breaks into a thousand pieces and when his fingers lift my hand, I'm limp in his grasp.

He brings my palm toward him and for a moment, I don't understand what he is doing. Not until a firm and steady repetitive beat thrums underneath my fingertips.

His heartbeat. I can *feel* it. And the strange thing about it is that the longer I focus on it, the more I can hear my own pulse thrumming in my ears, moving at the same pace, moving to the same beat.

"If I marked you, you would understand. You could tell that what I say is true," he continues. "But I can't."

My throat's thick and I fight to say something. But nothing comes out. Maybe because I want this more than anything I've ever wanted in my life, but it feels almost as if things have moved too fast and none of this is real.

"Sylsylla mentioned that," I whisper, noting that he's moving my hand, moving it upward to the slit in his tunic at his neck. My fingers touch his skin and I inhale at the same time that he does. He continues moving upward, bringing my fingers up his neck, his chin, his lips… There, he pauses before tilting his head slightly downward. My fingers slide into his mouth and I swear he groans.

"Sylsylla was being nefarious. I've always thought she wanted to be queen…I just never realized she wanted *me* to be the one to give her that title."

"What do you mean?"

"She has spent much time becoming close to my father. I believed she wanted him…but now I realize, her efforts were to be in his good graces so she could manipulate me."

I hear what he says, but I can't respond. Heat's pooling in my center as Da'red licks my middle and pointer fingers before he sucks one into his mouth. His mouth is so hot, the heat sends spasms right through my hand and I gasp as he rolls his tongue over the digit.

"I never explained, Rissa, but let me tell you this now. You are my mate," he says. "I know you don't feel it yet. You don't feel the way my life organ yearns to beat with yours. You can't feel the heat coursing through my veins with the need to mount you at every passing moment. You can't feel the possessive obsession growing within me at every click that passes. But *I* can feel it. You are mine, and I will spend the rest of my existence proving it to you if that is what it takes for you to understand."

My mouth falls open at his words as he stands with my fingers still in his mouth. I track his movement, tilting my head till it falls back on my shoulders. He's tall. So frickin' tall.

"But I can't be your mate," I whisper. "You're a prince…and I'm a girl from Earth. *Lower* Earth." My heart wrings. "Da'red…How can I be your queen when I am like this?"

"Like this?" He pauses. "What do you mean, little bloom?"

"I can take care of myself, but your people…they will expect—"

"Forget what they want or expect." One hand caresses my cheek as he leans down and places a kiss on my nose. "Rissa, where you lack, I will provide. Where you can't see, let me be your eyes."

I shake my head. "I don't want to be a burden. Never a burden. All my life I've fought to become independent. I live on my own on Lower Earth and I'm darn good at it. I do my art. I pay my bills. I can survive—"

His nose presses against mine as he breathes deep. "I don't want you to *survive*," he growls. "I want you to *live*."

"I—"

What can I say to that? Isn't that what I've been doing so far? Surviving? Have I really been living? I mean, I have my artwork that I sell to provide for myself, but apart from that, when's the last time I felt free enough to travel the streets of Lower Earth on my own? When was the last time I wasn't worried about earning enough credits to pay my apartment fees? Worried the guards who patrolled the lower levels wouldn't raid my space at any moment.

"I will leave Atar if that is what you want," he says. Words that make me freeze, my breath stopping in my throat. "I will leave the palace. I will leave the crown. We can go to a homestead planet in the outer reaches. I will make a farm, just me, you, and our kits."

A family? Kids? Those are a dream and this male is telling me he will give it all to me.

I grip the hand that's still caressing my cheek. "Give up your princehood? I couldn't ask you to do that."

"You wouldn't be asking. It would be my decision. I've never been happy here, and if leaving is what will give you peace, I will gladly do it."

I'm shaking my head even before he completes what he's saying. It won't happen. I could never do that.

Da'red releases a slow breath, his hand gripping my jaw a little firmer as he tilts my head so my mouth meets his lips.

His kiss is slow. Soft. Yet, in that slight brush of our lips is a promise of so much, much more. Enough to make my knees weak.

Da'red growls against my lips, the sound vibrating against the soft flesh.

"I need you to feel the bond. I need you to feel it like I do. Right now, my life organ reaches out to your own, but the cord is untethered."

I gulp. "You'd have to bite me," I whisper, and Sylsylla's words repeat in my mind.

If he doesn't want to bite me, maybe her words had some truth.

"I want to…more than anything. But I cannot."

I digest his words slowly. "Why?"

Da'red releases a breath and eases upright. "The other human, Aqnar's mate, nearly died before they realized there's a foreign device inside her that interferes with the bond."

"Huh?"

"An implant," he whispers. "Something buried inside your womb by your world leaders."

"Yes," I reply, thinking of the implant I'd been mandated to get surgically implanted even before I reached puberty. "I have one of those."

Da'red grunts. "We have to remove it."

I nod. I mean, what's the worst that could happen? If he removes it and the bond doesn't work, then that means I'm not his mate and we can save ourselves the heartache.

"You approve?" his voice has changed again to that deeper timbre than usual.

I nod again. "Yes, remove it."

Da'red is suddenly so close, his nose brushes against mine. He growls again, and it's almost like anticipation permeates from him so strongly that I shiver in hopefulness. "The moment it is removed, I will take you back here and make you mine, Rissa," he says. "I will claim you with my bite as I sheathe myself within you over and over again. You will shiver as I bury myself into you and flood you with my life spirit and my seed."

I shiver again at his words.

"Rissa," he whispers.

"Yes?"

"I can't wait for you to be fully mine. I want nothing more." He eases back suddenly. "We should go. Before I lose control and mount you now."

With trembling fingers, I hold on to the hand that grasps my own.

"Let's go."

---

Da'red

Leading my mate down the corridors to the medical wing of the palace, I can't help the pride I feel bubbling inside me.

Rissa is proving to be stronger than I even first realized. She is trusting me to do this. To remove something from within her body so that we may solidify our union. My life organ swells at the thought.

If she has taken any of what Sylsylla said to mind, she has not dwelled on it. She wants to try removing that device from within her so she can judge me for herself. I couldn't have asked for more.

And, as my cock swells in my trou, I am reminded of something else. The fact she has agreed to this can only mean one other thing— she feels something between us. Something more than simple attraction or sharing on furs.

Earthkin might not have the instinct for mate bonds...but maybe they are not completely unaffected by it either.

She can feel something, and that's all I need to know.

Pushing the door to the med bay open, the medic on duty turns, his eyes widening as he lays them on us.

"Ah, P-Prince Da'red. To what do we owe this visit?" His eyes widen some more. "Is your father in need of assistance?"

I shake my head, leading Rissa inside the room. Walking a step behind me, I note that she always keeps one hand discretely outstretched to brush against items as she walks past. Noticing that, I deliberately walked to one side of the corridor, keeping her close to the wall. I watched as her head tilted toward any sounds, her lips slowly moving as she counted steps, and my life organ swelled with joy.

I have no doubt that if left on her own, my Rissa would survive. The only thing is...she doesn't need to. Because she's never going anywhere without me ever again.

"No," I say to the medic, "I'm not here about my father." I gesture to Rissa. "I am here for my mate."

"Your *mate*?" For a moment, he forgets that I'm right before him. Schooling his features, he clears his throat. "At your service, Prince and Princess."

Rissa stiffens and I almost break my composure and smile. She already hates the title as much as I do mine.

"Da'red is fine," I say to him, watching as he straightens the spotless arzentus-trimmed tunic the medics wear. On the chest is the arzentus insignia of the palace, labeling him as being solely employed by the crown.

"And you can call me Rissa."

With Rissa's sweet voice, the male obviously relaxes and I notice his covert glance in her direction. The skin at the back of my neck tightens and I have to roll my neck to ease the pressure. With Perthru's help, Rissa is even more stunning than before. Wearing a flowing white robe, she looks even more like the goddess that she is. The soft material glides over her curves in a way that makes me want to grip her hips and pull her flush to me. She's delectable and my fangs drip just looking at her.

The medic clears his throat again. "Just this way, Prince Da'red."

I fight to push the feelings of possession away but still end up moving my hand to the small of Rissa's back as I lead her into the examination room.

It's like when I killed that Parsno. This need to keep her to myself can only be a result of the mate bond.

I need to mark her.

Soon.

The medic leads us to a spotless room and gestures to the hovering examination bed.

"If Princess Rissa could just lie down here," he says before turning to the vid screen beside the bed and calibrating it.

I only have to lead Rissa's hand to where she needs to go before she hoists herself up on the bed on her own. Resting back on it, she turns her head in my direction and I lift her hand to rest on my chest, to let her know where I stand.

The medic turns to us, a question in his golden eyes.

"My mate has two devices within her. One is a tracking device put there by a Zedeshi. The other is an implant."

Rissa licks her lips before speaking. "The implant is in my womb. My, uh, my government put it there a long time ago."

The medic nods. "I will do a scan."

Rissa's hand tightens on my chest as the medic completes the scan, a frown marring his brow.

"I can see the tracker the Zedeshi implemented," he says. "It's currently burrowing deeper into her tissue. We should remove it now."

I watch him closely, noting he hasn't said anything about the other device. "And the other implant?"

His eyes dart to me for only a second. "I…need to run more tests."

My brow furrows but I can feel the beat of Rissa's pulse in the palm she has against my chest. Even through my garments, her pulse beckons to me and I focus on it.

Everything will be alright. The fates would not have put us through so much to take it all away before we've even begun.

"Do you think something's wrong?" Rissa whispers, her head tilted my way.

The medic's gaze darts to her before he forces his eyes back on the device he's scanning her with.

I lean into her, brushing my lips against the soft skin at her temple. "Everything will be fine. I'll make sure of it."

The medic makes a small sound, wincing a little as he does. His gaze finds mine and I know there is a problem.

"What do you see?" Rissa asks. There is fear in her voice, and I hate to hear it.

"You are on the cusp of your estrous…" the medic says.

Her head turns my way. "Estrous?"

"When you become fertile," he says.

"B-but," Rissa stutters. "I can't become fertile."

The medic makes a grunt of assent. "Affirmative. The device appears to block the reproductive organs from performing as they naturally should. You will release no cells that can bring new life. Your womb will not shed. The device is performing well, doing those things, but it cannot block everything. You will soon produce chemicals that will indicate that you should be bred. To an Atari like the Prince…your mate…and every Atari male who comes near you, you will smell like prime mating material."

The immediate growl that rumbles from my chest is only dampened by Rissa's exclamation.

"What?!"

My fangs lengthen, the skin at the back of my neck tightening. "Are you saying, in a short while, males will scent my mate and want to mount her?" I ask. "*Breed* her?"

The medic goes even paler, his bronze skin taking on a lighter shade as his hands rise in defense. "A-Atari females don't experience this. Once they are mated and marked, their chemicals only affect their mate. B-but the Princess is not Atari." He turns to the data processor and looks over the scans. "Her chemical levels are different."

My nostrils flare, signaling my rising anger. "Can *you* scent her?"

The slight darkening of his face is all the answer I need and a low rumble develops in my throat.

*Rissa is mine.*

The medic gulps, eyes darting to me before going back to the scans. "The implant she has is an old one. Outlawed for use, actually. I'm surprised it was allowed. The data here says it has been illegal for use for several tens of revolutions."

I growl again and he pales even more.

"How do I stop the estrous?" Rissa speaks and her voice pulls me back to reality. She leans into me, calming me, but all I can think of is other males trying to take her away from me. She can reject the call of the bond between us. As it is…there is hardly a bond at all because I haven't marked her yet.

With this information, my mind is quickly becoming a chaotic place filled with unsurety.

"How do I stop the hormones?" Rissa asks.

"W-well," the medic begins, "there is one way."

"What do I need to do?" Rissa presses, and through the rage and jealousy clouding my mind, I realize the medic seems to be hesitating.

"It would not be wise to stop the chemicals. It is a necessary process your body must complete."

"Then what do you suggest?" I growl, my tongue flicking against my fangs. They almost hurt. A pain derived from need.

"If you mark the Princess and solidify the bond, the chemicals she releases will only affect you."

"To mark my mate, I need that implant removed."

The medic releases a slow breath, tapping on the data processor before him frantically.

For more than a few moments, he continues tapping on the screen, his lips tightening as the seconds go by.

"What's wrong?" Rissa asks. "Why isn't he saying anything?"

Lifting her head, she eases up on her elbows. "Something's wrong. Tell me what it is."

The medic's shoulders tighten and his jaw clenches as he squeezes his eyes shut. He is young. Possibly he doesn't know what he is talking about. Maybe he read the scans wrong. But even as I try to reason with these ideas, I know none of them is true.

Only the best medics can get a spot working in the palace. He is one of the best Atar has to offer. The fact that whatever news he has is causing him to behave like this sends prickles of ice all along my spine.

"Speak, medic." I can feel my life organ thumping harder and I wrap my arms around Rissa, leaning into her so her back is against my chest. Her hand slips down to grab on to my wrist, and she holds it tightly, tension in her veins.

"I have found the implant that is causing the trouble..." the medic says.

"And..." I prompt.

"And it is...your mate is..."

Rissa grips my wrist tighter.

"The device," the medic says, "has burrowed so deeply into her tissue that removing it may present a risk to the princess' life."

My world stalls...

"What?" Rissa whispers. I can't find the voice to speak. All I can do is stare at her, my life organ feeling like it is curling in on itself, the muscle atrophying as the life essence is wrung out of me.

"Your life, Princess," the medic says. "If we remove the device... you may not survive the procedure."

# 17

Rissa

The Atari believe in something they call the fates. Well, the fates must be kidding me. Playing a joke on me that only something completely inhuman and unfeeling would find mirthful.

Da'red refuses to let me walk back to his quarters. Instead, he carries me and silence descends upon us.

I wonder what he's thinking. Wonder what his next move will be. For, if the fates intended us to be together, why would something like this happen? The very thing implemented to stop me from any sort of fulfilling relationship is doing its job well and good—even though I'm far away from New Earth.

My belly cramps and not from any physical reason, but just from the fact that this is happening. I feel like I'm about to cave in on myself and disappear into a crumpled pile of pain and desolation.

"What now?" I finally whisper. My heart splits and cracks at the sound of my voice. I don't want to say the next few words. But what's the use in hiding away from the facts? "This means you were wrong, doesn't it?"

Da'red only makes a low rumble and pulls me closer to his chest.

"It's probably best if I make preparations..." I continue. "That refugee housing—"

Da'red stops walking so suddenly that I jostle in his arms.

"Rissa," he growls. "Why would I send you to the refugee quarters?"

I swallow hard. "Well...you heard what the medic said...maybe your fates were wrong."

"Even without the fates, *I know you are mine*. I'm not letting you go."

When a door whooshes open, I know we must be back at his quarters. Bee makes a sound in his throat as Da'red storms in and the door whooshes closed. Climbing on the bed, he shuffles on his knees across it before he sets me down, positioning me so he's straddling me. My hands rest against his trou, his thick thighs underneath my palms.

"Touch me, Rissa."

His command isn't one I expect. I expected him to be upset, a little bummed, possibly embarrassed that he'd declared so much when he was wrong about it all. But he's not. Instead, that deep timbre has gone to dangerous levels and I've been around him long enough to know what that means.

When I don't move immediately, Da'red bears down over me, his arms pressing into the bedding at my side.

"Touch me, Rissa," he repeats.

My hands tremble as I lift them upward. As soon as my palms make contact with his tunic, a breath shudders through him.

"You can't still believe..." I whisper.

Da'red leans closer and my fingers slide upward, traveling along what feels like only hardened muscle. Another breath shudders from him.

"I know what I feel," he says, "and I know what I want. And I want *you*, Rissa."

It's my turn to shudder, and as my fingers continue moving upward, I release a shaky breath. They brush over skin, velvety and smooth. The muscles in his neck move as my fingers skate over them to reach his jaw. Da'red stills as I continue, following a path over his chin to his mouth. His lips part, and my fingers brush over a fang. He releases a breath like a hiss.

"You want to bite me," I whisper.

Da'red doesn't answer; he only makes a soft sound like a whimper when I brush a finger over the other fang.

"I want to do more than that," he growls, his teeth moving against my fingers. "But I refuse to lose you."

Another breath shudders from me as he dips his face into my palm. I feel his breath against my skin. Feel how it vibrates through him. And I can't help but release a little whimper of my own.

There's an urgency brimming within me. Making my skin pebble with goosebumps. Causing need to pool between my legs. And causing my heart to swell and thump so hard in my chest that I wonder if he can hear it.

"You put your faith in me without knowing who I was." His words awaken my attention and I hang on to them, my throat tightening as he continues. "You trusted me with your *life*, not because of my station, but because you thought me worthy to fight for you."

As Da'red dips his head to my neck, inhaling deeply, the feel of his breath against my skin sends a delightful shiver that spreads through my being.

"You mourned for me, Rissa, when you thought those Parsno took me down. You *mourned* for me. No one has ever cared that much when they did not know who I was. But you did."

He grips me to him, pulling me impossibly closer as he buries his face into my skin. Da'red grunts, inhales deeply, and lets out a short breath against my neck as a rumble goes through him—one so deep it vibrates across my entire frame.

"You have no idea how much I want to claim you right now. It sends me into a trance."

I want to say something to him, something of meaning, something that will let him know exactly how much I'm feeling for him right now. But the words don't come to my lips. Because Da'red is telling me something that I wish—I've always wished—I heard. For someone to accept me just the way I am, without barriers or ideals, without stupid rules and laws and regulations. Just pure, raw emotion straight from the heart. It's exactly what I've wanted. He's opening himself to me. This Prince of Atar, someone so far above my rank, is opening himself to me, is bare right before me—baring his heart. And all I have to do is reach out and touch him.

I realize now that this man has been a lonely man. It's why I never realized just who he was before.

It was told to me back on New Earth—those that live on the upper levels flaunt their status. People like them could never fit in, never pass as just someone normal. But Da'red, Crown Prince of Atar, passed as a lowly Uulvian warrior just so he could rescue me.

*He did it all for me.*

Emotion swells deep within me, so much so that I reach up and pull him closer. I shift underneath him, and a moan rumbles up through his frame.

"Rissa," he groans.

I have not known him for long, but this undeniable pull makes it feel like I've known him forever.

For once in my life, I feel that I can be more. I want to be more. I want to be everything that he needs. But just like all my life, I've been held back by these stupid rules of my world. Here they are, still preventing me from my dream.

"I want you so bad," I whisper, but the heavy thought on my mind is the fact that even though I'm opening myself to him now, and even though Da'red is telling me everything he wants, we might never come together—not with this implant deep inside me.

"I'd surrender my life, Rissa," he groans again as my fingers slip down his shoulders, running over the taut muscles in his back. Da'red is perfect. I'm almost afraid to want him as much as I realize I already do. I'm almost afraid to let myself go, to wish, to hope that this perfection could be mine. My fingers dip down his back as if they have a mind of their own, slipping underneath his tunic, down, down into the waist of his trou.

My body prickles with need at the sensation of his tautness underneath my palms. "Rissa," Da'red groans a warning. Yet I can't seem to help myself. Reaching between us, I slip my hand lower until I palm the base of his cock. Da'red hisses, stiffening immediately.

"Rissa," he warns again as I move my hand up his thick length. He shudders for me again.

Fuck, he's so big. He's so, so big. I don't know how I took him the first time, but just the feel of him against my skin makes me want him again and again. I wish this man would hold me down. This prince to hold me down and pound me into oblivion. And it is at this moment that I know for certain that if taking out this implant will give me even just one chance at having Da'red forever, I will gladly do it.

My desire grows as I continue to stroke him, just the thought of him pressing into me, sheathing this thick rod deep inside me, makes need pool between my thighs.

"Rissa." It's almost a plea as he shudders above me and a surge of another strong emotion goes through me.

Da'red buries his face even deeper into my neck, his breaths coming hot and hard as he struggles to control the heightened emotions my fingers create. And it is I who is doing this to him.

Me. Clarissa.

I have control over him so much that his fangs bare against my neck.

Da'red pants, huge breaths coming from his mouth as he breathes against the spot, his fangs pressing gently into my skin with such precision he will nick me if he makes a mistake.

And the thought should make me pause. The sensation of those sharp fangs should send some terror inside me.

He could rip my throat out. Kill me in an instant with those things.

And yet, I stroke his cock, taking away his control little by little with the complete confidence that Da'red won't hurt me.

Because I am at my most vulnerable with him. I've always been.

Since the first moment we met, I've been in his care. And not once has he ever made me feel unsafe.

Even when I thought he was my enemy, he touched me with care. He protected me.

I'm afraid of many things. Life in a world where you have no sight comes with fears even your mind creates. Demons. Monsters you cannot see but imagine, anyway. But even though I've fought those fears they've always been present around me.

Only now…they are gone.

With Da'red, I am not afraid.

As I slide my hands to the base of his shaft, gripping him with both palms and working my way up again, a whimper of need releases from my lips.

He's totally at my mercy, and I've never wanted someone more than I want this male right now.

He shudders against me, and his whimper seems to snap something within him.

Without a word, Da'red grips my hands with one of his, a growl in his throat as he eases up.

Disappointment floods me immediately, but I'm suddenly gripped by the waist and spun as if I'm a rag doll.

I land on my belly, a soft yelp of surprise echoing from my lips as Da'red grips my hips with both hands and pulls me up on my knees.

The gown Perthru dressed me in is promptly lifted, baring my backside and the thin underwear she'd provided for me to wear.

That underwear is no more as Da'red flicks one finger underneath it and pulls, ripping it off me.

"Da'red?" I'm almost surprised my voice is so full of need. It's so clear, that when I hear myself, a spot of wetness swells in my center, leaking through my folds. I clench when he grips my ass with both hands, kneading and squeezing the flesh, spreading my opening as he takes me in.

"Qef," he growls. "Rissa, you're the most beautiful thing I've ever laid eyes on."

His words make me bloom like the flower he's always referring to me as.

"I may not be able to mark you, but I cannot resist from claiming you like this."

That's all the warning I get before I feel the heat of his cock pressing into me. A moan slips from me into the bedding as my eyes roll over the moment he spreads me for him, opening me further as his thick shaft pierces my softness.

I cry out into the bedding, so full but wanting more. *Needing* everything he has to give me.

Da'red slides into me, sheathing himself completely as he pierces my center.

A low, guttural moan is all I can utter as my eyes roll back and my face presses into the bedding.

Da'red rolls his hips, hitting all the right spots deep inside me as my lips quiver with pure need.

He moans, and it's the sexiest sound. Knowing I'm the reason he sounds so obsessed, taken to another world, only heightens my pleasure. And when he slides out, only to seat himself once more, I surrender to him too.

Da'red pounds into me like a crazed man, and even when I collapse into the bedding, an orgasm crashing through me that makes my knees go weak, he continues to spread me, fucking me raw as he fills me to the brim.

I pant into the bedding, gripping it between my fingers as need makes me lose my senses, and for once I'm happy for the darkness. Happy I cannot see. For here, in this place, I am lost and all I can do is feel.

Feel the way he grips my ass with one hand, squeezing and kneading tightly as he claims me, while the other hand reaches for me in all the other places I need to be touched.

In this darkness, there is a perfect place, and I don't wish to leave.

When Da'red presses down into me, forcing my body flat as he grinds his hips against my butt, thrusting that thick rod so hot and hard inside that the squelching noises create a harmony with my breaths, I'm caught unaware as my legs quiver, another peak rising and crashing through me.

Boneless, sweat moistening my brow, I whisper his name as he comes close.

Da'red takes my lips in his, sucking lightly before he releases and trails a path across my jaw to my neck. There, his fangs brush against my skin as he whispers my name.

"Rissaaa…resehfuhl my ari. Kanishta ma goorul, banakeh ginahdah."

I have no clue what he's saying but the way he says those words makes me melt underneath him. They sound almost like sacred chants. As if this Atari is worshiping me.

"I refuse to let you go, my ari. I won't stop until you are completely mine."

Tears well in my eyes as he pounds into me with renewed vigor, stretching me, and filling me to the brim yet again before he roars.

I'm sure the entire palace hears him, but I don't care.

Da'red is not ashamed of me. He wants me just as I am.

And that feeling…is priceless.

# 18

Da'red

Rissa is surely approaching her estrous. My skin itches just thinking about it.

As I stare at her now, watching her sleep nestled in the center of my bedding, an almost overcoming surge of protection and need goes through me.

I can scent her and it's stronger than before. Like the thread of something sweet coming from her skin that's beckoning me to climb on top of her once more and claim her again.

My fangs extend and ache, the need to mark her a physical pain that pounds in my skull.

Pacing the floor of my quarters, I run a hand through my hair.

Bee grumbles at my feet, tilting his head so he can look at me and I almost see the concern in the quud's eyes.

He must be wondering what I'm doing here. Why I haven't left the palace after returning. This is the longest I've stayed ground-side in many moons. And it's all because of Rissa.

I don't want to go out into the cosmos fighting my father's wars.

I want to stay in her arms, where it's warm and, for the first time, where I feel like I can make a home.

Bee grumbles in his throat as I pass him once more and I stop short, my gaze slipping from my sleeping mate to the animal at my feet.

"What?"

He grumbles again and if he could frown, I suppose the slight twist of his maw is what it would look like.

But I know exactly what my trusted companion is trying to tell me, and he's right.

I'm wasting time here.

Every moment that passes, my mate is in more danger. I have to fix this. But I cannot force her to put her life at risk for the sake of a bond she can't even feel.

Qef.

The fates to have denied me of anything genuine for so long. And now they flaunt what I've dreamed of right in front of my eyes, but just out of reach. It's like a curse from the gods themselves.

I want to roar.

I want to tear the place apart.

But I remain silent. I release my frustration with pacing, burning tracks into my flooring, because my mate is resting and I do not want to wake her.

For a moment, I pause just to stand and watch her. Again, I wonder if she knows just how beautiful she is. Has anyone ever told her?

She is so soft, and round, with so many perfect places for my palms to rest. She is short, small compared to an Atari female, but it doesn't take away from the fact that Rissa is perfect.

Without realizing I've inched closer, my knee depresses the bedding as I lean in, running my nose along the smooth skin of her arm.

A soft moan escapes her lips and she shifts in her sleep, her rounded ass swaying with the movement, and making me stir again.

The medic was right. Her scent is so much stronger. It beckons me. And this close, it is hard to ignore.

Pressing against my trou, my cock jerks and fights against the fabric, wanting a way out.

I want her again.

No, *I need her forever.*

"Da'red?"

Rissa's eyes blink open and right at me, her gaze focusing on nothing.

"You're here," she whispers.

I don't know how she knows of my presence, but she reaches right out to me, her fingers pressing against my chest.

"How did you know…"

"I can smell you."

My brow shoots up as I gaze at her face, cheeks rosy from sleep.

"You smell good." Her fingers run up my bare chest, causing little shivers to go through me. Never in all my revolutions has any female had this effect on me. "Your scent makes me feel safe."

My life organ thumps at her words and I want to tell her I will do everything in my power to always ensure she is safe. Taken care of. Happy.

She deserves it all.

But those words are almost overpowered by need when her fingers skate down my torso. My thoughts change to something else.

I want to tell her how much I want to claim her.

How my fangs are dripping, sending life spirit down my lips as I watch her lying sated and filled with my seed in the center of my bedding.

And I want to do it all over again.

I want to spin her and take her over and over and over again until she is boneless. And then I want to have her some more.

The thought of sinking into her sweet slit makes a groan rumble through me and her fingers pause on my skin.

"Again?" she whispers. "So soon?"

I can only push a grunt of pained laughter through my nose. If she only knew the thoughts going through my head, it would scare her.

But no matter how much I take her, no matter how much I sink into her softness, it will never be enough. And I will soon go mad, insanity claiming me from the life spirit brimming in my fangs.

"I will always be ready to have you, Rissa. No matter the time or the place."

Her cheeks grow rosier and her lids dip, hiding those beautiful deep pits from me. I could fall into Rissa's eyes and stay there forever.

She clears her throat, her fingers leaving my frame as she eases up on her elbow.

"Would it be okay if I see Marion and the others?"

Her request catches me off guard.

"The other humans that were rescued?"

Rissa nods.

The thought of letting her out of my sight for even one second makes an uneasy feeling go through my entire being. But who am I to alienate her?

If it were up to me, I would attach her to me wherever I go. I never want to be out of her presence. But that doesn't mean she feels the same about me.

I have to remind myself my mate is human. Humans don't feel the bond like we Atari do. Rissa is learning to like me.

To feel for me.

Qef. She probably only enjoys it when I'm deep inside her and nothing more. I cannot force her to enjoy my presence too. I will have to wait.

Follow the mating laws of the Earthkin. Hope she feels for me even a quarter of what I already feel for her.

"It's just," she whispers. "I'd like to meet with them. I don't know if that will be too much trouble for you. I don't mean to demand anything after really just arriving here—"

"Rissa," I stop her immediately. "I'll contact Aqnar and Bhihan. I will bring you to their mates. Your Earthkin. Whatever you need, I will give."

Leaning closer, I pull her hand into mine and brush my lips over her skin.

Big mistake.

Her scent makes me want to pull her toward me and cover every inch of her with every piece of me.

Her smile is bright enough to rival the stars.

"Thank you," she whispers, and my life organ lurches.

Her soft voice and utter gratitude for something so small, when I could give her the world, makes warmth melt inside me.

Gods know, I am in trouble with this female.

***

Rissa

Perthru supplies me with shoes that make my feet feel like they're in a spa. And even though I stress there's no need to give me yet another gown that feels fit for a princess, she scolds me in much the same way she scolds Da'red for not yet showing me "my chambers". Because, apparently, they've prepared a whole huge room for me to call mine, fit with my own walk-in closet with countless princess gowns and lavish items.

That and Perthru's gentle chiding are almost two shocks to my system that are hard to get past. She's quickly taken the role of the mother I lost after I was banished to the Lower Levels after the officials realized I was blind.

It's almost comforting.

Now, dressed in yet another robe that feels superior to even the fabric available to the elite on Upper Earth, I walk with Da'red's warmth on my left and Bee's on my right. Like my two guardians, I step with confidence that almost feels surreal as we move through what Da'red describes as a shopping tower.

The floors are smooth. I don't have to worry about bumping into anything—not that my two protectors would allow it. Where Da'red's gentle hand on my elbow guides me, Bee's sturdy frame on my other side does as well. Bee leans into me like a gentle nudge that helps me to navigate through the many people walking around us.

Being out in a new space like this feels like a dream. Gone is the anxiety that always followed me when going new places on the Lower Levels.

There are sounds of laughter instead of the deep music of Lower Earth's nightclubs and fight pits. There's fresh purified air...

There are no off-putting smells or sounds. Everything is as perfect as the man by my side and to think that one day he will be ruler of this world.

But I shouldn't be surprised. Da'red is the exact definition of honorable. It would only make sense that his world is like this.

My fingers brush against Bee's fur as my other hand grips the folds of the dress I wear. It sways as I walk, whispering over the floor beneath my feet.

There are other whispers too. Voices saying words I can't understand, almost too low to hear.

My senses become heightened as we go on, my back stiffening a little. I might not be able to see the people around us, or understand what they're saying, but I can sense their gazes. I *feel* their attention. And when I lower my head, keeping my gaze low out of pure habit, Da'red suddenly stops walking and, at his cue, Bee does too.

I have no option but to halt, ears perked to try and figure out just what's happening that's caused the sudden stop.

When Da'red shifts, I feel him move to stand before me and then his gentle fingers against my chin, prodding me to tilt my head up to face him.

"You look beautiful, Rissa."

Is that why he stopped walking? To tell me that?

Warmth spreads across my cheeks as a smile I can't hold back stretches my lips.

"If they are making you uncomfortable, I will make them leave."

For a second, what he says doesn't register. And then it does.

"Wait, what?"

"I will clear the market towers of everyone except your Earthkin friends who are awaiting your arrival."

My mouth falls open. "N-no, you don't have to do that." My cheeks grow even hotter as I imagine him ordering everyone to leave simply for my sake. "I don't mind the people here. It's nice to be out in society for once."

He leans closer, close enough that his scent wafts into my nose, making me want to lean into him.

*"Isn't that the Prince?"*

*"Where?"*

*"And who is that with him?"*

*"Is the Prince mated?"*

*"Was there a declaration from the palace?"*

The words filter through to my ears with the harsh whispers and I'm suddenly aware of everyone around us.

"Rissa…" Da'red's voice pulls me back like a tether. "I should have warned you this might happen. But I have not been on Atar for so long, I doubted they would recognize me."

"Are you uncomfortable?" I ask. I didn't think about him being recognized either. I keep forgetting just who he is, because he feels so *real* to me. "Do you want to go back?"

I almost feel like warmth develops in the center of my chest, something invisible there reaching out to Da'red as he breathes a soft laugh through his nose and strokes my chin.

"I am only concerned about *you*, my ari."

In a bold move in front of all of these people, I press a hand against his chest and lean in. Da'red doesn't pull back. He allows me to touch him like this, to draw closer to him even though we're in public in front of all of his subjects, and it sends a delighted shiver through me.

"I'm okay," I whisper.

And as surprise to me, Da'red leans forward and places a soft kiss on my brow.

"Come, my ari." He takes my hand this time, and I lift my chin despite the rise in whispers around us as we walk. When I hear the distinct voices of the two people who I came here to see, another part of my heart rises and swells.

"Rissa?"

"Rissa!"

Marion and Mona are suddenly in front of me, their hands grasping mine even as Da'red reluctantly lets me go.

I want to tell him thanks for giving me this opportunity but emotion swells within me so much that all I can do is gulp back a sob as the two women embrace me.

"Oh my god, I thought I'd never see you guys again." I sob into Marion's shoulder as Mona pats my back.

They sniffle, just as overcome with emotion as I am, and I'm barely aware of their husbands, no, their mates, in the background greeting Da'red.

This is all so strange, and yet so perfect.

I can't see these women, or their mates, but I can feel the envelope of love that surrounds us. We've been through so much.

When I first met these women on that cruise, I wondered if I'd make any friends. I had no idea what would happen next. That a tragedy would rip us apart yet stitch us back together with an experience that will stay with us for a lifetime.

As Marion and Mona disentangle their arms from mine, they coo at the dress I'm wearing.

"I feel like royalty." I breathe out a laugh. Warmth fills me just saying the words and knowing I have this amazing male by my side.

"And that's because you *are*." I can tell Marion's grinning.

"Girl, you already know what I think. Get it!" Mona snickers and it's so great to hear the laughter and smiles in their voices.

"I'm happy you two are alright," I say. "I'm happy you made it."

Marion rubs my arm. "I'm glad you made it too."

One of the males clears their throat and Marion giggles.

"This is my mate," she says, directing my hand to those of a large male. "Aqnar."

As soon as we touch, there's a rumble at my back that I think is Bee before it dawns on me that it's Da'red.

Reaching back with my other hand, I find him immediately. He hasn't left my side and I grasp his arm. My touch seems to stop that rumble in his chest.

"It's a pleasure to meet my ari's Earthkin family," Aqnar says.

"It is also my pleasure," the other male says.

"This is Bhihan, my mate." The way Mona says it makes me smile. As if she's incredibly proud of the male the fates have given her, and as I rub my hand against Da'red's arm, I can't help but allow that feeling to affect me.

I am also happy he's in my life.

# 19

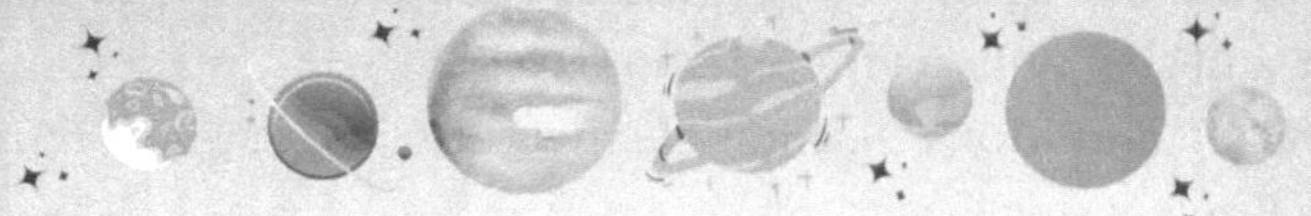

Da'red

Patience. Control. Those have never been my strong points. And as we walk through the various shopping plazas, resisting the urge to throw Rissa over my shoulder and take her back to my quarters is almost impossible.

I barely manage it.

Aqnar and Bhihan glance my way now and then. No doubt they sense what the females cannot. They see what I do.

The way the males around us are at attention.

The way some linger close.

The way they stare at our females. *My* female.

Rissa's scent is beckoning them and I have to remind myself they don't understand why they're inching closer to our position.

Or why the flesh at the back of their necks is throbbing, their cocks rising with need.

The thought makes my fangs extend in a growl that catches the attention of our females and even Bee.

He reacts to my mood and growls as well, causing Marion to send a questioning glance in Aqnar's direction.

When she tilts her head, I see the mark on her neck where he claimed her.

I have to force down the lump in my throat as I stare at it, my fangs aching. I want Rissa to wear my mark in much the same way.

She's a beauty as she walks alongside Bee, following her friends as we enter a garment store.

Her smiles were non-existent when I found her, and now they are so bright and full of life. Those smiles are worth more than a thousand moons.

Bhihan growls when a male comes too close, his eyes on the females who don't seem to notice what's going on around us.

"I know they're not Atari and I know my mate is like temptation walking, but I cannot promise I won't hurt a male if they get any closer to our females," he says.

"Agreed." Aqnar's brow dives, his gaze flashing to a male close by us who quails even as his fangs descend in a snarl.

Stretching my neck, I fight to control myself.

*Breathe.*

Control.

This is for Rissa. She needs this. She needs normality after what she went through.

I could have easily kept her on the palace grounds and invited her friends there. But that would be nothing like being out here, on the streets of Atar where there is life.

And Rissa needs life. She deserves to experience the freedom she deserves. Not tied down by the foolish laws and shackles of her people, or the ideals of the crown.

But her scent.

It's affecting me too.

I can't keep my eyes off her and I'm happy that Bhihan and Aqnar are already mated. Rissa's scent does not affect them, but I and every other male in our vicinity is being called toward her.

The more minutes that pass, the more I become obsessed. I want her beneath me, sinking into her over and over again.

Her estrous hasn't even fully begun yet, and the beckoning is already this strong. I'm not sure I will survive it.

And the more males that scent her, the more rage builds in my veins.

But I don't own this female. Not yet. I will never own her, but I want her to be mine. Completely. In every way possible.

And I want her to want me too.

"Da'red, is this one nice?"

I'm drawn from the thoughts clouding my head when Rissa turns in my direction as if she can see me.

Is she as aware of me as I am of her?

She holds up a red semi-transparent fabric and a lump forms in my throat for a whole other reason apart from the distaste these hovering males are causing.

Bhihan growls, fire igniting his eyes when his mate, Mona, stretches a purple fabric of the same material across her frame.

"What do you think they use these for? Maybe curtains?" Marion asks, unaware of the way Aqnar's muscles are suddenly tightening beside me the moment she lifts a black stream of the same fabric.

"Too nice for curtains. It feels like silk," Mona muses.

"I know, right," Rissa grins and my life organ stops. "I could wrap myself in this."

And she does. She pulls it around her and I don't miss when several hovering males swallow hard.

That's it.

I want to rip their throats out.

I'm at her back in the next second, arms circling her as I grasp the fabric in my hands, my chest pressing into her back.

"This fabric," I growl, dipping my head to her ear so only she can hear me, "is used during mating." The thought of seeing Rissa wrapped in this red almost makes me groan.

"Used during mating? How?" Still holding the cloth, she twists it in her fingers and it runs over her arms.

My breath stops in my nose.

I can see those arms tied and pressed back against my sleeping space, every word that comes from her mouth an echo of the ecstasy I'm sending through her veins.

"For those females who wish to be restrained during the rut," I growl. My nostrils flare as I pull her scent in, my cock hardening against her and I know she feels it when those cheeks of hers grow warm.

They grow even hotter as I allow her to paint the picture in her head.

"Could we use it too?"

What?

I blank.

The image of Rissa tied and waiting for me to ravage her is all I can see. And even when she giggles and follows her friends to purchase the items they chose, I stand there like an idiot, my cock straining in my trou and my life organ thumping hard in my chest.

---

Rissa

Shopping with Mona and Marion lasted for a few hours but it felt like only minutes.

The entire time, I felt like a girl living on Old Earth, completely removed from my reality. We were out together, laughing and making jokes, not a care in the world. No fear of Lower Earth guards stopping us and checking our papers. No fear of being robbed, beaten, threatened. No fear that we could be venturing into class D zones where the air is toxic. No restrictions caused by our disabilities.

It was freeing.

And Da'red...

He was by my side the entire time.

The whispers didn't stop. In fact, they got louder, or maybe I got better at listening. People talked about us and I'm sure the other women heard too. They didn't say anything, and though I tried to ignore it, I couldn't help hearing the people's words.

These are his people. His subjects. And I am just a human who has come into their realm. And yet, Da'red stayed by my side, almost as if he couldn't bear to not be close. He and Bee kept to me like my personal guards, and though that might have seemed suffocating to those people looking at us, I basked in it.

He laid his claim over me in public without having to say a word.

The ride in the hover vehicle back to the palace is silent, but words don't need to be said. There's tension between us. Sweet, sweet tension I could cut with a knife.

Little shivers crawl all over my skin as the seconds tick by and I'm afraid that if I even open my mouth, I'll let out a squeak or a moan.

As Bee moves to plop down at my feet, his warmth spreading through my robes and over my legs, I nibble on my bottom lip.

I might not be able to see Da'red but I can feel him. I know exactly where he's sitting, directly across from me, and can feel his gaze focused on nothing else except for me.

It's the reason these tiny little shivers are moving across my skin, almost as if he's undressing me with his eyes.

My thighs clench, the memory of his hardness pressing into my back resurrecting thoughts of how he felt deep within me.

I want this male.

I want him more than I've wanted anything else in my life.

My palm squeezes my belly and I know I've made the decision even before saying the words to myself.

I need to get this implant out. Even if it kills me.

All my life, I've been held back by things outside of my control. My sight. The laws of New Earth. The restrictions placed on Lower Earth. Even the stupid cruise.

But this.

This is something I can control.

And for the first time in my life, I'm going to reach out and grab it.

# 20

Da'red

The moment I step onto the landing pad, I know something is amiss.

Perthru stands at the bottom of the pad, looking up at me with a face that betrays nothing—to most. But like a child that can sense when things disturb its mor, I see right through her.

The slight furrow of her brows. The way she takes in a deep breath of air as soon as I appear, her shoulders stiffening as her chest rises. And, perhaps the most telling, a few strands of her hair filaments that have escaped their restraints at the back of her head.

My brows dive immediately and no words pass between us. At my back, I can hear Rissa speaking to Bee as she steps onto the landing pad, and just the sound of her voice makes an aura of protection surround me.

I must keep her safe, because I could bet my life on it, but whatever is bothering Perthru has something to do with my Rissa.

"Perthru?"

"It's your sire, Prince."

Any expression I had on my face disappears as I wait for her to continue.

News from my father has never been good. Never been welcomed. And now, I doubt this instance is any different.

"He wishes to seek your presence."

This time, I frown a little.

"For the first time in many moons, the king has left his chambers to venture the halls."

I cock my head, eyes narrowing as I stare at her. But Perthru doesn't lie. Never has. Even when it would have benefited me as a kit. And why would she lie to me now?

"Father has left his chambers..."

Perthru blinks at me, her lips tightening. "He has visited *your* chambers, Prince."

My brows shoot up this time, at the same instance that I feel Rissa's presence at my back. No doubt she's listening to this conversation. Possibly, she's even wondering why I haven't introduced her to the king.

I want to tell her I'm not hiding her. That this is all to protect her. From *him*.

"He wishes to meet the Princess."

Perthru's words make the air go hard in my lungs at the same time that I feel the slight tightening of Rissa's fingers at the back of my tunic.

She's been doing that the entire time we were in the market towers. Little touches as she reached out to make sure I was always still standing there, still by her side, as if I would be anywhere else in this universe.

Now that I've found her, she will never get rid of me.

Her slight touch sends warmth and protective feelings all through me, and all I want to do is turn around and pull her into my embrace.

There is no full bond between us, and I know not if it's fear that she's feeling at Perthru's words, but just the thought of it makes me unable to ignore her slight touch.

Turning away from Perthru, I pull Rissa into my arms. Her slight gasp is buried in my tunic as I hold her close.

"Da'red?"

A million thoughts swirl in my head as I hold her, none comforting.

The only reason the king wants to meet her is to decide whether this bond between us should take root.

All these revolutions, and he must have not understood why I spend all my time away. Why I have shirked my duties as Crown Prince planetside. Why I have taken every mission to leave this homeworld as much as I can.

If he thinks he can sway my decision, it's a clear indicator that the male who should know me better than anyone else, knows not one thing about me. If he did, he would know Rissa is all I need.

Denying the bond between me and this female will never happen.

"The king wants to see me?" Rissa tilts her head so she's facing me. "Should we go now?"

I pull her a little tighter, stiffening at her words. My throat moves as I stare down at my beautiful mate.

What should I tell her? The truth?

I cannot lie.

"Rissa...the male that seeded me into my mor's womb is like an insidious disease. No good will come from him meeting you. Moreso, not when..." I stop myself, but my mate is no fool.

"Not when what?"

Qef.

I haven't had time yet to convince her that I am worthy. That I want nothing more than to have her by my side at every waking moment. For her to be mine in all respects. But most of all, I haven't returned to that medic and threatened his life yet. For he must find another way for me to join with Rissa. I will not put her life at risk just for her to wear my mark.

"Not when we're not mated yet..." Rissa whispers and something aches deep inside me. There's something in her tone that I've never heard before. Something that pulls my attention.

"The king wants to meet me because he's heard about us, hasn't he? He wants to meet the Prince's mate." She blinks several times, clearly consumed by thought. "And I'm not really your mate yet, am I? Because I can't be..." She grips her midsection, head dipping as her brows furrow. "Because of this."

I gulp, understanding what she's referring to.

Gripping her hand, I realize she's digging her fingers into her skin.

"Rissa," I pull her hand up to my lips, stopping her, "I will fix this, somehow."

I want to say more, but Perthru makes a sudden noise, a grating of her throat that makes me glance over my shoulder.

We are at the landing pad closest to my quarters, and there, walking along the palace balconies, I see the procession that follows the king everywhere. A stream of unnecessary guards, as if anyone on Atar would dare harm the ruler of this world and in his own palace, no less.

He is heading this way, though he has not yet spotted us. I will have to intercept him.

Rissa stiffens at my side and I can tell she's caught the chill in the air that precedes that male I call my kin.

"Perthru." I nod to Perthru and she's already moving.

Turning to Rissa, I bring her small fingers to my lips once more. "I will meet you in my quarters. There's something I have to…deal with."

I wonder if she will protest. I expect her to. But Rissa surprises me.

She smiles and nods, leaving me momentarily speechless as Perthru appears at our side.

When Perthru opens her mouth to greet Rissa, she's stopped when Rissa turns and smiles her way too. It's so radiant, I don't think I will ever need the light of the star to guide me another day.

"Perthru," Rissa says, and Perthru's eyes widen slightly, her mouth opening and closing in surprise.

And this is why my mate is much more than she seems. Much more than the king or anyone else can see. She's survived so long on her own and she's already adapting here.

"Yes, Princess," Perthru regains her bearings, "it is I, Perthru at your service. I will escort you to the Prince's quarters."

Rissa nods, her fingers slipping from mine as she flashes a smile my way.

"See you later," she whispers and that lump in my throat is hard to push down as I watch them walk away, Perthru on one side, Bee on the other.

There is a sense of calm with this female that I don't realize until she is no longer in my presence. With Rissa, I don't have to be anyone or anything other than myself.

Maybe because it's something I've always yearned for. Something my life organ and the spirit circulating within me have always needed. This calm. For now, as I watch her walk away, everything around me slowly frays and twists.

At my back, approaching just as quickly as the king, are those same feelings that made me flee this world at every chance possible.

Rissa is the only reason I've even spent a day here...and one that I enjoyed.

She is...*everything* to me.

As I turn to face my father, I know that like a rock, I won't be moved. Not from this newfound feeling, and definitely not from this female.

Shoulders squared, I'm ready to take on the one person who has stood like a sentinel in my way all these moons.

---

Rissa

Perthru is quiet as we walk. A non-judgmental sort of silence. As if she's simply enjoying the soft pitter-patter of our shoes against the smooth floors.

"You've known him a long time, haven't you..."

The only reason I know she's heard me is the soft sound she makes through her nose.

"I was the one who raised him, if I may be so forward. The Prince's mor passed shortly after he was birthed." She pauses. "She gave us the sole heir to our world in exchange for her. The life of a brilliant being."

I tilt my chin down, my fingers brushing into Bee's fur as we walk.

"It sounds as if she was a great person."

"The best. She's the greatest queen Atar has ever had."

Her words make me smile. I might not have met Da'red's mother, but if the sense I'm getting from his father is anything, I'm sure that the male I'm falling in love with is everything like the woman who birthed him.

"And you will be too."

Perthru's words knock me out of my thoughts just as Bee begins to slow down. We must be arriving at Da'red's quarters.

"I'm sorry, I will be what?"

I don't know why I get the sense that Perthru is smiling.

"A great queen."

She stops walking beside me and so does Bee. We've arrived, and I hear the whoosh of the door as it opens. But my mouth's hanging open as I wait for her to repeat what I obviously misheard. When she doesn't, I stutter.

"B-but you hardly know anything about me."

"I know enough, Princess. Many females have been at the feet of the Prince, yearning for his attention."

My belly curls, but Perthru continues. "But none have ever rekindled the light in his eyes that died when he was just a kit. *You* have. And that is all I need to know."

Her words make something flutter deep in my chest as she excuses herself, mentioning that she will be back later with something for me to eat.

And as I step into the room, the door whooshing closed behind me, I can't help but grab on to that feeling and hold it tight.

# 21

Rissa

Perthru's not gone for very long before I hear someone outside the door again. As a matter of fact, she's not gone hardly long at all. I'm still frozen by the door, gripping my chest as her words reverberate in my head and when the door whooshes open, I turn expecting Perthru to be there. But the scent that catches my nose and the presence that comes with it, one that sends a chill across my arms, tell me I'm mistaken.

Sylsylla.

"Princess!" I can tell she's beaming. Or pretending to.

"Hello, Sylsylla."

"Princess, we apologize, she forced her way—" The guard's distressed voice only makes me feel sorry for him. He speaks so quickly, it's as if he believes I'm about to send him to the gallows.

"It's okay. Let her in." I give my best smile, even though my skin crawls with the brush of air as she enters the room. By my side, Bee grumbles with discontent.

They always say animals are great judges of character, and she's the first person I've heard Bee grumble at in the space of time I've known him.

"Actually, Princess. I'd like you to come with me." Even as she speaks, she walks to my side, circling me like some vulture. I wonder what the look on her face is, how she is regarding me with her eyes. But I don't need sight to tell me she's not looking at me kindly.

I can feel it just like I can feel the vibration go through Bee's fur as if he's trying hard not to bite the female's leg off.

"Oh, come with you? Where may I ask?"

"The Prince requires your presence, with the king."

I fight hard not to let my brows furrow.

I just left Da'red outside a few minutes ago. If he wanted me to meet the king, why not let me stay alongside him?

When he'd told me he'd see me later, I'd welcomed the time away from him, because there's something I need to get done. Something I'm sure he'll never ask me to do, but a process I need to undergo anyway. And it would be my choice, wholly and completely.

"I believe they are waiting." She speaks sweetly, yet there's an undertone that puts me on edge.

"Fine. Show me the way." I smile again, fingers tightening in Bee's fur. "Come on, Bee."

Funny how I've gotten used to this big furball. Maybe because Bee hasn't tried to swallow my arm since that first time.

Sylsylla makes a sound in her throat. "Do you *have* to bring that creature? The king would rather not have it in his chambers."

Again, it is hard to keep my face straight. "I'm not leaving this little furball all by himself. He's such a loving little thing." I smile to take any edge off my words and when I don't move to follow her, I hear the slight sound of annoyance she blows from her nose.

"If you must have it so," she says. "It's this way."

By the sound of her voice waning, I can tell she's already exited the room and I dip my head, running a hand through Bee's fur.

"You'll protect me, right?" I whisper to the huge animal.

Bee grumbles and I know he understands.

"Good. Let's go."

I've never been to the king's chambers but even then, I'm almost positive that's not where Sylsylla is leading us.

Why?

Call it a hunch.

As we walk, she says nothing and it's not like when I was walking alongside Perthru. This silence isn't comfortable. There's no softness about it. Just a cold hardness that sends chills down my spine.

Memory of what Perthru said, of all the women who have been at Da'red's feet just waiting for him to shed his light on them but being unsuccessful, all that comes back as I keep my hands steady on Bee.

The animal's calm energy is just like Da'red's and it gives me strength, as if I'm surrounded by him.

Being around Marion and Mona with their mates, I realized one thing. When an Atari bonds, he bonds for life.

And Da'red wants me.

He…loves *me*.

A smile develops on my face, knowing that whatever this female before me is trying to pull, it won't derail us.

I might not know the intricacies of life in the palace yet. I might not know what it takes to be queen yet, either. But I'll do it all for him. I'll do anything for him.

My smile grows bigger when I hear his voice. My Da'red, and I almost hasten my footsteps, until something twinges in my senses. Something that makes my steps falter instead of move forward.

Something I wish I never heard.

---

## Sylsylla

I've spent countless moons in this cold, lifeless palace waiting. Waiting for the day the Prince would come to his senses and realize that I'm the perfect female for him.

I was born to be royalty. The only female of my clutch, I was treasured on my homeworld. And when I came of maturity, the golden track that appeared on the back of my head, creating a pattern that runs down my back. It all signified one thing, the oracle had said. I was different. A female to be treasured.

So when I went to my first mating only to be used and imprisoned by the male who chose me, I knew there had to be a mistake.

I, Sylsylla, am special. I deserved more than what the fates were giving me. And that is when an Atari came to my world.

His bronze skin was adorned with golden trinkets that mimicked my birthmark. A prince. Da'red. And I knew I was looking at my birthright.

He was supposed to be mine.

He *would* be mine.

And when he rescued me from that harem, from the mate that wasn't meant for me, I knew the fates were finally smiling at me.

Except, this Prince…had no interest in mating.

No matter how hard I worked to get a position in the palace, finally working my way up to walk freely, freer than any attendant after befriending the king. Even then, in all the lavish garments and friendly gestures I've bestowed on this useless Prince, he has not found favor in me.

I believed he was infertile. That his masculine urges were dead.

Except, one day he returned…and not with the usual scowl and distaste he has for his own father, or the world the fates have given him to rule.

He returned with a mate.

I turn to glance back at the female as she stops short, the slow lingering smile that I've pasted on my face curling into disgust as I set my eyes on her.

She's a short, unshapely thing. Where I am lithe and embody the grace of a queen, she is round and filled with soft curves. Big eyes widen as she hears the Prince's voice and the momentary loss of happiness that disappears from within them, snuffed out like a dying flame, is almost as pleasurable as the Prince will be once I get her out of the way.

This ugly, useless thing is what he believes the fates have given him? He is mistaken and I will not allow it.

I stare at her, not having to hide my disgust because I know her little secret. She is without sight.

She cannot see that we are not really before the Prince and his father. That I have led her to my quarters so she can fall right into my claw. And like a puppet, I will use her. I will make her reject the Prince.

I will make her leave.

"I...never wanted you." Da'red's voice echoes in the space and I keep my gaze on the female. She stands almost at the entrance to my quarters, her legs seemingly frozen as she stares in the direction of his voice.

A smile curls my lips even more as pain shoots in her unseeing eyes.

Yes.

That same pain is the pain I felt when the Prince said those words to me. To have never been wanted by the one you want the most...it's a pain that can shatter a being.

*And it will shatter her.*

As the recording continues to play, I grip the sides of my robes, watching the human as she takes it all in. Every word, as if it was meant for her.

"I have never wanted you. When I rescued you and brought you here to the palace, it was only because you'd been through too much. No female should have experienced what you had. You were almost forced to breed...you would have been just one female in that scum's harem and you would have eventually died. I took you here because I knew your life would be better."

I release a breath, knowing the fates have smiled on me with this. And when the female before me shatters, I will know the fabric of reality that was torn because of her arrival has been mended.

"That was all," the recording continues, "nothing more. I know on your homeworld the males are different. I am sorry to have misguided you in any way."

I watch her, enrapt and waiting for her reaction, but there is none.

For a moment, in the silence of the recording's end, I am left dangling.

Perhaps her species shows sorrow in ways I am not accustomed to. But, picking up the play, I rush to her side, gripping her hand in mine.

She promptly pulls it away, snatching her hand back to her side in a manner that would have upset me under other circumstances. But at this moment, it gives me the greatest pleasure.

She is breaking apart inside.

"Da'red..." she whispers.

I almost cackle.

Foolish human.

The fates did one thing right. Her disability is exactly what I needed to make this work. And when she suddenly turns, pulling the annoying creature along with her, I know I have succeeded.

She will think he rejected her, and she will run back to the hole she crawled out of. She will reject him and the pain of it all plus the untethered bond will drive him to insanity.

And I will be there.

I will be there to lick his wounds and take his life spirit. To ease his pain and he will realize that it is I who the fates intended for him.

Not the useless meat sack that is the female running away from me now.

# 22

My hands tighten in Bee's fur so hard, I'm afraid I might have hurt the gentle creature, but he doesn't protest as he leads me away from wherever that bitch brought me to.

Gripping my chest, I force back the pain and all the insecurities that threaten to rise and come to the fore. Because I know better than that.

Even though I heard the words, even though I know Da'red said them, I refuse to believe them.

I refuse to believe it was him telling me he doesn't want me, even though it was his voice. I refuse to believe he would do it this way.

Because even though it hurt like hell, something was not right.

"And I'm not an idiot. I may not be able to see, but I'm not a fool."

Rubbing Bee's fur with harsh strokes, I release a breath.

"Take me to the medic," I whisper to the animal. I'm sure he can understand me. I'm sure he's not mindless. Bee's somewhat intelligent, and I'm banking on that now. Because he has to be my eyes.

"You know where that is, right, big guy? You know where the medical wing is?" He makes a low sound in his throat, which I assume is a yes. "There's something I need to do there."

My breath feels hot in my nose as I walk, doubt making me want to stop, turn back, and just curl into a ball.

What if I'm wrong about this?

What if this leap of faith is just that, a leap of faith, and there will be no one to catch me when I come falling down?

Bee navigates the halls with me by his side like an expert guide dog, and I don't know how I make it all the way without collapsing. It feels like my heart is breaking. Like it's being crushed, despite what I've made up my mind to do.

And when Bee suddenly stops, nudging my leg gently and I step forward through an open door, I know I'm either about to make the worst mistake of my life, or the thing that will change everything for me from here on out.

---

Da'red

I look nothing like the man approaching me.

We may have the same color skin. The same color eyes.

But that is the same with all Atari.

Nothing about this male tells I'm related to him. His kin. His heir.

His voice reaches me even before he does, and I wonder if it has always been this way. The unease that writhes over my skin at just hearing him speak. The urge I have to leave this place not coming from my discomfort in the palace, but from my father himself.

"You're alone again, son."

He's still behind the double line of guards preceding him. They approach and disperse, forming a V that spreads along the edges of the landing pad and closes on the other side, while in front of me, the space opens up to reveal none other but my dying begetter.

"I am always alone." Even as I say this, I know it is no longer true. I have Rissa now. I'll never be alone again. Even just that thought sends warmth through me.

I stare down at the male who seems to have shrunk with time.

I remember him being a formidable warrior. One that towered high above many other males in his day. Everywhere he walked, he commanded respect and authority. But now, the remnants of such a time do not seem to have lingered in this male before me. And for a moment, looking at him, a sense of guilt passes through me.

A lot has changed in all those moons I've spent away.

"You have never been alone. I have given you everything you've ever wanted."

But nothing I ever needed. And yet, he has never understood.

He comes to stand before me, his gaze flicking over me for only a moment before moving to the hover vehicle at my back.

"Where is the female?"

I'm tempted to ask "which female" but we both know who he's referring to.

"Why do you seek her?"

His gaze flicks to mine.

Seeing him out here, under the natural light of the star, is strange. I cannot remember the last time I've seen him outdoors. But even with the brightness of the day, there is hardly any light in his eyes.

"There were reports that the Prince has found a mate," he begins, observing me as he speaks. "That you were sighted with this mate by the watchful eyes of the Atari public."

"I fail to grasp your point, my king."

His eyes narrow.

"How dare you make a public appearance with a female I have not approved."

Whatever I've been holding back swells in my chest and I fight to keep it down.

But he's not done yet.

"You will mate with her, rut her if you will, and sate yourself with her flesh. Get her out of your system. Then you will take her to the outer reaches. Give her a nice farm. Leave her there." He turns, looking out over the palatial city and seemingly oblivious to the rage that has bled into my eyes. "I have chosen a female worthy of you. She is waiting in my chambers."

My fangs descend, cutting into my lips.

"Let me guess...*Sylsylla*?"

The king snorts, hard enough that if I wasn't slowly going out of my mind, I would wonder how his frail being managed to release such a sound.

"Sylsylla? She was supposed to be a plaything for you until I found a female suitable to carry the crown, but you never engaged. You've ignored her for so long I wondered if a male might have stirred your loin. But," he finally turns to face me, seemingly unperturbed by the fact my gaze has most likely bled to black—an obvious display of my rising aggression, "you did something unexpected. You brought home a female." His head tilts slightly as his gaze drops to the line of lifeblood running from the wound where my fangs descended into my lip. "The female waiting for you in my chambers is much nicer."

I see black.

The urge to reach forward and snap my own father's neck is as real as the pain of my claws biting into my closed fists.

This is just like before. Just like all those times as a kit when my life was ruled, controlled by laws I did not understand. So much so, existence became unbearable. But I'm past that and I'm no longer a kit.

"Where is the female?" he asks again, eyes narrowing slightly and even with his now slight frame, a semblance of what he once was lingers through his being. "In your chambers I suppose."

I take a step forward, standing face to face with him.

"She is mine, and she will always be mine. You have never listened to me as your heir, only as your general. And as your general, let me tell you this. I will raze all of Atar if you try to take my female away from me. If you step in our path, I will burn everything dear to you and crush it to the ground. Take her away from me, and I will search to the edges of the universe until she is back in my arms.

"There is nowhere across the stars that I won't go to ensure she is safe. Step against me, father, and I promise you this, you will lose *everything*. But perhaps, most of all, you will lose your son and any chance you have of this lineage continuing its rule of Atar."

For the first time, I see hesitation in his gaze. It flashes there long enough for me to straighten my shoulders and turn my gaze away from him.

I've wasted enough time here. My Rissa needs me.

And I need her even more now after this conversation.

I need to feel her tighten around me. Need to be reminded she is mine.

The king curses. "You are just like the female that bore you. Stubborn. Illogical."

A smile develops on my lips as I make my way from the landing pad.

"You'll regret this." His voice is like an ominous warning, but I refuse to look back. "One day you'll wish you'd heeded my words."

I halt, ice on my spine as I turn toward him. "I will *never* be the male that you are. I will never fail to protect the one thing that means anything to me, let her die all alone, and then live life pretending she never existed or I didn't care. Because unlike you, father, I know what *real* is when I see it. And Rissa is real. The only regret I have is that it took me so long to find her."

His face tightens as I walk away, unease surrounding me as a pain develops in my chest.

I need to mark my Rissa and I need to do it soon. I need to place my claim on her. Let the whole of Atar know once and for all that she is mine.

# 23

Da'red

Rissa.

I need my Rissa.

I don't know how I reach the corridor that leads to my room so quickly, or how I even got here.

I can hardly see outside the concoction of rage and lust thrumming through my veins.

Eyes still bled to black, I'm dimly aware of all the palace attendants taking a wide berth as soon as they see me, eyes wide, trembling as I walk past.

Even on the worst days of the Great Wars, I have never been like this.

So unhinged.

So close to shattering into a million pieces.

I need Rissa, for I know that as soon as she takes me into her arms, it will all be better.

My calm will come.

But even before I reach my quarters, a growl goes through my frame.

The guards standing there are male.

Considering my father's sudden arrival, I'd forgotten they were still stationed in front of my quarters. They would have scented her. Yearned for her. Wanted to sink inside her and I was not here to snap their necks for even breathing her air.

I growl at them, letting the sounds vibrate through my throat as I approach and they wither before me.

"Forgive us, sire."

Already apologizing?

All manner of restraint flies through the window at his words.

*"What did you do?"*

He's pinned against the wall, my fist around his throat before he can blink.

He sputters as the other trembles helplessly at his side.

"We couldn't stop her and the princess went with her willingly, sire."

For a moment, his words make little sense and it only makes more rage rise inside me.

"What?"

"The princess. She willingly went with Sylsylla, sire. We could not stop the velushan from barging in."

"Sylsylla?"

Where would Sylsylla take Rissa?

I must have said it out loud because they both begin speaking at the same time.

The king's quarters.

More ice develops over my spine.

Was this his plan all along?

He knew I would not yet present my mate to him, so he bet on me sending her away with Perthru while he distracted me. Meanwhile, Sylsylla was to take her to his quarters, only to be forced to see the female he prepared for me there.

I growl again.

Rissa.

I can't let her think I would hurt her so.

I release my grip, ignoring the guard's desperate gasps for air as I move away from my door and head toward my father's chambers.

Even taking the secret network that gets me there quickly, it still feels like the distance is forever. By the time I'm standing before my father's chambers, I've thought of every single possibility I can conjure.

To see Rissa's expression. To see her face contort with hatred and pain as she believes my father's lies is almost too much to conceive.

But nothing prepares me for what greets my eyes when I pull those doors open.

Nothing prepares me for the horror before me.

For a moment, I stand and look, unable to reconcile reality with the image of red before me.

My life organ stops as my gaze follows a wet trail of lifeblood that leads from the door across the room.

There, soft robes lie crumpled on the ground, lifeblood marring the delicate fibers and staining them like a cruel painting.

Rissa?

My heart shatters and I cannot move.

I cannot see her face with half of her body out of view from how she'd fallen behind the king's favorite chair. And a part of me doesn't want to see it, for it will make all of this real.

A part of me wants to close the doors and open them again, rewriting the scene inside as if it never happened.

I can take her hatred and her scorn, but not this. *Never* this.

Someone moves, and that's the only time I realize I am not alone.

The guards that usually stand inside the chambers are missing, but one person is present. Standing there, a dagger in hand, lifeblood dripping from its edge.

Sylsylla.

My whole world comes crumbling down the moment she turns to face me.

I don't even know when I move, or how I get my legs to cross the distance, but as I turn my gaze from the velushan in my presence, the only person I can think of is my Rissa.

Falling to the floor, my hands hover over the unmoving body lying there.

There's so much lifeblood. Too much.

It's soaking the robes that cover her frame and my fingers shiver as I lift them toward the fibers surrounding her head.

This can't be happening.

I can't have lost her before we even begun.

I can't have lost the one thing that's given me true purpose in forever.

I can't…

As my fingers touch the fabric covering her face, they freeze, unable to go further. Unable to pull back the cover and reveal what I am too afraid to see.

Because in all my life, in all the wars I've fought, I've never feared anything more than I fear this moment right now.

Not even the threat of death and disembowelment sent tremors through my frame as the sight before me now.

My whole being feels like it's being shredded and ripped apart, and I hardly hear the arrival of someone else in the room.

There's a gasp and a voice that sounds like Perthru's.

"Summon the guards," she orders, but her words sound far away and inconsequential.

For I cannot breathe.

There's a new pain in my chest, one that's different from any other pain I've felt before. This one comes from so deep within me, it feels like I'm being ripped apart from the aspect of my very existence.

Nothing matters as Perthru rushes closer. Nothing matters anymore.

And as I finally lift the robes, my fingers soaked in my mate's lifeblood, my vision almost blacks out when her face is revealed.

For a moment, time stops once more.

There is confusion.

Then relief.

So much relief, my chest heaves and I can breathe again.

For the face before me isn't my Rissa's. The female lying motionless here isn't my beautiful mate.

This woman is Atari.

But right on the tail of the relief comes my rage.

I cannot see or hear Perthru desperately grabbing on to me as I turn my attention to the trouble that's been in this palace all this time.

When my eyes land on Sylsylla, she takes a step backward. But not fast enough.

I'm moving with a fluidity I only use in war and I'm before her before she can even think of running. My hands close around her throat as I lift her and slam her into something. A wall. A piece of furniture. I don't qeffing care.

Females are to be treasured, not treated like this, but there's just one problem. My female is missing and Sylsylla is here with a weapon in her hand.

She is here and *where is my Rissa?*

*"What have you done to her?"* I don't recognize my voice. I don't care that her eyes widen as she stares at me. I don't give a qef that I'm scaring her. "WHERE IS RISSA?!"

There's a flurry as guards rush into the room, pausing slightly at the scene before them before Perthru takes charge and directs them to the female lying motionless on the floor.

But my full attention is on the female in my grasp.

*"Don't let me ask again."*

Sylsylla sniffles, her nose holes widening and flattening as moisture fills her eyes. "Why do you care about that useless, ugly thing? Look what I've had to do? Look what you've made me do for *us*?"

I snarl, my fangs lengthening. "For *us*? Whatever you did, you did only for *yourself*, Sylsylla. Now tell me where she is. I swear to the gods and the demons that haunt our ancestors, if you hurt Rissa…"

Sylsylla laughs. It begins low, then morphs into something maniacal. "I should have," she laughs. "It's her throat I should have cut. If she didn't come to this place, you would have bonded to me—"

I release my grasp and she falls to the floor as I step away.

Her words sound like poison I don't want to hear and she's already told me the most important thing. She didn't harm Rissa.

I just have to find where she is.

"Arrest her."

I barely note Sylsylla's cry as I leave the room. Guilt weighs down on my shoulders like a silent, invisible presence damning me to the fires of oblivion.

When I took Rissa to this place, I considered it to be one of the safest in Atar. I thought I was rescuing her, not bringing her into more danger. And, consumed by my own problems with this palace, I didn't consider someone would target another so completely pure and without blame.

Rissa is missing, and I have no idea where she is.

She could be anywhere.

She could be in distress. In pain. Bleeding.

All alone.

My life organ thunders against my chest, hitting every bone in my ribs as I search every room I come upon.

My movements become frantic, air seeming like a commodity I can't afford as I force myself to breathe.

This palace has always been cold and desolate, but never have the halls felt so empty.

I make it all the way to Sylsylla's chambers with no one in sight, and when I get there and tear into the room, all that greets me is…nothing.

The room is spotless. There is no one within.

I turn, about to make my way back when something resting on the bedding catches my eye.

Whatever god is leading me pulls me toward the object and I pick it up, brows furrowed as I stare at it.

It's a communicator. The same one Sylsylla carried that day.

As I press play, my own voice speaks back to me.

I stare at the device, hearing myself repeat the exact words I told Sylsylla. Why she'd recorded me…no…why she'd even kept the recording in the first place sends a shiver down my spine and a sour taste settles in the pit of my gut.

Rushing from the room, device still in hand, I head back toward my quarters. I get there, only to throw the door open and see an empty space that's as cold and uninviting as before Rissa was in my life.

For a moment, I threaten to shatter.

She's here somewhere.

I have to find her.

"Where is the Princess? Have you seen her?"

The guards by the door glance at each other, shaking their heads in unison.

I *have* to find her.

I'm about to turn and continue my search when something hits me deep in my chest. But unlike before when pain was like a constriction covering and stifling me from the inside, this feeling is different.

I stagger, hand grasping the wall as my eyes widen.

Warmth blooms all across my chest and I can…I can *feel* her.

I can feel my mate.

"Rissa."

Lifting my head, I know exactly which direction to take, for deep within me, that untethered cord is reaching out. Stretching. Straining to connect with its other end.

I know where Rissa is.

I can find her.

But as I rush in her direction, something else makes my life organ halter and thump.

Because I'm heading toward the medical wing.

And that can only mean one thing.

Rissa isn't safe.

## 24

Rissa

I can hear the medic gulping and get the sense he's terrified of me.

Maybe it's the way his fingers tremble when they skate over my belly, as if touching me is a crime and he'll get his fingers chopped off.

Or maybe it's the way he keeps whispering prayers to the gods under his breath, so low I should probably not be able to hear them.

"Did you get it out?" I whisper.

He's been working on me for a few minutes, the soft whirr of the machine he's using to extract the devices from inside me the only thing apart from the sounds he's making.

Guilt edges on my conscience that I had to threaten him and make him help me. It was the only way to convince him I really want the procedure. Removing the implants from within me is the first step to making everything okay.

And even then, after he finally acquiesced, I wondered if he was playing me for a fool.

The entire procedure has been painless so far, and I've been conscious.

It feels more like a visit to the dentist, except he's working in my gut. There is no wound, just a slight incision he used to gain access, and I wish I could get a better sense of what he was doing.

"You said that second one, the implant I got on New Earth, was dangerous to remove, didn't you? Do you think you can reach it?"

"I-I have, Princess."

My brows shoot up as he continues.

"I am extracting it as we speak."

I gulp, fingers tightening in the bedding beside me.

A hot, coarse tongue flicks over the back of my hand, and I smile. Bee's been great emotional support through this entire ordeal.

The medic releases a slight breath.

"Is it bad?"

"I-I do not wish to harm you, Princess. If anything happens, the Prince will take my life."

I shake my head. "Da'red would never do that."

The medic releases another nervous breath.

"I may not know him for long, but I know him enough to gather he isn't a mindless bloodthirsty fool."

"Pardon my forwardness, Princess, but you haven't seen the way he looks at you. I'm Atari and even I have never seen a male look at any mate the way the Prince looks at you. I am most certain he will end my life if I harm even a filament on your head."

More guilt consumes me as I bite hard on my bottom lip.

I feel bad for forcing him to help me do this, but I had no other choice.

"He won't harm you."

The medic makes a sound almost like a whine.

"I promise. I won't let him. *I'm* the one that asked you to do this. If anything happens, I'm to blame."

But I pray nothing happens.

I pray he can get the devices out with no side effects.

For the first time in a long while, I close my eyes and pray. I pray to the gods of New Earth and I pray to the fates of Atar.

There must be a reason I survived the massacre. Why I was brought here to this place. Why they led me to this man that's changed my life in more ways than I know.

I...I can't continue after this without him. Now that I've had a taste of Da'red, how on earth am I to continue living without him if this blows up in my face.

Or maybe, I won't even be able to keep on living anyway. Not if the medic doesn't succeed with taking this thing out.

Bee whimpers as my fingers dig into the bedding below me, but I don't have the strength to give him any words of assurance.

I've got too much riding on this.

Too much—

The medic lets out a breath and it sounds as if he staggers back.

"What? What is it?!"

"I...did it."

A beat passes between us where everything freezes for me, his words taking effect.

"I removed the devices."

"Both of them?"

"Yes, Princess. Both."

My chest heaves with short breaths as I force my lungs to work.

He did it.

A smile spreads across my lips at the same time that a loud sound reverberates in the room as if the doors have been flung in.

"Rissa?"

It's the voice I've been longing to hear, but instead of the joy that's coursing through me, my face contorts as tears fill my eyes.

He's before me in an instant, arms enveloping me as he pulls me into his warmth.

Da'red's breath is hot on my skin as his chest heaves in much the same way mine does.

"*Rissa*."

He says my name like he's filled with pain. As if he's about to shatter to pieces and clutching on to me, pulling me into him, is the only thing keeping him together.

"Are you hurt?"

I shake my head. Speech not a thing I can manage.

"Are you positive?"

I nod, swallowing hard at the concern in his tone.

"Rissa, I thought…"

He shudders against me and I can only wrap my arms around him and hold him close.

"Thought what?"

"I thought…"

He only grips me tighter, dipping his nose to my head as he inhales deeply.

"I couldn't find you. I looked everywhere. I thought…" Da'red swallows hard enough that I feel the movement of his throat against my crown. "There are a lot of things I can lose in this life, Rissa. But not you. Never you."

His words make something break inside me and mend again. More tears swell in my eyes as I face the reality that I was right to take this leap. That I was right to trust in us.

Da'red loves me more than anyone else ever has.

He's the best thing that's ever happened in my life.

As he eases back, no doubt looking me in the face, I manage to smile yet a tear escapes and rolls down my cheek.

Da'red freezes.

I lean into his hand as a finger rises to wipe my tear away.

"Rissa, there are waters in your eyes." He pauses. "What has caused you pain? Why are you here?" And then his voice wanes as if he turns his head away from me. *What have you done to my mate?*

If I wasn't clinging on to him, if I couldn't feel pure peace while in his presence, just hearing the way he said those words would send pure terror into my veins.

Da'red's pulling away from me and I hear something clatter and the scurry of feet as the medic tries to put distance between them.

"Wait!" I clutch his hand and it seems to be the only thing stopping him from going after the poor male. "I asked him to." I gulp. "No. I *forced* him to."

I sense when Da'red turns to look at me. "Forced him to what, Rissa?"

His voice is so gentle when he speaks to me, it only makes more tears form in my eyes.

"Rissa…what…"

There's a tremor in his tone as I feel him come closer.

When the air above my belly tickles my skin, I can tell his hand hovers over me. Over the incision.

Da'red doesn't say a thing. I doubt he's even breathing.

So I reach down and grip his hand.

My throat works, smoothing over the lump that's risen within it as I stroke his skin.

"I forced the medic to remove them."

"Remove what, Rissa." His voice is a mask. I have no clue what he's thinking and I wish I could get a better sense of his state of mind right now.

"The implants."

He stiffens in my grasp.

"He succeeded. He took them out."

For a few moments, the only sound in the room is the soft beeping of some of the instruments and Bee's huff of hot air through his nose, as if he's getting comfortable.

The only thing that moves is a breath that shudders from Da'red's chest, vibrating along my arm as he sways a little.

"Rissa, you did this all alone. I should have been beside you. If you had died I—"

"I had to." I grip his hand tighter. "And I had to do it without you, because I know it's something you'd never ask of me. After Sylsylla tried to trick me I knew it was time."

Da'red stiffens some more. "Sylsylla tried to trick you…"

I gulp, nodding slightly. "At least, I think she did. It was your voice but…" Even remembering what was said in that room makes a pain develop in my chest. "I'd like to think you'd have said such things in private with me, to my face, rather than in front of an audience. That if you rejected me, you wouldn't need to do so in front of anyone else and that you'd have at least cared about me enough to know that I wouldn't protest, if that's what you really wanted."

A gentle hand presses against my cheek, tilting my head so I'm facing him.

"It was a recording. I never said those words…at least, not to you.

She recorded me saying them to her. Rissa, I'd never turn you away from me."

I nod in his grasp, a slight smile spreading my lips as another tear escapes my eye. "I know," I whisper. "I knew you weren't there. I didn't smell your scent."

"My scent?"

I can feel my cheeks heat. I've never really told anyone I identify a lot of people by the way they smell.

A deep rumble comes from his chest as he chuckles, right before his breath brushes over my nose.

When Da'red kisses me, it's soft and slow, and yet it sends heat all through me.

My eyes roll back as he groans into my mouth.

"When can my mate leave this place?"

His question throws me for a loop before I realize the medic is still in the room with us.

"Th-the Princess can leave at any time. She will need some rest. Th-there might be slight discomfort." Something clatters to the ground as he seems to back away even more, just as Da'red leans forward.

His arms envelop me as he lifts me against his chest.

"Bee."

More clattering as Bee growls and follows us out the door.

And as I bury my face into my mate's tunic, I can't help but smile. My entire body is singing and I realize I don't even care to ask where he's taking me.

I just want to be with him.

# 25

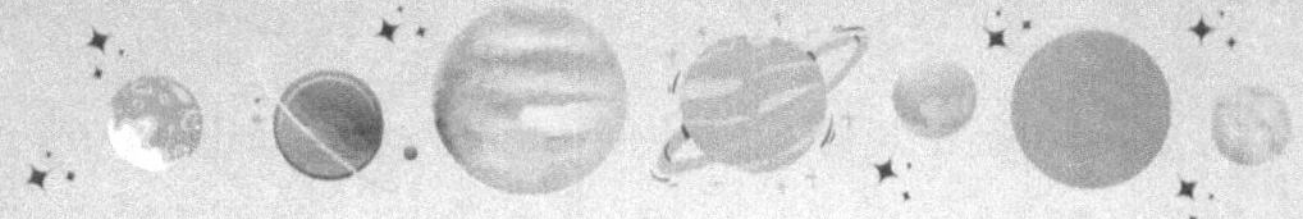

Da'red

"Evacuate the wing."

It's all I have to say to the guards by my door before they glance at each other and nod, hustling away at my command.

For I want no one close by. I want no one to even get a whiff of my mate's scent, for I intend to claim her for the rest of the night and make her scream my name for the gods to hear.

My door swooshes open and I turn to nod at Bee outside the entrance.

"Stand guard."

He growls in affirmation, turning his back and plopping his rump down as the door swooshes closed once more. For added security, I engage the locking mechanism.

I want no interruptions.

"Da'red?"

Rissa's voice is so soft, it does two things to me. It makes me want to protect her with my life…and it also makes me want to spread her legs and fill her with my seed.

Unable to answer her, a slight growl rumbles in my throat as I head directly to the bathing room. There's a section she hasn't discovered yet and one that I know she will enjoy.

"Where are we going?"

I stop in the annex to the bathing room and switch off the lights. Immediately, the area is filled with the reflections of only the crystals that line the walls.

"Oh, Rissa," I groan. I wish she could see this. "In here, in this room, the light shines on you in a way that makes you look unreal. Like a figment of my imagination."

"Light?"

"There are crystals in here. Iridescent." My gaze falls to my mate as I watch the light play over her skin. She really is the most beautiful thing I have ever seen.

And to think she put her life on the line for me. Just so that we can be together. *She* decided on her own.

She wants this as much as I do.

I will not let her down.

Moving over to the small waterfall running in the center of the room, I kick my boots off and check the temperature before stepping in.

Rissa yelps slightly when the water hits her skin, and I pause, waiting for her to adjust.

"A bath?"

"Waterfall."

"Indoors?"

I grin. "I have so much for you to experience, little bloom."

As I set her back against the coming spray, I lean in and do what I've been dying to do the moment I set eyes on her in that med bay.

My lips crash against hers, taking everything she has to give and yet yearning for more.

I want to consume this female. I want her very being to be melded with mine.

I want to breathe Rissa, and only Rissa for all my days to come.

My cock hardens even more than it was, pressing painfully against my trou as I bring my hips down and press into her.

And Rissa moans. She moans into me. Giving herself to me. Surrendering to my lips and the hardness pressing into her. All I can think of is the feel of her gripping me tight. Her heat enveloping mine, and how I can't wait to sink inside her again.

"Da'red," she whispers. "I can't wait."

And neither can I, little bloom, but I must. For if I don't force myself to take it slow, I will claim her too hard. I will rut her like a rabid uncontrolled beast.

"I want you to mark me."

Her words make my fangs ache.

"I want you to mark me. Will you?"

My breaths come harshly as Rissa writhes against me. Now wet, her robes form little resistance between the heat of her center as it presses against my length.

And Rissa moves, bringing her body up against mine in a way that makes me feel every contour and every curve.

I can't help the groan that goes through my frame.

"Rissa." I want to take this slow, but already I am aching beyond what I can bear.

Rissa pants, her arms coming up to wrap around my neck as she spreads her legs and I settle between them.

The warm water rushes around us, cascading against the curve of her round bottom as I grip her cheeks and spread her apart.

She moans, throwing her head back and baring her sweet neck to me.

The sight is enough to cause life spirit to flow from the tips of my fangs in a gush that sprays over her.

"Now."

Reaching between us, Rissa grasps my cock and I can feel my heat in her hand, burning through even the wet fabric that clings to me.

She strokes me, causing my eyes to bleed to black as her fingers glide along my length. I throb in her hand, pre-spend seeping into the wet garment.

With one hand, I release my mate for a moment to rip the trou and I bob free, slapping against her palm.

Rissa licks her lips and I groan again.

Everything she does, every slight movement, drives me crazy.

And then she does something that makes me almost release my load right there and then.

Rissa reaches down and parts her robes, slipping the thin undergarment she's wearing to the side as she brings my flared tip to her delicate folds.

Steam radiates from my skin as my body heats just at the feel of her.

"Mm." She moans as she runs my tip against her, grinding her pink flesh into me in a way that makes me want to pin her back and pound into her with all the strength I have.

I take everything within me to simply grasp her round ass and hold her there while she tortures me slowly.

Her face is flushed, her eyes closed as she bites her lip and rubs me into her, taking pleasure from the feel of me.

And then she says words that take every ounce of my control. Whatever I was doing to keep myself still, to let her take this slowly, it all disappears when she moans.

"You feel so fucking good, Da'red."

That's it.

A growl rumbles from me as I grip the hand that's clasped around my length and direct my tip to her entrance. With one pullback of my hips, I surge forward.

Rissa cries out, her neck baring even more as she throws her head back and I dip forward, sucking on her soft lips as she tightens around me.

Fates know, I have felt nothing sweeter than this. Nothing sweeter than this soft pussy milking my shaft for everything I'm willing to give.

I go mindless, slamming into her as she accepts every inch of me.

Qef me. She's beautiful.

And just as I hear her scream my name, tremors going through her walls, I growl her name right back.

"Rissa." My fangs descend as I pierce her neck, sinking them deep.

Rissa cries out at the sudden wound and I lick the spot, my tongue swirling around my fangs as I pound into her, giving her everything I have.

Because this female has complete control over me.

Qef me. She accepts my cock so well, her little whimpers as her fingers dig into my arms almost send me into overdrive.

The moment the last of my life spirit seeps inside her veins is the moment she screams my name once more. I extract my fangs, licking and sucking on the wound to ease the sting as Rissa trembles against me.

Her body heats as the life spirit takes effect and I lift my head so I can look at my mate as my cock slides in and out of her. So I can watch her take every inch of me as she becomes mine, wholly and truly.

Rissa reaches for me, hands closing around my neck as she pulls me closer till we're face to face. Our breaths entwine as I stare into her unseeing eyes while knowing that this female is the first person to truly "see" me in a long time.

And then I feel it. Deep within me where that cord sways untethered lights up like a spark. My thrusts falter for a moment as my chest heaves. Heavy breaths release from my nose as Rissa's brows furrow slightly.

I swallow hard as the sensation grows, and I feel when our cords connect. The moment we join as one sends a shockwave through me that makes me shudder.

I don't know whether it's the bath or if there are eye waters in Rissa's eyes but she pulls me even closer and whispers against my lips.

"I can feel it. *You*. I can finally feel *you*."

It's the best thing I've ever heard.

Rissa takes my lips as I slide deeper into her, taking everything she can give me and feeling through the bond just how much she wants this as much as I do.

"My female," I growl. "Rissa, you're mine. Forever mine."

# 26

Rissa

Two days later and I still feel boneless.

At least, I think it's been two days.

Since Da'red brought me back to his quarters, we haven't left. It's been one endless session of lovemaking that's been sending me to the stars and back.

Sitting up in the center of the bedding, I pant, shaking my head to gain some clarity.

"Da'red?" He must be gone again to wet the rags he's been putting over my skin to help cool me down. For I'm heated like I'm having a fever. Except, I'm not sick.

Unless this is really an ailment and his dick is the only cure.

Reaching down between me, my hands come away with slick and I groan just at the feel of it. I don't think Da'red has spent more than a few minutes without his cock in one of my holes. And I don't want him to ever stop.

Even when I feel I can't take anymore, one mere touch and my thighs clench again.

And he's insatiable.

This is the first break of clarity I've gotten in days.

"Da'red?"

Plus, there's this new feeling. Something strange and warm in the center of my chest that thrums and glows every time I think of him. It's like having a second beating heart that connects with the person I love most in the entire universe.

I sense him even without using his scent. I feel him as he approaches, first in my chest and then when his fingers skate over my thigh.

"You're awake."

That sexy voice, that irresistible timbre that makes me shiver, runs all across my skin to coalesce like a deep vibration at the center of my thighs.

I gasp as Da'red swipes his tongue and licks at my sensitive flesh and just like that, I'm suddenly ready again.

My thighs clench, holding his head in a vise as he dips his tongue inside me and groans into my pussy like a starving man.

"This is how I always want to start my days."

"It's morning?" I pant as Da'red lifts his head.

He rumbles a growl that vibrates against my clit, making it hard to focus.

"The star has risen and, unfortunately, we must leave these quarters. There are things…things I must tend to. And…there is someone you must meet."

I gulp, some of the intense feelings rising from my core dimming as reality hits me full-on.

"Your father."

"Unfortunately."

I release a slow breath. I knew this day would come sooner or later. I knew I'd have to face the man who obviously wants me to have nothing to do with his son. I just…hoped I could hide away from that fact for a bit longer.

Da'red grips my thighs, squeezing them gently before he crawls between my legs. Fangs whisper across my lips before he kisses me gently.

"Perthru will be in to assist you in getting dressed."

I nod as he dips his forehead to mine, before easing off the bedding and even though I would give anything to remain in this dream-like state, I know we both have to face reality.

A reality wherein I'm a princess. Living in a palace. A prince, my mate, and the best partner I could ever have by my side.

Da'red describes everything he's doing as he moves around, painting a picture for me. It's a thing he's taken to doing now as if it's second nature to him and I can't help but smile as I sit up and pull my legs toward me.

When he's dressed, the bed dips as Da'red climbs towards me once more. The cord that tethers us thrums as his lips find mine and I try not to question if all this is true.

What if I died on that cruise and these are my last moments dreaming of a life that will never be?

As Da'red pulls away, a sense of loss envelops me immediately.

"So, I'll see you later, sometime?"

Da'red growls. "My mate, do you think I can survive outside your presence? Perthru is waiting by the door. I will let her in and wait while she tends to you."

My eyes widen as the door swooshes open and Perthru's scent permeates the space.

Hers is like mint. Cool and collected like she is.

"Princess."

My cheeks turn into a furnace as I recall that I am naked in bed. Wrapping my arms around me, I try to hide myself but Perthru only makes a sound in her throat.

"I may be larger than a human, but I have already seen what you have, and it is all beautiful. Now, now." The air in the room shifts as Perthru begins to move about. "We must wash you, prepare your hair, and choose a suitable garment."

I huff a laugh through my nose as my arms relax.

I don't have to hide here.

I am safe.

As we walk down the corridor toward the king's chambers, it feels surreal. The gown I'm wearing swishes around my legs as Bee guards me on one side and Da'red guards the other.

I've never felt more at peace…or more loved.

But as we walk, something is different.

Other times I've walked these corridors, the palace felt like a cavernous place. Empty almost. Yet now, every few seconds, attendants greet us.

"Happy rising, Prince, Princess…"

"What's going on?" I whisper.

"I've increased the staff in the palace," Da'red simply says. "There are more guards, for your safety. More attendants too."

My brows rise and I open my mouth to speak but he continues.

"After what happened a few cycles prior, I'm never taking any chances when it comes to you again."

My mouth slams shut. He must mean that whole thing about the medic.

Gripping his arm that I've been holding on to as we walk, I rub it gently, shamelessly enjoying the muscles I feel underneath his tunic.

"It's ok." I smile. "It all worked out exactly as it should."

"But there's a chance it would have all ended in chaos and loss." I sense that he tilts his head my way, not breaking our pace. "I haven't told you yet, Rissa, but that day when Sylsylla took you and tried to deceive you…she could have taken you away from me forever."

I smile again. "I never believed her. I didn't trust her from the start."

"Rissa…that day, my father prepared a female for me in his chambers. One he thought suitable to be the next queen." His words send a chill down my spine. "Sylsylla…ended her existence."

I almost stumble over my dress. "What?"

"When I think about it, think about what I almost lost, I want to put forth my proposition again, my mate."

I shake my head a little in confusion. "What proposition?"

"I will leave this place, this life, if it means keeping you safe. If it means you are happy."

Da'red slows down and I realize we must be arriving in the king's presence. And he's telling me this now because whatever happens next will determine our future.

I hear the doors open, I feel as Da'red leads me forward, and the sudden silence as the doors close is almost deafening.

I can tell we're in the king's presence even before Da'red speaks.

"Your Excellence..."

"My one and only heir...and his mate."

The voice is so rich, and so much like Da'red's, that I take a few moments to process the fact that yes, I am in the presence of the king. My mate's father and my father-in-law, if I want to think of him like that.

A lump forms in my throat and I'm suddenly frozen, not sure what to do. But then my brain kicks into gear and that person I always was comes to the rescue.

The one that could pretend she had sight even when she didn't. The same person who overcame unbeatable odds and survived a massacre, survived the dungeon, and will keep on surviving.

The brilliant smile that appears on my face as I execute a curtsy is one that I pull from the depths of my soul.

"Your Excellence..." I bow.

Beside me, Da'red's warmth is like a column I lean on as the bond thrums between us.

"It's a pleasure to finally meet you."

As I rise, I expect the king to scoff. Maybe say some derisive words. But all that happens is silence.

"You've marked her," the king finally says. "Solidified the bond."

"Aye," Da'red responds.

Silence again and the unease in the air makes it thick and heavy.

"Your name, female."

Surprising even myself, I push past the lump still in my throat and tilt my chin upward, eyes pointed in the direction the king's voice came from.

"Clarissa, Your Excellence. I hail from Planet New Earth." I bow again and the king grunts.

"You've mated my heir, Clarissa." Da'red steps forward slightly and the king pauses before continuing. "Surely you know, he is the next regent of this land. I've built Atar with my bare hands from a fledgling world in the outer reaches to what you can see now." He pauses again. "Well, I suppose that statement isn't entirely true...you cannot see. Of course, the only heir I have will be foolish enough to—"

My spine stiffens at the same time that Da'red growls, air brushing against my face as he blocks me by stepping in front of me completely.

"If you dare to continue, it will be the last words you say to me. You don't deserve to be in her presence, much less to receive her kindness. Do not take any liberties with me."

I press a hand against Da'red's stiff back, feeling the fact that his muscles are all bunched as if he's ready to throw his fists.

But for the first time in all this, I don't need him to fight for me.

I've spent all my life being subjected to nasty comments regarding my disability. What the king has to say won't affect me. But what he says about my mate will.

I step from behind Da'red and face the king as Bee comes up on my side.

Drawing strength from them both, I direct my face at the king.

"You're right. I can't see. But even me, who has lived without sight all my life, can tell when there's something precious before me." I can almost feel the king's attention. "I'm talking about your son."

The silence that ensues gives me more courage than it probably should, but now that I've started there's no going back.

"Da'red and his men searched for me and my friends, fought for us when they didn't need to. We were strangers to them and this world. There was nothing to gain, yet they fought anyway." I take a step forward, releasing the man and the animal I've been drawing strength from and relying on my own. "And you know why? Because they're selfless. *Honorable.* Despite what you think about me, despite who I am, I know without a doubt that this male, this Atari, will be the best king that this world has ever had."

The bond between us thrums as undeniable love and warmth flow from Da'red.

Gripping my chest, I continue facing the king. "And I know this, because in here, right here," I grip my chest tighter, "I can feel your son. He doesn't tell me, but I feel his fears, his worries, and despite all that, he holds his head high and faces them head-on. I know your problem is with me...but what more could you want in a son? What more could anyone want?"

My words end in silence and for a moment, I wonder if I've gone too far.

That's before a clap sounds not far before me. Then another. And another as the king applauds slowly.

"I understand now why my son has held on to you so tightly."

At my back, Da'red growls again and I reach back and grasp his arm, rubbing it slightly, letting him know I'm fine and it'll be okay.

The king releases a breath. "Fine," he says.

Fine?

"Even those in the far reaches of Atar are already speaking about you and your mate. There is not much I can do," he says. "The coronation is on the morrow."

And then his voice changes as if he rises and comes slightly closer. "If you wish to be queen," he says, "you will stand up like you just did and rule this land alongside my son."

His voice changes slightly, as if he turns his head and I realize next that when he speaks, he's directing his words at Da'red.

Da'red stiffens.

"Your mor was a lot like this female," he says. "Small, soft, but she had a fire within her when she needed to fight for what she believed in." He grunts, and it's a sad one. "Contrary to what you think, my heir, I *did* fight to save her. I brought the best medics from across the stars and I never left her side, not even for a moment. Your mor was very special to me. She was...the essence that made me whole. I was never the same after she left. She was...and will always be...my ari."

Whatever was making Da'red stiffen slowly leaves his bones as he relaxes underneath my hand and I realize at this moment, that what his father is saying is something he's always wanted to hear. Something he'd *needed* to hear.

When the king's cold fingers suddenly close over my arm and I jerk, Da'red growls again, his hand pressing into my back.

"I mean no harm," the king says, but the silence that follows has me wondering what the hell's happening.

The king sighs. "Even I can admit she's a beautiful thing, Da'red."

He releases me, his voice waning as he turns away. "Take care of her."

A breath releases from me slowly as Da'red pulls me into his chest.

It's over?

I doubt it, but despite the tension still in the air, I can't help but feel that we made some progress. That his father opened up to him even just a little gives me hope.

Da'red pulls me into him and presses his nose into my hair.

"I'm sorry, my ari. That is not something I wished for you to endure."

I shake my head, burying my nose into his chest and accepting his comfort.

"We can leave this place. I found a world far from this one—"

"No." I shake my head, directing my face at him. Lifting my hands, I trace his handsome face, my fingers moving over the sharp lines of his jaw and chin. "I don't want to leave here. This is your home and it will be mine, too."

"On the morrow…"

"The coronation…"

Da'red tilts his head in assent.

"I'll do it." I spread a smile on my face.

"You'll do it for me."

"Anything for you."

"Oh, Rissa."

I grip him tighter. "I really want to stay here. You're here and…my friends are here too." I smile. "For the first time, I have a family…you know. It's what I've always wanted."

Da'red skates a finger up across my jaw.

"My little bloom," he whispers. "My ari."

His words warm me from the inside out.

"My love," I whisper back.

"I have a surprise for you."

# 27

Da'red

"Oh my God…Look what you're wearing! Please tell me I didn't miss the coronation!" The female with the dark hair wheels forward on a motorized chair.

"Trudy?"

Just the look on Rissa's face is enough to let me know this was the right decision. Bringing her Earthkin here, so I wouldn't be her only support after being in the presence of my father.

Rissa's smile warms not only the bond thrumming between us, but my very being. I can hardly pull my eyes away from my human as Aqnar, Bhihan, and Qhenno greet me, thumping their chests with their fists as they grin, fangs and all.

Because I have a mate now. I've marked my female, and she is mine.

I grin back at them, hardly believing the fates chose us four to take care of these precious females.

I let Rissa go and her Earthkin embrace her in much the same way that my Atari friends embrace me. The room is warm and full of laughter. Life.

And that thing Earthkin call love.

She's whispered that to me before, my Rissa.

That she *loves* me.

I cannot fathom what the word means, but I feel it. I feel it in the way my life organ swells when she is close. When her fingers skate over my skin and I rest my head on her bosom as she strokes her hands through my hair.

In those moments, I am most content.

And now, I am at peace.

I was right about this sensation. About this palace no longer being that cold, cavernous place it usually was now that Rissa is here.

Now, there is hope for the future.

"And you must be the *Prince*." Qhenno's mate maneuvers forward and stretches her hand toward me. I stare at it before remembering the human custom of touching palms.

I glance at Qhenno, ensuring he won't go ballistic from me touching his mate, and he inclines his head slightly, giving assent.

"I'm Trudy." She smiles at me and I notice there is not a trace of sadness or distress on her face. And neither are those emotions on the faces of the other females. The struggle these females went through seems erased, and I have my men to thank for that.

"Thank you for what you've done," she continues. "Thanks for letting Aqnar, Bhihan, and Qhenno complete their mission. Thanks for not giving up on us."

I open my mouth to say I had nothing to do with it all, but Aqnar slaps me on the back.

"The Zarzenius finally has a family again," he says.

A family? A crew.

My brows furrow. "Surely you do not mean…"

Bhihan crosses his arms and tilts his head back, that cocky look on his face that I'm so used to, only it's usually accompanied by a bowl of floosh in his hands. "What, did you expect we'd leave her alone and empty, to float the void like a ghost vessel?"

Qhenno shrugs. "Certainly the Prince hasn't lost his gonads…"

The dark-skinned female, Bhihan's mate chokes on a laugh and I realize everyone's been listening to our conversation.

But what they're suggesting is that we should travel the stars again.

My eyes fly to find Rissa's head inclined my way and her lips slowly spread into a warm smile.

"Surely you weren't thinking I'd want you to give that up too? Just for me."

I'm at a loss.

This was supposed to be a surprise meeting for her, yet, it feels like I'm the one being surprised.

"I want to go out there with you too." She reaches toward me and I step into her embrace, loving the feel of her touch.

"A warrior princess." Aqnar's mate, Marion, grins.

"A p-princess." Rissa clears her throat and coughs, cheeks growing warm.

"Hey, get used to it, Your Highness," Mona says before her eyes bug out. "Wait, does that mean I'm technically related to royalty?" She grins. "You know you three are like sisters to me now."

Rissa turns, tears in her eyes, and the other two females, Trudy and Marion, all pout, tears filling their eyes too.

"Oh fuck." Mona releases a huge sigh, her grin disappearing as she quickly wipes her eyes. "I shouldn't have said that. You three are going to make me cry."

As they embrace, a resounding boom echoes from outside the door and I squeeze my eyes tight.

Mona loses all sense of the tears that were supposed to be falling from her eyes as her head pops up from the huddle they're making. "What the fuck is that?"

Qef. I'd forgotten about Bee.

"Bee!" Rissa turns, panic leeching off her in a wave. "Poor thing, we shouldn't have left him alone waiting out there. I'm sure the girls won't mind."

Bhihan groans. "Don't let him in."

At his utterance, Qhenno starts chuckling and Aqnar can't help but join in.

"I swear on the gods on Atar, if you let him in, I'm leaving," Bhihan continues.

"What is it?" Trudy's concerned face immediately draws Qhenno to her side. She grips him in much the same way that Rissa grips me without even realizing she does. As if I am her rock. Her strength. And I'm tempted to move back into her embrace.

But Rissa's turned toward the door, heading toward it and I only manage to wrap my arms around her waist and pull her into me before opening the door myself.

Bee bounds in immediately.

"Oh my fucking god, you have a lion?!" Trudy screams.

"That's not a lion. It's more like a…what the hell is it, anyway? A dog? He seemed tamer the last time we saw him."

Bee sniffs Rissa, licking her arm and causing a giggle before his eyes widen as if he's smelled his favorite treat.

From somewhere behind me, I hear Bhihan groan before cursing, just as Bee's head snaps in his direction.

"Don't let him—" Bhihan's words are cut off the moment Bee dashes toward him.

"Qef!" He curses as Bee launches himself in the air. Bhihan barely catches him before they both go crashing into the floor.

Bee snarls, catching Bhihan's arm in his mouth as he shakes his head as if playing with his favorite soft toy.

Bhihan growls and curses, shaking the quud while everyone stands frozen looking, not sure what to do.

"Qef you, Bee! I have no floosh! I ate it all already." Bhihan's utterance cuts through the air right before his mate collapses, holding her belly as she points at him and laughs. "This is why I didn't eat any floosh hours before seeing this beast at the markets the last time. He's addicted!"

"*He's* addicted?" Mona's cackling so hard none of us can't seem to hold it in as laughter fills the air.

"Now I know why he's called Bee. He's obsessed with floosh just as much as you are!"

"Female, I'm dying here." Bhihan's brows dive as he glares at his mate, but even with his serious look, the warmth in his eyes makes it almost comical.

"Here, Bee," Mona calls, pulling a small packet from her pocket. "I carry these around so I can keep him in line. You can have some."

Bee's ears perk as he releases Bhihan and pads over to Mona instead, and unlike the roughness he just displayed with Bhihan, he's unbelievably gentle as Mona feeds him the treat.

"Look how sweet he is," she whispers.

"Only when he's got something he cares about on the line," Rissa says, her smile warming every corner of the room.

She squeezes my hand and I get the impression her words hold more meaning than the obvious.

As the other females circle Bee, rubbing his fur and feeding him floosh, my gaze travels around the room.

Their words from earlier float in my mind, and a sense of peace and warmth envelop me as I wrap my mate in my arms.

These cold walls never felt so warm before.

And this feeling, these beings that surround me now, this…family.

It's all because of her.

Lowering my chin, I press a kiss on Rissa's forehead.

She smiles. "What's that for?"

"For everything," I whisper, rubbing my nose against her skin. "I love you, my ari."

Rissa's throat moves.

I don't expect her to say it back, but she does, pulling me even closer as she rests her head against my chest.

"I love you too, my prince."

# EPILOGUE

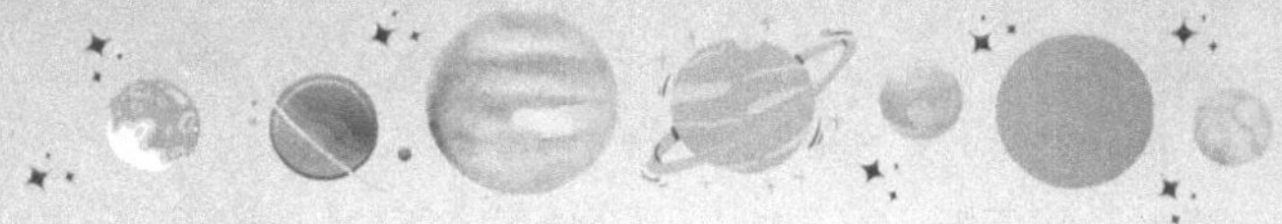

Rissa

Sitting here on this dais, over the thousands upon thousands of Atari seated before me, my heart should be thumping hard like it usually does.

It isn't.

I've never been surer of anything in my life.

That I want to be by his side. That I want to give him the life he never had.

Before us, the king addresses his people and the crowd hushes as he speaks.

As I sit here, I wonder what the Atari see when they look at me. Was I what they expected their next queen would look like?

Of course not. I doubt it.

But I'll be the best queen I can be. When the time comes, I will do my best to support Da'red. I'll do my best to give him every opportunity I can because that's exactly what he did for me when he risked his life to come save me.

His fingers tighten on my hand as he rubs them in his, completely uncaring of what the crowd of onlookers might think. Completely uncaring that we must be the center of attention.

He loves me.

And it's that assurance that's making me so brave.

"Citizens of Atar...I present to you, your new Princess. Rissa, of New Earth."

I gulp, rising on legs that didn't feel like Jell-O until this moment.

By my side, Da'red stands and I follow his lead as he walks forward.

The gown Perthru dressed me in flows with a long train behind me as I walk and I realize as I move forward, that in the next few moments, I will find out just what the people of Atar think of me.

There's a whistle in the crowd and someone screams in English.

"Girl, you look fucking amazing! Whoo!"

Mona.

Only Mona would be so brave in a sea of strangers.

I press my lips together to stop from grinning, but my cheeks grow red anyway.

To know that my people are out there watching me, supporting me, it's more support than they'll ever know.

Da'red's fingers tighten in mine in silent support as I feel the cool fingers of the king on my brow.

The crown is thin, light, and as soon as it settles on my head, there's an eruption of noise that's so unexpected, it startles me.

The whole of Atar screams my name in unison and praise.

"Rissa of Earth, we welcome you," the king says. "May you bring blessings to our land."

As the crowd erupts, I grip Da'red's hand like a vice and he rubs my fingers in his.

They've accepted me as their princess.

This is my life now.

"Come now, Rissa." Da'red dips his head to my ears and I feel the drag of his fangs over the soft flesh. "There is much to attend to."

*Back in Da'red's quarters*

"When you said there were things to attend to, I thought you meant princess and prince stuff." I giggle as Da'red lifts me and deposits me in the center of the bed, with enough roughness I know we aren't about to go to sleep.

The entire journey back to the palace, he's been whispering in my ear. Telling me how beautiful he thinks I am.

How I'm the best thing that's ever happened to him.

The gown I'm wearing pulls against my chest before I hear the cloth rip.

I startle. "Da'red, that's—"

"Perthru won't mind."

I open my mouth to protest but his lips crash against mine, stifling whatever I had to say.

Da'red kisses me as if I'm the air he needs to breathe. And as his lips crash against mine and my robe's discarded somewhere in the room, my body sings as I lie bare before him.

Soft fibers that feel like silk wrap around my hands as Da'red rises and I'm momentarily open-mouthed with surprise as my arms are brought behind my back.

"Da'red, this is…"

"That fabric you bought in the markets."

My skin heats at the memory and what he said it was used for.

The cloth is so soft as he wraps it around my wrists once more before bringing it over my shoulder.

With slow precision, Da'red brings the cloth over my breasts, making it rub against my nipples as he fastens a harness, bringing the fabric around my back and over my other shoulder.

It rubs and slides as he moves, tickling my nipples and forcing them into peaks as he grasps one of my legs.

"Oh!" I gasp as my ankle is brought up and secured, the fabric creating a knot that keeps my leg suspended above my head.

"Fates know, Rissa," Da'red growls and the sound of his voice makes me clench.

"Qef."

When my other leg is brought up and fastened, I lie helpless before him.

My legs are spread, and my arms are secured behind my back.

I'm completely open to the male.

"Is this...what you wanted?" I lick my lips as I hear my mate growl.

"More than anything."

As Da'red dips, his tongue piercing me immediately, I cry out.

I want to squirm but there is nowhere for me to go. I can't do anything but remain at his mercy, hips bucking shamelessly into his face as he takes me to ecstasy.

I don't know how many times I climb that mountain or how many times I come back down only to climb it again, but when Da'red finally eases back and a feel his flared tip at my entrance, I know I'm always going to be wanting more. More of him. More of this. More of our everything.

"My ari!" I scream his name as Da'red leans forward and seals his lips with mine.

"My ari," he repeats, and the bond thrums between us.

He is mine.

I am his.

Forever.

# ABOUT THE AUTHOR

A. G. Wilde is an avid reader, a gamer, a lover of all things space, alien, and sci-fi.

She is addicted to intense romance, irresistible heroes, and deliciously naughty things.

patreon.com/agwilde
facebook.com/agwilde
twitter.com/authoragwilde
instagram.com/authoragwilde
amazon.com/author/agwilde

# AFTERWORD

♥ This concludes Guarding His Mate. ♥

I hope you enjoyed reading Rissa and Da'red's story as much as I enjoyed writing it. These Atari have opened up a whole area within my soul where I'm now craving obsessive, possessive, marshmallow-centered males.

Da'red was interesting to write because I didn't want to get too deep into the politics of being a prince and palatial life. I wanted him to be as normal as possible, or maybe that was just the character himself speaking to me. After all, that was his wish too.

And Rissa. Writing a blind heroine isn't easy for an author who writes from the POV of the character's gaze. That was a thrilling change in concept for me and I loved writing her character.

Writing heroines that are different from the norm really opened my eyes to a few things. One, it made me realize just how much of my readership is underrepresented! I hope that you could relate to at least some part(s) of the heroines in this series. And, two, I realized just how much I enjoy writing about characters that can overcome, despite their challenges.

Lots of love and happy reading!

♥ A.G.


Scan the QR code below if you want to ☞ Join my mailing list, ☞ Find me on Facebook , or ☞ Join my Patreon (exclusive access NSFW character art, ARCs, sneak peeks, and more!)

He has two options: Let her go.
**Or let her in.**

Other books in the series: Sohut's Protection, Ka'Cit's Haven

———

**Ajos: The Restitution Book One**
She didn't move to the big city just to be kidnapped by aliens.
That wasn't even possible...
Right?
*WRONG.*
When Kerena wakes up, she's not on Earth anymore.
Heck, she's not even in the same galaxy, and the face hovering so close
she can make out every detail? That face is definitely...not...human.
But before she can really figure out what's going on, Kerena realizes
she's caught in the middle of a war—one she was thrust into as soon as
she was ripped from Earth.
She's surrounded by aliens in a rebellion, but there's one—the one with
the strange golden eyes, minty-teal skin, and rippling muscles—that
holds her attention.
His presence is magnetic and his heated gaze makes something stir
deep within her.
He's battling something that has nothing to do with the war and his
warning that she should stay away does not go unheeded.
He's a dangerous rebel fighter. She gets that. So...why is he still
hovering so close? And why is he growling at everyone that so much
as looks in her direction?
*Most of all, why does he keep looking at her like she belongs to ... HIM?*

Other books in the series: V'Alen

———

**Arrival: Captured Earth Book One**

ADIRA
The machines came, and they trampled us all.

I have nothing left. No family. No friends. No home.
They harvest us. They breed us. They feed from us…
There is no hope…Not until one fateful moment when my eyes open
and I see something streaking across the skies.
What appears is like a demon before my eyes…
But can they be worse than the evil already upon us?
I will just have to wait and see.

FER'RO
Sailing across the stars for what feels like eons…we have followed our
enemy to a little blue planet.
We had wanted to arrive before them…now I think we may be too late.
But when we kill the first Scrit and I see the being drowning within its
depths, I know I have to save it.
And *it*…turns out to be a *her*. **A female.**
This planet has hope yet. I will save her and her kind.
…Little do I know…she's the one who ends up saving me instead.

*Dark. Steamy. Gritty. A thrilling romance intertwined in a plot that will give
you chills.*

Other books in the series: Base Zero, Cataclysm, War

———

**Claiming His Mate**
**Fated Mates of the Atari**

**When I get a once-in-a-lifetime chance to go on a luxury space cruise,
I jump at it.**
This cruise is the beginning of something amazing, and nothing is
going to stop me from going.
But when things go wrong shortly after departure, it's clear I have
made a mistake.
Suddenly thrown into a world where I have no way of defending
myself, the last thing I expect is an Atari warrior coming to my rescue.

This cruise has been full of surprises…but the Atari is the biggest one of all.

He's tall, growly, possessive, and he sends my pulse into overdrive with just the slightest look.

Why the heck is my body reacting this way to this stranger?

*And did he just declare that I am his mate?*

Other books in the series: Craving His Mate, Fighting for His Mate, Guarding His Mate

———

Scan the QR code to view all books